A MOMENT MORE SUBLIME

Stephen Grant

A MOMENT MORE SUBLIME

A NOVEL

UPPER WEST SIDE PHILOSOPHERS, INC.
NEW YORK

Published by Upper West Side Philosophers, Inc.
P. O. Box 250645, New York, NY 10025, USA
www.westside-philosophers.com

Copyright © 2014 by Stephen Grant
Cover Photograph Copyright © 2013 Kathrin Stengel
Author Photograph Copyright © 2012 Geoffrey Onyett

Upper West Side Philosophers, Inc. provides a publication venue for original philosophical thinking steeped in lived life, in line with our motto: *philosophical living & lived philosophy.*

All rights reserved. No part of this publication may be reproduced, stored in a retrieval system, or transmitted, in any form or by any means, electronic, mechanical, photocopying, recording, or otherwise, without prior permission in writing from the publisher. For all inquiries concerning permission to reuse material from any of our titles, please contact the publisher in writing, or contact the Copyright Clearance Center, Inc. (CCC), 222 Rosewood Drive, Danvers, MA 01923, USA (www.copyright.com).

The colophon is a registered trademark of
Upper West Side Philosophers, Inc.

Library of Congress Cataloging-in-Publication Data

Grant, Stephen, 1963-
  A moment more sublime : a novel / Stephen Grant. -- 1st edition.
      pages cm
  ISBN 978-1-935830-19-1 (pbk. : alk. paper)
 1. Philosophy teachers--Fiction. 2. Schools--England--Fiction. 3. Labor unions--Fiction. 4. London (England)--Fiction. I. Title.
  PR6107.R376M66 2013
  823'.92--dc23
                              2013007988

For Mona Grant

CHAPTER ONE

"Consider this. Do all humans aim at happiness? Is happiness broadly similar for all humans? Must you read philosophy to be happy? Must you be morally good to be happy? To answer yes to these questions is to commit yourself to the ethics of Aristotle, and I hope this is what you will come to do." He looks up at them. "Who would answer yes?"

Inevitably, it is Maya who is the first to respond. "Would that mean that happiness is the same for one of us as it was for a twelfth-century monk?"

"Yes."

She starts in disbelief. "They were happy reading and praying, but no one here would be happy doing that."

"The easiest way to understand this would be to consider the terms we are using. 'Happiness' is the most common translation of the ancient Greek word 'eudaimonia'. Many now feel this is better translated as 'a flourishing life'. Aristotle believed that all humans shared a common nature, and we could describe, at least in outline, the flourishing life for all humans because in each case it would be fulfilling a range of natural capacities that we all have. He would have said that, although the monks may have believed they were leading a flourishing life, they would have been mistaken. Humans naturally appreciate pleasure, and the best life will include many of the pleasures that the monks refused. They therefore could not lead the best life."

Other hands are now raised, but Maya continues on the assumed right of follow-up questions. "Are you saying that you can't be happy if you don't read philosophy?"

Smiles all around. They sense that this is so improbable it's actually amusing that anyone should have made the claim at all. This in turn creates the opportunity for point-scoring against the philosophers. They have all studied Plato in their first year and find an arrogance in the idea of the ideal state as one ruled by philosophers, which they also detect in their teachers of the subject.

"At some stages Aristotle appears to go as far as suggesting that the best life is not simply one where you study philosophy but one where you focus purely on the most abstract areas such as the fundamentals of logic, mathematics, and physics. Even subjects such as ethics would no longer be a part of what one does. He suggests that the gods are pure conscious thought, and as the gods have the best possible existence and no practical concerns, the best possible existence must be one of pure thought for its own sake. He thinks abstract philosophy is like that."

"Does anyone believe that now?" Joe's first contribution of the year. He is looking down and drawing some sort of machine as he says it, pressing the pen down on the paper with excessive force. Aside from Maya, he is the only student of the five with mental health problems of which Tom is aware. The ever-present symptom is that he sits with his ankles clamped tight and moves his knees apart and together with metronomic regularity over the entire seventy minutes of every lesson. His concentration is so sporadic it is extraordinary that he has made his way this far through school, benefitting from only the short episodes of attention which punctuate the general, swirling storm of his mental energy. Tom takes this to be an indication of what Joe could have achieved if capable of focusing for more than a fraction of any class. This thought fights for supremacy over the extreme irritation Joe causes by constantly drifting into conversation with others around him, but Tom has never seriously considered having him withdrawn from the class.

In December of last year, there had been an inspection. The aging little Ofsted man with the shirt-splitting belly and the incongruous Paul Smith designer glasses was already sitting in the room when Tom entered two minutes late and saw him tick a box indicating the class had not started on time. Tom began by asking a series of questions based on the material covered in the previous session. Joe's hand shot up at the first question, and he answered using precisely the words Tom had used two days earlier. The same happened with the second question. Other students quickly understood that Joe had studied and memorised that entire lesson in preparation for a possible inspection. They also began to respond with unusual enthusiasm. The inspector commended the "positive learning environment" and awarded the lesson the second highest of the four possible grades. So Tom lets Joe sit there with his knees knocking and his bad drawing and his constant talking.

"No one who counts himself an Aristotelian today would accept this. There are differences of opinion over whether or not Aristotle himself really held this to be the case. Most believe that he was committed to the view that the best life for all of us would involve philosophy as a means of fulfilling the intellectual potential that all of us have. But he also stresses the value of developing the moral virtues, such as being charitable, and talks of the importance of friendship. It is better to think of the best life as one which involves developing a range of capacities, including our philosophical ones."

Tom now gives each of them an extract from Book I of *Nicomachean Ethics* accompanied by several questions, answers to which they must extract from Roger Crisp's new translation. This is not the one that the exam board specifies, but it is more readable than the Penguin version. This in turn makes it easier for Tom to sit down and daydream as the students try to decipher sentences which are longer than most paragraphs. It is many years since his expanding laziness overcame the professional obligation to circulate among the students, checking their progress and helping them. He now sits quietly as they get on with it and reflects on other matters. He calculates that, as he will provide the right answers at the end, it makes no sense to dilute their enthusiasm by correcting them as they go. Once he has gone through the text with them, he writes some notes on the whiteboard summarising key points. The board is still annoyingly stained down the right-hand side from where rainwater used to leak through the roof. The leak was fixed as part of a mass of decorating and repairs which preceded Ofsted's visit. Prior to that, on rainy days, he could use only the left side of the board because the constant drip of water would wash away anything written in its path.

After the lesson, Maya follows him to his office to pick up a list of secondary texts she has asked for, some of which he has read himself. Although she is in a second-year course, she is in her third year at the college. She arrived with eleven GCSEs, ten of them at A*, pretty much the best any British sixteen-year-old can do before progressing to two years of sixth form study, followed by university.* She then took five AS courses in her first year instead of the usual four, picking up an A for each of them, as well as re-taking the eleventh

---

* Note to American readers: 'sixth form college', in the British educational system, is more or less equivalent to 'senior high school'.

GCSE to ensure the full set of perfect grades. In January of her second year, she re-sat an English lit paper in which she had scored only a B, despite getting an A overall. When the result came back as another B, she dropped out of the college and returned the following year. The email from Learning Support said she now had a better counsellor and better meds, but to monitor her carefully. Going on past experience, Tom judges it unlikely that she will suffer another breakdown if she fails to get the place at Cambridge which has been held over from the last year. He has taught many more fragile than her who have survived the grades they didn't want. He is theoretically required to consider whether she might be at risk of suicide, but he believes the likelihood of that to be vanishingly small. Then again, you never really know.

When she leaves, he sits in uncomfortable anticipation of what awaits him. He will have to wait fourteen minutes between switching on his computer and being able to use it. It will take another four minutes if he wishes to open his work emails, though he will have just about enough time to check his Hotmail before his mule of a machine fully revives for the day ahead. This is the unavoidable consequence of the college lacking the money to buy new equipment while having to upgrade the software without which attachments sent by anyone from first-year students to funding bodies cannot be read. In practice, this means that, if he wishes to prepare some work at home to print off for his first lesson, he needs to take an earlier train in order to have time to both print and copy it.

The irritation of waiting for the computer to finally kick into life each morning always needs to be balanced against reprieve from opening the emails he knows Barry has sent him. These are from either late the previous evening or at eight in the morning when Barry has arrived at his desk in the English department with a series of new ideas on which urgent action might be required. In a moment of breathtaking misjudgement, Tom had agreed to stand for the position of branch secretary for the Union of College Lecturers two years earlier. The thought of representing the staff's interests had figured somewhat less prominently in his reasons than the attraction of having four teaching sessions removed from his timetable to carry out his revolutionary responsibilities. He had anticipated meeting with management once a fortnight, helping to chair branch meetings twice a term, and plenty of general discussion about the uselessness of the college's senior managers.

What Tom had not understood was the Castro-like enthusiasm of Barry Egham, branch chair of fifteen years. Barry had approached him on the back of two questions raised in a branch meeting, asking him if he would be interested in "getting a bit more involved." It emerged that the then secretary would be leaving the college, and Barry decided that it would be good to enlist someone from outside the English department. The position of secretary carried little importance in itself but came with a much higher status because whoever took up this post also became a lead negotiator. This in turn meant engaging in hand-to-hand combat with management, which elevated the holder to the rank of local hero. Barry persuaded the only other person interested in standing for secretary to think instead of the great work to be done as health and safety officer, thereby neatly matching the available candidates to the range of posts and avoiding the need for elections.

Tom's relief at avoiding the possible humiliation of defeat dissipated when it became clear exactly what working with Barry was to be like. There would be meetings at eight-fifteen every Tuesday morning in which they would discuss all ongoing union-related issues with the other seven members of the branch executive committee. Tom's role included preparing the agenda for any meeting and recording all action points. In order to maintain branch unity and strength, the two of them would visit two of the college's programme areas each week to meet with their members for an hour. This allowed them to detect all rumblings in all areas of the college. Barry insisted that a newsletter must go out twice a term, and Tom was expected to draft at least two or three articles for each one. On top of this were the individual cases which periodically came his way, in which he might have to spend hours with a member who was accused of incompetence, or who was taking out a grievance against his manager for bullying. But Barry had further ways of extending the work beyond the official hours. He was also a member of the union's national and regional executives and thought it essential that Tom should find out where they stood in the context of the wider issues facing the sector. He would check his voicemail to hear, "Tom, it's Barry – there's a regional meeting on Saturday from ten till one, I'll see you in front of Boots at Kings Cross at nine-thirty"; or "Tom, it's Barry – there's a conference on strategy for defending pensions in a couple of weeks, I think we both need to be there, and I've sent our names to the national officer who's running it." Only once did Tom ever dare to refuse, claiming that he had a longstanding commitment to take his mother out for her birthday on the weekend of a demonstration to save a college in Essex from partial closure. This felt more justifiable than the real reason of having organised a key tennis match which he needed to win to avoid sinking into league three for the first time. Barry didn't like tennis.

The problem Tom found in dealing with Barry was not that he was fearsome or intimidating so much as that he was so enthusiastically committed that any refusal resulted in the sense of guilt one might have at disappointing a child. Barry wasn't naïve, but he had the belief normally associated with youthful idealism, and it was uncomfortable to know you were letting him down. It also generated an unpleasant self-awareness in Tom, a sense of the distance between his philosophical critique of policies which damage education and his readiness to oppose. He never quite knew which motive was the stronger, but every time he got up on Saturday morning to travel up the Northern Line for some excruciating trawl through the woes of London's secondary education system, he knew it wasn't virtue which lay behind it.

The eighteen minutes pass, and the second of his six new emails is from Barry.

```
Tom,
Dickie wants to meete. Droop inot my office
and lets hav a word.
Cheers,
Bary
```

Tom is relieved that his weekend remains intact, but he rolls his eyes at the thought of meeting with the principal in the first week of the academic year. Whenever Dickie asks to see them it is a bad sign. He has an unconcealed loathing for the union, which he must overcome for the regular fortnightly meetings. He never meets them more often unless he has to. Given all the jobs being cut elsewhere across London, Tom fears this may be the only reason he would summon them. Better to find out Barry's thoughts on this sooner rather than later, and he walks down the two flights of stairs to the English department.

Barry habitually sat in only two positions. The first was when he had his face four inches from his monitor as he belted out some message to the union members or a press notice so replete with misspellings that only a former journalist could have written it. The second was when the chair was in the reclining position as he marked the essays of his communications students or provided searing Marxist analysis of contemporary events. At sixty-two, he still retained hints of the physique of a former near-athlete who had failed a rugby league trial for his local professional team when he was seventeen. Now he never even mounted his exercise bike, but there was a smooth efficiency to his movements and no sagging excess visible on his face.

When Tom enters, he is playing with his reading glasses and smiling at the report he is reading on the BBC website about a Conservative donor caught by an undercover journalist advising her not only on how to set up an account in Cyprus but also offering to take her out for dinner to explain the details.

"Hi, right, let's go," says Barry in a Yorkshire accent uncorrupted by thirty years of life in west London.

Tom follows him out of the room, but instead of heading towards the union's office, they turn towards the management offices, and Tom stops him.

"We're going to see him now?"

"Why not? He said to come along for a quick chat just to sort out a couple of issues before term starts. Let's see what he wants."

"Since when is he this informal?"

"Never. That's why we need to see what's up."

They enter the outer office where four secretaries coordinate the meetings of the principal and the vice principal. This room is trying so desperately hard to look like a sophisticated office that it never does anything more than advertise its own cheapness. The unpleasant, hard-wearing carpets and the oak-effect furniture are home to four women whose dress sense is far more influenced by the casual indifference of the teachers than they realise. None of them ever achieves the business-like sharpness they seek.

Bella, Dickie's secretary, greets them and opens the door into the principal's office to tell him they have arrived. Tom can't hear the response, but she comes back out and has them sit down on the Ikea sofa for ten minutes before Dickie opens the door himself and asks them in. Tom isn't sure if this is a strategy to emphasise his power or if he just wants to give the impression of being busy. It never even occurs to Tom that there may be a genuine reason for the wait.

Dickie's expensive, tailored suit hangs remarkably well from the sloping shoulders of his five-foot-five-inch frame. Jacket and trousers taper neatly around the various bulges, almost hiding the improbably round potbelly. He asks them about their summer breaks and welcomes them back with all the conviction of someone who doesn't mean a word of what he says.

In two years of meetings with Dickie, Tom has only ever had one exchange which came close to relaxed. During a delay when Bella was hunting for a file, it came up that Tom was working through a box set of *The Sopranos*. Dickie had watched it all first time around on his new fifty-inch plasma set with his full Sky package, and they had swapped views on why it was so compelling. The goodwill lasted until Bella returned with the file and it emerged that Tom had correctly remembered an offer made at a governing body meeting in which Dickie had promised to include all the unions in the development of the college's new strategic plan. They realised this would mean allowing the people Dickie most hated to enter discussions over the future of an institution which he felt he possessed with the same degree of ownership as those expensive suits and his two homes. At the end of the meeting, in an apparently casual return to the subject of *The Sopranos*, Dickie talked about the subtlety and cleverness of the finale, providing a helpful interpretation to guide Tom through it.

The office door opens again and Sally Field walks in, pausing in the doorway. "Bella, please stop what you're doing for a moment and bring us some water."

She is rarely present at these meetings, but Tom loves it when she is. She had started twelve years earlier as Dickie's secretary, a Sarah Ferguson lookalike. Rumours began circulating after a couple of years, but final confirmation only came late one Friday night at The Garden, when Dan Corporal, the vice principal, was buying rounds of Jack Daniels for three heads of department. He had come to the outer office after receiving an email from Dickie saying that his budget for ESOL was to be cut, and one of the other secretaries told him to go straight in. He entered to find the office empty and was about to turn around and go out again when he heard a grunt of pain from the neat little ensuite, and he realised Dickie might be having a heart attack. He moved towards the bathroom but stopped on seeing events through a crack in the door. Sally was leaning over the sink, gripping each of the taps for dear life, as Dickie bounced back and forth behind her just as fast as his little legs would carry him. Dan's shock was soon succeeded by the panicky dilemma over whether he should quickly exit the office, even though the other secretaries had seen him, or stay and pretend he was unaware of events in the bathroom. This second option was compromised when he looked back in the direction of the bathroom, inadvertently glancing at the mirror just above the basin, and found himself staring straight into Sally's eyes as she gazed into the same mirror. For reasons he could not explain, he then sat down and waited. There was the sound of two people trying to dress quietly, some whispering, and the flush of the toilet.

Dickie then emerged, greeted Dan, and offered him the only increase in ESOL funding for any college in greater London in that academic year. In a letter to the *Education Guardian*, a senior union leader singled this out as an act of great humanity and foresight.

Sally moved from being secretary to head of personnel without ever wasting time on either relevant experience or appropriate qualifications. The full extent of the advertising for this new post was a card placed on the notice board in the personnel Portakabin. She was the only applicant, and Dickie chaired the interview panel.

Opinions vary over whether this promotion was a reward or a sign that Dickie was displeased when she started putting on weight. But whenever Tom has to sit through meetings filled with the tension of dealing with a man who despises him, he is always able to take refuge in imagining what must have been going through her mind when she looked into that mirror and saw Dan looking back. His amusement at this will soon be overwhelmed to a degree he would have believed impossible.

"I'd like to start with news which I think will be welcomed by all and which will be a relief to many. Psychology is no longer NTI. Nor are biology, engineering, and media studies. Indeed, there remains not a single subject at this college which we shall be obliged to formally describe as under 'notice to improve'. This is a tribute to the fine work of so many staff, and it vindicates the great faith senior managers have always shown in the middle managers and lecturers who deliver these crucial subjects."

Whenever Dickie speaks, he always gives the impression of trying to deliver some Churchillian address to the millions who hang on every word of the only man who can save them from peril. Yet the estuary accent and the pompous tone inevitably make him sound like the modest little man that he is, always slightly overreaching as he tries to find the words to give himself the credit he thinks he deserves. NTI is the latest means of trying to measure the quality of the college's performance in a neat, numerical return. If the pass rate in a subject falls too low, the college must write to the funding body to declare this. If performance does not rise above the minimum standard within two years, funding for the course will be reduced. This is intended to motivate staff to do a better job. In reality, everything carries on as before, but the college presents information differently in order to avoid any problems. Thus, if Dickie is smiling, it is partly because he has found some means of achieving this, but mostly because he wants everyone to know. It is tempting to deny him the pleasure, but they need to know, so Tom asks him how it has been done.

"Quite simply, we were being punitively harsh on ourselves. We were treating our AS exam results as the results of one-year courses, whereas this grossly distorts the true picture of our academic world."

"AS courses are one-year courses," Barry remarks.

"On the contrary, Barry. They last only from September to May, which Sally tells me is a mere nine months. Only when students move from AS into the second year of their course have they entered what will become a course which lasts over twelve months. Instead of counting our AS results, we have therefore entered the more appropriate results from our A2 courses, and these reveal that not one subject at Sandford is NTI."

At the end of the AS courses, all those who fail are told they cannot go into the second year, and all those who don't like the subject drop it anyway. The upshot is that virtually no one ever fails at the end of the second year. Using the second-year results will show results leaping from pass rates of around sixty percent to well over ninety. Psychology is in the same department as philosophy, and Tom shares a room with one of the teachers. He knows that their results have actually declined again, yet the Department of Education will see them as a model of improvement.

Barry mulls this as Dickie beams. They have a lot of members teaching all of the affected subjects, and funding cuts would raise the possibility of job losses. Getting out from under this threat by any means is welcome.

"Is this way of looking at it within the guidelines?"

"Barry, we have followed the guidelines religiously. We are clear. But there are also some other issues I wish to raise. Specifically, I wish to ensure we avoid any repeat of our photocopying shenanigans of last term."

One aspect of Dickie's commitment to the free market in education was to introduce an internal market into the college. This hasn't really affected the teaching side, as his policy has been simply to cram as many students as possible into every classroom, and they can in turn study anything they want for all he cares. No point in getting the departments to compete against each other if they can all have as many as they can fit in. But he felt there would be more scope on the administrative side of the college, so he broke up various parts of the college into autonomous business centres with their own budgets.

One of the centres was Procurement – the only part of the organisation permitted to purchase and distribute outside supplies of basic materials – and one of its cost-saving measures was to reduce the amount spent on paper by cutting supplies to the different academic departments. This was intended to make the latter use paper more sparsely. Instead, they started running out by Thursday afternoon of each week, and no one could produce any worksheets for Friday classes. The departments could buy more paper from Procurement out of their own budgets, but at three times the price you would pay in a shop.

Under pressure from teachers, the only solution which the heads of department could come up with was what Dickie is now raising. It was cheaper to get paper from Reprographics, but they couldn't buy it, as this would be procurement. So they had to take a blank piece of paper and have someone run off a thousand copies of it. Procurement tried to put an instant stop to this, but as Reprographics was a separate business centre enjoying an unexpected boost to its income, the process carried on for the final month of the academic year. Dickie refused to intervene as he wished the market to assert its authority, but when the Art department cancelled its entire order from Procurement in order to go exclusively with Reprographics' second-hand alternative, the college was heading towards the point at which it would soon be photocopying its entire supply of blank paper before sending it out to the teaching staff to be photocopied again. All of this was taking place without reducing the amount of paper being used, while massively increasing costs for additional ink for photocopying.

Dickie spreads his arms on the table. "I think we need common sense to win a victory for Sandford. I am going to increase the supply of paper for each department, but each lecturer will have his own code for photocopying, and each programme manager will be responsible for monitoring the use of each lecturer in their area. Serial offenders need to be spoken to, whilst the sensible majority will be able to continue on their responsible path."

"Very sensible," says Barry. In practice, this means nothing will happen.

The academic side of the college is divided into four departments, each of which has ten programme areas with a programme manager at the head of it. The four heads of department answer to the two vice principals, and these are all Dickie's people. They don't like him, but they rarely try any resistance. Those who do are summoned to his office to see him either on his own or with some more obedient soul such as Sally, and there is perhaps an hour of sneering cross-examination to identify the causes of their failure. But below head of department is union territory. Thirty-eight of the forty programme managers are members, and to devolve anything to them is to ensure that no one will face any undue sanctions. This is the closest Dickie has ever come to acknowledging defeat.

"One more issue must come before you. The governing body will meet tomorrow to discuss the building strategy." Up until a few years earlier, there had been the prospect of a steel-and-glass cube rising out of the car park and football pitch. This was now an expensive memory, with two million pounds in architects' and consultants' fees wasted before the government decided it needed new college buildings less than the country's financial institutions and ended all school building projects in favour of bank bailouts. So they were stuck in their leaky seventies block until the next boom came around to finance something they could all fit into. "I and the governors wondered if you might like to attend in order to discuss how we hope to repair and maintain Sandford's walls for the next generation."

If Dickie is inviting them, it means he is absolutely sure there is nothing of interest to be discussed, and he can benefit from the illusion of including the union in a key meeting without any danger that it might challenge the path he wants to take.

Barry draws a deep breath. "Will there be any discussions concerning the terms and conditions of employment at the college?"

"Barry, the discussion will be about maintenance."

"In which case, please thank the governors for their invitation, and tell them we would welcome attending future meetings when the issues are more directly related to the concerns of ordinary working people at this college."

"Barry, you're not being invited to join the governing body, but I will pass on the message." He usually manages to restrain himself because he can't bully the union in the way he is accustomed to dealing with his managers, but the combination of Barry refusing him with the suggestion of greater participation on the only body which has any real authority over him causes the tone to sharpen. "At any rate, I hope we can look forward to a year of cooperation and progress." He smiles broadly at them.

Meeting over. Sally's minutes will contain a pale imitation of what has been said, but as long as the substance of what affects the members is preserved, who cares? They go down to the union office, a coffee-stained cupboard between the staff toilets and the canteen. The radiator operates at sauna-like temperatures, or not at all, and the window looks directly onto one of the main arteries linking the humanities to the sciences.

"Fuckin' twerp," says Barry. "So pleased with himself at being clever enough to jiggle the figures you'd think he'd won the Nobel Prize for maths. Right, I think we should call a branch meeting to update people on the national initiative on pay and the local struggle for better London salaries. See if you can book the music centre for next Thursday."

Tom says nothing.

"What?"

"Why did he meet with us? All of this could have been done by email."

"Showing off. He likes to think he's clever, and the best people to prove it to are your worst enemies. Book the music centre for Thursday and set up a meeting of the branch executive committee for Wednesday so we can vote on strategy." He sees Tom is still uncomfortable. "Look, the price of freedom is eternal vigilance. I've a meeting with the national negotiators on Saturday, and I'll ask them if they know if anything's up. Now set up the branch meeting."

Maybe Barry is right, and it is only later in the day that it comes to Tom why he is suspicious. Dickie never smiles at them. He rarely smiles at anyone.

CHAPTER TWO

"Streatham Hill," she says.

"Why?"

"We can afford it. It's near Balham, which is gentrifying. It has good transport links and it has a high street."

"Is Streatham Hill part of Streatham?"

"Streatham is drug murders on ice. Streatham Hill is leafy roads with large Victorian houses, and the potential of being the next Clapham, but without the bankers."

"No tube."

"Clapham has the Northern Line. Worse than no tube, and it hasn't done them any harm."

"Where do you get all this 'potential to be the next Clapham' stuff from? Sounds like estate agent bollocks."

"Rightmove."

"They talk about drug murders on ice?"

"You have to read between the lines."

"So we might get to live next to somewhere which is next to somewhere nice."

Tom's problem with all this is not fear of taking on a mortgage but a horror at the effort it will require to start looking at places, arranging the finances, moving, decorating, and the countless other tasks he knows he will be required to perform. They have been in their current place for the eleven years since arriving back in the country. It is a near-perfect testimony to the traditional skills of Victorian house building. The windows may well be original, such is the ferocity of the wind blowing through them regardless of whether they are open or shut. In winter, each radiator will warm up a radius of about ten feet around itself but refuse to do any more. In the large lounge, the classic nineteen-seventies gas fire will augment the geriatric central heating so that visitors are also safe from hypothermia in the middle of the room. But anyone walking from the adjoining bedroom across the lounge to look out of the window will have to pass through up to four different temperature zones on the way.

They rent the semi-converted ground floor flat from the decent, old Irish gin queen who lives upstairs. Two or three times a month Tom has to go up, letting himself in with the key she has provided for such occasions, in order to lift her off the floor and guide her towards the bedroom. He can never tell if it's divine reward for years of confession or a heightened sense of self-preservation which survives the gallons she pours down herself, but she has never once fallen on her bottle. He also goes up once a month to pay the rent of five hundred pounds which she hasn't raised in all the years they've been there. The market would make them pay twice the amount for somewhere half the size. They don't much like the City types who line the rest of the street, but beggars can't be choosers. The problem is that the longer they stay, the more they find themselves literally papering over the cracks.

He puts his hands behind his head, and she rolls over in bed and lays her head on his chest.

He had met Sofia when they were both working at the same language school in Valencia. Tom was a full-time teacher, whereas Sofia worked only part-time in the recruitment office on a separate site. She took the job so that she could get the cheaper rates for employees wishing to study English, including the course which Tom ran for academic purposes. It emerged in one of the classes that he played tennis, and she approached him a couple of days later and suggested a match. She would always deny that she had pursued him, but he cared little. The long, dark, impossibly straight hair. The serious attitude. The nervous, polite manner. The careful preparation of essays on classic authors.

He had played women before and had already decided to focus more on just keeping the ball in play and to avoid at all costs humiliating her by playing as he would against men. When they warmed up, she looked quite well-coached, with the timing and footwork of someone who had had lessons when she was younger. On the opening point, he hit a second serve as his first, and she pushed the ball back so wide that he mishit his backhand into the net. On the second point, he hit another second serve after missing his first, and she pushed the ball straight back down the line for a winner. He then slammed down a first serve which she thundered straight back at him, causing him almost to trip as he tried to get the racket down to ground level to play a half-volley. She reeled off the first four games, in which she used a strategy of hitting with power only when he did. As this invariably resulted in instant defeat, Tom tried to move her around by carefully hitting into the corners. Her response was to use the same tactic but with immeasurably greater control. He found himself running back and forth along the baseline as she effortlessly peppered each corner of the court. "You're very good," he said at a changeover. "Thank you. You run very well," she replied without irony.

At four love down, he started hitting first and second serves as hard as he could. The first time he did it with a second serve, she was caught by surprise, and he aced her. He then hit two more big serves, both of which won him points. She thrashed straight winners of the next two but then hit a forehand into the net to give up her first game. She then began an arm-waving monologue in Valenciano in which she first asked herself how she could make such crass errors, and then answered by referring to her extreme idiocy. She didn't speak to him at the changeover and started bouncing around manically between each point, now hitting every shot with what seemed like steroid-driven force. He realised that up until his minor triumph *she* had focused on avoiding *his* humiliation. Losing a game had resulted in a corresponding memory loss of this noble aim, and she reeled off the next eight games with barely the loss of a point. They showered and had a glass of wine in the small pavilion of the neat little five-court club. She told him how, as a child, she had trained at a tennis academy when they were handing out scholarships to local kids. She rose to number three in Valencia for her age group but started getting rolled over by the older girls when she entered the national junior tournaments. By the time she was seventeen, she realised she would never make it as a pro and started to play only for fun and study harder. Within an hour, they had made love for the first time.

The excitement of such an illicit relationship was mitigated by the concern not to be found out, but not by any sense of professional ethics. This meant the thrill of rolling around in his studio during siesta before seeing each other in the afternoon class. Were the relationship to be discovered, it was difficult to know the consequences. He knew it was not permissible for him to be sleeping with a student, but such principles were weakened within the world of English language teaching abroad, where younger, foreign teachers taught older, foreign students. He used to get drunk with his director of studies, and they liked the fact that he was fluent in Spanish. Finding qualified teachers at short notice in the middle of a course was a headache these private schools would rather avoid, so switching Sofia into a different class, or even a blind eye, would have been the more probable outcome.

In any event, her completion of the course meant that their precautions could be set aside, and he was just another English language teacher going out with a former student. It also opened up the discussion about where to go. Sofia had a degree in European literature from Salamanca and had taken the EAP course to raise her English to the point where she might do a graduate degree in England. Tom loved the un-London pace of life in Valencia, but he could never escape the sense of not advancing. At thirty-one, ten years Sofia's senior, he found himself with someone who was moving forward in a way he was not. He had completed a joint degree in Spanish and philosophy at a former poly, a choice prompted by the double fact that Spanish had been his least awful A-level and that the admissions officer handling clearing enquiries had told him there were still places available on this combined course for people with his level of success. The shaming failure of his A-levels meant he worked harder at university, and he also found himself unexpectedly drawn into the philosophical half of his degree.

He mulled the option of a Master's degree but only committed when a tutor told him the University of Valencia was to open up an MA in analytic philosophy taught in English, and would be offering scholarships for suitable candidates. He was drawn almost entirely by the thought of returning to live in Spain, where he had spent the third year of his BA. Going back as a student would also help postpone the horror of work, and he found himself applying to an institution unaware of the lowly status of his alma mater and facing a field of competition populated largely by phenomenologists with second-rate English. It was the first and only scholarship he ever won. He just about managed to forge his way through the courses on Frege, Russell, and Wittgenstein, and found to his relief that he could choose a course in philosophy of the emotions as an alternative to the one in mathematical logic taken by every other student on the degree. His relief was only exceeded by that of the newly appointed lecturer, whose course could now run with Tom having signed up. They worked their way through Peter Goldie's book, and scales dropped from his eyes as he was taken not only with the theory but with the style.

The two years of studying for his MA were followed by five teaching English, the last of which was spent living with Sofia. But this latter period also brought on the affliction of that same fear which comes to so many who live abroad in their twenties. There is always that sense of delaying the more serious existence at home rather than truly evading it. When Sofia told him she had found a Masters course at Birkbeck in Victorian studies, he was relieved at being compelled to move on. He also felt uncomfortable at the thought of living with someone so many years younger who was en route to overtaking him academically. Tom contacted the same tutor from the University of Valencia who had schooled him in the emotions and who had now risen to become a professor with contacts at King's, whom he emailed even before he sent his reference in support of Tom's PhD application.

Tom went back in July to find a flat, and a neighbour of his mother's told him about the one in Clapham South which they now rented. Sofia moved over in late August, and they both started studying part-time in October. They also became colleagues again, with Tom teaching English and Sofia Spanish in one of the language schools in South Kensington. Three years on, and they caught a break which rocketed them out of graduate-student, hourly-paid, seasonal-work poverty and into part-time, public-sector-low-pay-with-a-pension poverty.

Tom saw a job at Sandford College advertised on a notice board at King's, asking for someone to teach A-level philosophy. He called and was asked for an interview the next day, where he was up against a logic nerd with no teaching qualification, who had seen the same ad. He had to work off his one week's notice in South Ken and was made full-time a couple of years later, just as he completed his doctorate. Sofia got a part-time post in the Birkbeck Language Centre and then moved up to full-time when the centre expanded. She was now earning more than Tom and halfway through her own doctorate.

They started going on holiday three times a year, working in a week at Easter, another at the beginning of July, and a couple more at the end of August. This came on top of the visits to Sofia's mother in Valencia. Instead of last-minute package deals on Greek islands which were undiscovered because there was nothing there to discover, it was get-away-from-it-all in a national park in Portugal with a hire car and regional wines. They bought better clothes, and he bought better tennis rackets. They had started together in London earning twelve pounds an hour, claiming housing benefit when the language teaching dried up in the winter. Now they are full-time, permanent, safe, and still paying the same five hundred pounds a month in rent.

He knows that she must have carried out countless web searches across various parts of London. "Have you found some possibilities already?"

"Thirty-five. But only twenty-six are west of the high road and sound as if they need only a bit of redecorating. We can see the first three on Saturday morning."

"I think I'm playing a league match."

"I checked your online bookings. You don't play till three."

In the space of twenty minutes, he has moved from long-term tenant to first-time buyer. He has partially succeeded in drawing Sofia into his own world of minimal effort, but once she has decided that certain actions are necessary, it becomes a practical impossibility to slow any progress without risking a dispute of such monumental proportions that it is more attractive to concede.

"Ok, set it up. But only three appointments, and I want to be back here by two."

She kisses him, and he rises to prepare for the lightest of Friday routines. Preparation means showering and dressing. Lightness means only two sessions, with the first at eleven-twenty, and the second at two. On days when Barry doesn't snag him for a meeting, he can finish at three-ten and be back home for four. Alternatively, he can mark the rare essays he sets and spend a night drinking at The Garden and eating at The Empire of the Mughals. Living in Clapham has the advantage of proximity to the Junction, from where trains run to Sandford every ten minutes.

He has long since stopped using the quiet compartment, finding it no less noisy than the others but made more irritating by the fact that any invasion is not only unpleasant but ignores rules specifically designed to protect people like him. This retreat came some time after the earlier one of no longer politely asking people to reduce their sound levels. Some would do it, but refusal made the noise particularly humiliating. On one occasion, he thought the woman opposite was listening to an exceedingly long voicemail on her speaker, before realising it was a fire-and-brimstone sermon by a fast-talking saviour. When Tom asked her if she would mind using her headphones, she looked from side to side in genuine disbelief and told him he was to burn in Hell. This at least had anecdotal value over the dinner table.

On another occasion, he had the prime seat at the front of the upper deck on the bus and turned to ask someone halfway back if he would mind turning down his Nirvana. "I fuckin' would akchullee." The beautifully concise reply came with a fixed stare of such malign intensity that it was clear any further requests would be treated less sympathetically. This lover of public music then began an impassioned speech to the two friends sitting near him about how much he objected to this sort of intrusion. "I fuckin' hate twats like that. Always sticking their noses in where they ain't won'id." He then increased the volume. "Oy cunt! Can yu hear aw'right?" The next fifteen minutes passed with his heart racing at techno speed. Mercifully, the three got off without the anticipated final flourish, but enough was enough.

What had struck him about both these responses was the reversal of values in which his attitudes, which would once have been considered an expression of conventional moral rights, had become an outrageous intrusion. Now he either resigns himself to the surround sound banality of mobile-speak or retreats into the world of podcasts and music downloads. He is more or less used to it at this point, and under today's assault from an architect's call to say he will be late, he simply turns to *Seize the Day*.

He arrives at his office with enough time to start the computer, read through any emails, and avoid the temptation of deleting any from Barry. While the PC is warming up, he will prepare the extracts he is going to teach, guaranteeing time to reflect upon homeownership in the relatively restrained atmosphere of the classroom.

His office was originally a tiny one belonging to the departmental secretary, with enough space to squeeze in just a handful of lecturers. Only Mike, his fellow philosophy teacher, is there when he arrives, so no need to ask Alan Frost, the head of religious studies, to pull his chair in so he can reach his desk.

Mike started at the same time as Tom. A logician, but not the one who had turned up for interview on the same day as Tom, and without the anti-social skills which disqualified such people from teaching anywhere outside the country's top universities. Both had responded to the same job ad and then moved up to full-time when the only other philosophy teacher got a head-of-department job in Bristol. Whereas Tom's failure to land a university post was a predictable consequence of his failure to publish more than the one article which had come out of his doctoral thesis, Mike's case was more curious. His record of a first degree in maths and philosophy from Cambridge, followed by a doctorate in the metaphysics of maths at King's, was practically a blueprint for success in a field where logic was revered to roughly the same degree as was once the case with the sayings of Old Testament prophets. Yet here he is, teaching Descartes to sixteen-year-olds instead of delivering conference addresses in New York.

Mike's vice is a perverse species of incontinence. The standard route to an academic post is via publications in peer-reviewed journals and references from a well-placed supervisor. The latter is not an issue, but when Mike begins to write he analyses each proposition for any conceivable response. Each one is then anticipated in the next round of claims, and the next series of possible counter claims emerges. The problem is that he sees necessary new lines of attack everywhere, and the most modest claim requires pages of defence against imagined critics, which in turn open up still more possible weaknesses. The top journals will consider articles with a maximum of six thousand words, somewhat shorter than the minimum of forty thousand which Mike tends to belt out on topics often viewed as relatively narrow in focus. On one occasion, he asked Tom to look over a draft which he had edited down to twenty-five thousand words and from which he hoped to cut out a further fifteen thousand. Tom agreed out of sympathy and found to his horror that only a third of it was in English. The opening line was: "Cantor presents us with, $Q(k) = \{1/n1 + \ldots + 1/nk \mid n1, \ldots, nk \geq 1\}$." He tried reading only the English parts and suggested removing some of the conjunctions. Mike hasn't shown him anything since.

His more interesting idiosyncrasy is a borderline paranoia concerning the levels of danger he incurs whenever he goes out with women. Whatever the root cause, his condition is a glorious triumph of emotion over reason. In so far as there is any sort of rationalisation available, it seems as though one former girlfriend was the daughter of someone who may have been hooked up to the Latvian mafia. As she lay in bed beside him, she would speak of how her father took seriously the importance of traditional womanly virtue, how he was reluctant to let her travel abroad for fear she may be corrupted, and how many heavily-armed ex-military types he employed at his import/export company on the docks. When Mike refused to make the trip east, even with the promise that her father would arrange an academic post for him at the State Electronics University of Riga, she swore that her family would never forgive him for using her in the way he had. Two weeks later a car pulled out from its parking place as he was coming out of his flat, with driver and passenger peering at him before accelerating away. From then on every car which pulled out was an object of suspicion. This often made life in London pretty heavy going.

His concern was expressed most spectacularly when he went to meet his next girlfriend at her offices off Bishop's Avenue. As he passed through the revolving doors, he looked down to see a beam of red light hovering over his heart and dived to evade the sniper's bullet. Looking back from the safety of the marble floor, he realised the light fell upon all those entering the building in order to activate the rotating doors. He picked himself up, approached the reception desk, and asked the dumbstruck Polish girl if she would be good enough to tell his latest belle that he had arrived.

When Tom sits down, Mike is banging away on his keyboard, the only way to ensure that striking a key will result in a letter appearing on the monitor. He doesn't even look up when he says, "Barry called, wants to meet for a couple of hours at three-thirty."

"Oh, for fuck's sake!"

Then Mike raises his head and smiles with satisfaction. Part of his appeal is that his own irrational fears give him a brilliant insight into those of others, and his naïve, boyish accent gives him the air of honesty which makes this sort of deception impossible even for Tom to discern. They share the four first-year and two second-year philosophy classes, with each of them focusing on his preferred areas. Tom teaches ethics and philosophy of art to the first years, while Mike teaches theories of knowledge and metaphysics. In the second year, Tom teaches Aristotle's *Ethics* as the obligatory text, while Mike does philosophy of science, and they split a philosophy of mind course between them.

Tom's first class is a first-year course, and he retrieves the overhead transparencies from his philosophy of art folder and makes copies of some extracts from Tolstoy. He has been planning to switch all his materials into an electronic format, but only half the classrooms have computers, and half of them are not reliably connected to the digital projectors, so he is better off with the humming overhead projectors as a primitive but reliable means of technological support. Most of the students will be seeing one for the first time, with their doubts tempered by the amusement of being taught using antiques. Well into the twenty-first century, the college is still using chalk, and if the manufacturers stop making replacement parts for the OHPs, then almost the entire teaching staff will return to simply writing stuff on the board for students to copy down. Tom typically employs the classic technique of the piece of paper covering most of the text, followed by the slow reveal. As he rarely bothers to look over the material he is about to teach, even he doesn't know what's coming.

His week finishes with 2Phil1, and he will use the same combination of OHTs, extracts, and discussion questions as in all his other classes. Friday afternoon always means more discussion and less writing. When he enters the room, he sees Joe's legs aren't moving, and he wonders if he is on something new. Then they start up and continue for the remaining seventy minutes of the class.

Tom plugs in the OHP and carefully places the piece of paper over it to ensure it is ready for later. Still, it is odd to have a class with so few students. This is an anomaly thrown up by the drive to stuff as many into each class as possible. The rooms are built for a maximum of eighteen students, so college policy is that the largest class can be no more than twenty-four. It becomes really tough to fit them in after that. Since first-year results in philosophy were better than expected, meaning more students made it into the second year, the section manager had no choice but to open up another set once student numbers passed the threshold of two dozen. The result is a small, additional class for those who couldn't squeeze into the first.

Tom looks up at his students and wonders what it must be like to teach in a private school and to know nothing more than this. "The best way to understand Aristotle's discussion of moral virtue is to start with his idea of the human soul. He claims it is divided into three parts. The lowest part, which he calls the vegetative, is concerned with nutrition and growth and does not interest him in this text. The middle part is called the appetitive, and this is broadly composed of emotion and desire. The highest part is the rational one, which distinguishes us from all other living beings. The rational part is further divided into two parts. We have theoretical reason, which aims at discovering eternal and unchanging truths about the world. And we have practical reason, which aims at discovering how we should live."

A hand goes up. Laura sits next to Maya, but they rarely seem close. She missed almost a third of his classes last year, and Tom sent four letters home as part of a campaign to remove her from philosophy. But she failed two of her first-year courses, and her C in philosophy was the higher of her two passes. "Problems at home." Without philosophy she couldn't do a second year, and because the college was funded by the head, she had to remain. She wasn't the annoying type who chatted and texted like most of the serial non-attenders, but Tom resented endlessly having to remain after work to provide copies of material she had missed the previous week. When Mike set up a philosophy department website and uploaded all of their materials, he no longer had to do this, and he disliked her less from then on. He didn't know what her problems were, and no flashing red flag appeared next to her name on the college's system, so whatever they were, Learning Support didn't know either. This probably meant that it was either no more than a shitty home life, or else something minor enough for her to be able to conceal it from her previous school and this one. She didn't speak once in class last year. Well, fresh start and all that. "When Aristotle talks about a soul, is it in the same way as Plato? I mean, does it leave the body when you die? Is it a sort of religious soul?"

"Aristotle's notion of the soul is more like a biological concept. Think of it as a description of the way in which each species is internally organised such that it can function properly. He thinks even plants have souls, and his views are therefore very distant from both Plato and most religious thinkers."

Maya now questions him. "So he agrees with Plato that reason is superior to emotion and that moral goodness is therefore based in reason."

"He implies at the end of the text that a life of pure philosophy is the best possible life for a human, but his account of moral goodness comes in his theory of moral virtue, and here he differs dramatically from Plato. For Aristotle, moral virtue means that you have had a good upbringing, which means in turn that the middle part of the soul, your emotions, have been trained such that you feel the right way at the right time for the right reasons. For example, you feel sympathy for those who deserve it, and you act in ways which are consistent with those feelings. So if a virtuous person entered the room and saw Laura lying on the floor in obvious difficulty, she would be moved to help because she believes that this is the right thing to do. This is because she has learned to feel this way in such circumstances."

"But aren't some people naturally good or bad?" Miles is the only black student in the class. He travels from Peckham, taking three trains, and arrives for the nine o'clock sessions before half the locals who walk. He is never on time, just not as late.

"He thinks that some people may suffer from some sort of natural disorder, but for virtually all of us you are born with the capacity to be either virtuous or non-virtuous, and you will develop in one way or the other depending on how you are brought up. If you have the right upbringing, then doing the right thing will be obvious. If you have a poor upbringing, then you have little chance of ever seeing the world as the virtuous person does."

"But I think if I came in and saw Laura lying on the ground I would help her, but I wouldn't have some sort of automatic reaction. I'd do it because I'd want her to help me next time round."

Joe looks up. "All right, let's say Tom scooped out one of her eyes and shoved his dick in the socket. Wouldn't you just instantly think, 'That's wrong!'"

"Oh my God!" Tom shouts, but the exchange between the two students continues as if Tom hadn't spoken. Miles is amused by the strength of the counter-example but will not give ground. "No, I'd just think 'I hope he won't do it to me.'"

"Come on, man. There's shit which is just wrong, and you don't stop and think if you can get something out of it later down the line."

Tom raises his arms and shouts at Joe. "Can we not use that sort of language and these sorts of examples, please."

"I was just trying to make your point for you."

"Thank you, but can we try to use more moderate language?" His struggle against bad language has weakened over the years, as it has moved so much into mainstream vocabulary that he has even found himself unthinkingly telling a student to 'fuck off' when he turns up late yet again, with no homework, no pen, no paper. But you have to draw the line somewhere.

Tom tries to bring the conversation back to moral virtue, but he now finds it difficult to shift from his mind the image of himself with his dick in Laura's otherwise empty eye socket. He avoids looking at her and hopes that neither she nor Maya will ask a question.

"The best way to understand how we acquire the virtues is to think of Aristotle's own analogy with a skill. No one is born knowing how to play a musical instrument, but we can learn after repeated practice, and it eventually becomes like second nature. This means that just as the skilled musician can pick up and play an instrument without thinking, so the virtuous person will react in the right way when circumstances demand it."

He hands out an extract from Book II and decides to string this out so that he can avoid the risk of any further discussion. When the class finishes, Laura stays behind after the others have left, but says nothing when he asks if there is a problem.

Three-ten. End of the week. No marking to do. As all the courses he is teaching are ones he's taught before, no preparation either. Time to check the *Guardian* for the latest DVD releases to pick out a couple to download for the weekend. This plan is erased when he enters his office to find Barry sitting in his chair, engaged in an impossibly serious exchange with Mike and Alan Frost. Barry looks up at him. "Better read this."

Tom looks at the email which is open on his computer.

```
Dear Colleague,

Sandford faces a challenge, and I am writ-
ing to inform you of the measures we are
taking and the policies we are implementing
to address this challenge.
```

As you know, we all must work in a building which is not fit for purpose. We had hoped that new government funding would allow us to erect a replacement for the current one, but this is no longer a hope to which we can cleave, and it is not feasible to avoid the unavoidable truth that we must find other means to provide for our own future needs and those of our students. We must now make some hard choices. In light of this, the governing body has authorised me to begin a round of cost-saving measures which will allow us to carry out essential works on our existing premises.

These measures must be ambitious enough to permit us to develop a modern site, and realistic enough such that the college remain in a financially sound state. I regret to say that we cannot achieve this with the staffing complement we currently have, nor with the relatively generous salaries which we now pay. I must therefore inform you that I and other senior managers will be drawing up plans for a restructuring of our staff which will involve a leaner workforce with a more flexible salary scale suited to a more austere set of circumstances.

I am aware that this may cause concern, but we are not in a position in which we can simply stand still, and if we are bold now, we can secure a future for this great college of which we can all be proud.

I will provide you with regular updates on our progress, and I shall be seeking meetings with representatives of staff associations in order to discuss these matters further. This will be a difficult time, but we are in this together, and I believe we

```
will emerge a stronger college at the end
of it.
Richard Kilman, BA
Principal
Sandford College
```

Barry looks at him. "He left half-an-hour before this was sent out. Said he had to go to a meeting with the local director of education to discuss the changes. Cowardly fucker didn't want to be around, and he won't give us a meeting until Tuesday evening."

Tom looks back at the email. Well, no longer any need to go flat-hunting at the weekend.

CHAPTER THREE

There is an enduring myth that unions are aggressive, rebellious, and unrealistic, and here is a myth which has fewer grains of truth than most. In reality, they are defensive, conservative, and pragmatic. Whilst there may have been a time when there was a greater bullishness about their ability to forge a workers' utopia using the stick of strike action, such a time, if it existed, has long passed. The constant of mass unemployment, layers of legislation, the crumbling of factories, and a steady, almost imperceptible ebbing of any belief in what any government will ever aim for, has left a shell of ultra realists who specialise exclusively in clinging to what remains of what used to be.

Nietzsche observed that the ultimate symbol of victory for Christian morality over the empire which used to crush it was that the Catholic pope sat in Rome. In two thousand and three, the British unions helped organise the largest demonstration in history when they marched on Valentine's Day to prevent a modern Christian's crusade. Two years into the war, they funded the campaign which returned him to power because he was less awful than the alternative. What made this defeat even worse was the crystalline, self-conscious awareness of it. Unlike the Romans, the unions never converted. They suffered instead the knowledge of needing to support their least dangerous opponent.

The irony barely concealed by the myth of aggressive unions is that they fight against managers who are the true revolutionaries, for whom goodness means breaking what is there to squeeze ever more out of those beneath them. The modern hero is the reformer, the moderniser, and the anti-heroes are those forces of conservatism which cling for dear life to jobs, pensions, and a longed-for dignity.

When Tom read Dickie's email, he was struck by how, even as he informed his staff that he wished to crush them, the planned misery of others was transformed into a testimony to his own virtues, his inhumanity into a symbol of strength. Yet this could not conceal a smallness which made him feel that this man was simply not someone who could defeat them.

There is a constant feeling that Dickie's viciousness cannot mask a profound stupidity, and this is fortified by a sense that the union is strong enough to beat him. UCL Sandford is starting out with a series of advantages which make self-defence highly practical. It is organised over a single site, and it takes never more than two to three minutes to see any member. They are in London, which means easy access for regional and national officials who come armed with advice and experience going far beyond those of the locally elected officers who receive four hours a week off their timetable to do all the union work which comes their way. Two hundred and seventy of the three hundred and fifteen lecturers are members, and whilst many joined on the off-chance that they may need protection from a bullying manager or a vengeful student, fending off redundancy will radicalise even the mildest among them. Within four days of the principal's email sixteen more lecturers have joined.

They face two disadvantages. All colleges were removed from the control of local authorities in the nineties, and power now resides in the hands of the principal and a governing body composed of volunteers from the local community, all vetted by Dickie before they join. If he follows the law, he can do anything as long as the governors back him. When the local MP, a junior minister at the time, was invited to speak at the branch's annual general meeting, Dickie had him marched up to his office by two of the security guards to interrogate him about his reasons for being there.

The second impediment to success is the supremely democratic manner in which a local union operates. All key decisions must be passed by the entire branch before any significant move forward. This often makes progress frustratingly slow against a dictatorship within which instant decisions are handed down to lieutenants who obey without question.

The key now is to establish the details of Dickie's plan of attack and to rain down a shitstorm of such intensity that he will compromise. Even from the start, the aim is to limit the damage rather than preserve the status quo.

Barry has called a meeting of the branch executive committee for five on Monday evening, anticipating that it might run so late that a morning meeting would be insufficient. This should also give him time to alert the regional and national officers, ensuring that they can start offering up some initial advice which he can then pass on to the others. The meeting with Dickie is set for two-thirty on Tuesday, and he has given them only an hour. There is not to be any discussion, just a few more details of what he has decided. The union will be holding a branch meeting on Thursday at which they are guaranteed a large turnout. Barry and Tom will then be able to give out further information and set out an initial strategy for resistance.

Barry told Tom to cancel his Monday afternoon class so they can meet before they see the other members of the branch executive committee. As Tom enters the union office, Barry is on the phone with the regional officer. He gets rid of him as soon as Tom comes in.

"Right, Colin Preston will be at Thursday's branch meeting. That's good. Immediately gives the impression that you're part of a wider group that's ready to support you." He looks at Tom before speaking again. "Have you ever done this before? A local dispute, I mean."

"No."

"Listen. If we are to win, it's large numbers of people acting in unison for a long period of time, especially with a wanker like Dickie. In order to pull that off we have to be absolutely decisive, and we have to look absolutely united. I don't care how big a twat you think I am, you never say anything in public which suggests we disagree. We hammer out what line we take between us and then we both stick to it."

"Does that include the way we act with the BEC?"

The BEC includes Tom and Barry, who have authority by virtue of being the branch's negotiators, as well as seven others local officers elected to more junior positions. Each of these carries a maximum of one or two hours a week of remission. Many don't even bother to turn up regularly to the weekly meetings, but if you have only an hour a week and Barry takes up forty-five minutes of it with a lecture on dialectics, then non-attendance is understandable.

"They will look to us for the lead, and we have to give it them. That doesn't mean we don't listen, but we have to start every meeting with a clear idea of what direction we want to go in. If it changes because of what we all discuss, fine. But everyone, the BEC included, has to feel that there's strong leadership which is worth fighting for and which is capable of winning."

Barry invariably treads the line between clear-minded practicality and terrible cliché, but the latter never offends because one always has the sense that the former is present in sufficient force. The division of labour that the two of them have agreed on is that Barry will rouse the troops and Tom will provide analysis of what the union can expect and how they might respond. This suits them both. Barry sees all disputes in purely psychological terms. They are not won by a management with greater power on its side or by a union with greater numbers. The outcome is determined by who is tougher, and if the UCL is to win here, it must be because enough of them are ready to outlast the enemy.

Six of the remaining seven members of the BEC turn up, with one unable to as she has to pick her daughter up from nursery. Barry immediately launches into the need for constantly giving the impression of strength, of belief and of confidence. If they are well-organised and remained committed, then their weight of numbers can prevent more or less any policy from being implemented. But maintaining commitment over months is going to be the key challenge. Dickie need only amble carefully towards his destination, knowing that in the end his teachers have to work. The union will need to break his stride by making life so uncomfortable that he will falter. Barry turns to Tom for an initial series of ideas on how to proceed.

"His email suggests he wants to do two things. He wants to make some people redundant and cut the pay of others. We don't know how many or how much, and he may not even know himself at this stage. We're in September, and it probably won't be until next May that he gets rid of people. That way he'll have plenty of staff running out the door to take up new jobs, and if he's lucky he may get away with no redundancies, which is cheaper for him. We know he wants a better building, but we don't know how much he plans on spending or exactly what he has in mind. He's probably counting on cutting a good deal with some major builder who needs the work."

"Is it legal for him to decide to do this without some sort of formal consultation?" Jim Hollander is the representative for middle managers. He has been at the college since it was created in the late seventies and takes the same train as Tom each morning.

"It's legal for him to announce that he wants to make redundancies, but he has to engage in formal consultation after he's announced his aim. The upside for us is that we will have plenty of time to stop him. We think that there are four different lines of attack we have to use. Only the governing body can overrule him, and even if they're mostly his people, we have to start chipping away at them. We need to get to parents to tell them he wants to wreck the college their children are at, which will be a big deal for the first-year students who are still planning on being around for an education in what's left of the place next year. We need to have a press campaign. We're thinking of something along the lines of 'Greedy, overpaid, little fat man slaughters innocent teachers and destroys education.' If we can liken him to bankers or MPs who fiddle expenses, it will help win public support."

He hesitates before continuing. "We also need to think in terms of strike action. We've spoken to some of the officers at other branches, and they recommend starting with negotiations, and if they fail then moving to one-day strikes once or twice a month. They reckon that on average management will wish to negotiate a settlement after a maximum of three strikes. Apparently, there's a tendency for people not to realise just how much they hate it when we come out. Looks like a general failure of management if you let things get that far."

After this, each person is given responsibility for working on each strand of the proposed defence, with Tom and Barry focusing on the possible strike action and the press campaign. Tom has moved from a state of disbelief on reading the initial email to fear of what it might mean to a sense of irrational optimism generated by Barry's rhetoric and the unqualified anger of all those around him.

When he stands on the train platform on his way home, he finds himself near a group who have been in a physics staff meeting. "He can't cut any more science posts unless he cuts student numbers, but then what would be the purpose of a better building? It will have to be jobs in areas where there are small classes already."

One of the perverse aspects of these developments is that almost all of the normal activity in the college has to continue as if nothing had changed. All teachers have to come in to teach all of their classes, set work, mark it, arrange trips and send letters to the parents of difficult students. Anyone turning up to observe what takes place inside a classroom would be unaware of any change to normal life. Yet in offices, the canteen, in corridors, every moment becomes either focused on what is to happen or else comes to feel like a short-lived escape from it. The largely unconscious sense of security which had obtained until just a few days ago has been replaced by an invasive feeling of instability, in which no one yet knows what awaits them, but everyone knows that whatever is coming is worse than what they have. One feature of this is that, whereas the classroom used to be a locus of pressure, it has now become the most effective relief because it forces everyone to think and talk of something else for at least seventy minutes.

When Tom enters the room for his nine o'clock session on Tuesday morning, he finds only Maya there. The other four arrive over the next eight minutes. The college rule is that students cannot enter class if they are ten minutes late. There is a train from Clapham Junction which arrives at Sandford Station at eight fifty-three, meaning that those travelling out from the centre can just make the ten-past-nine deadline. Students never heed the request to take an earlier train. In the days when half the college's students received an education maintenance allowance of thirty pounds a week, those who travelled furthest were often there first because they needed the money to pay for their train fares, and if they missed any class, they would lose the money for that week. The year after the EMA disappeared, attendance for the first class of the day dropped forty percent. When Tom sees all five students he cannot believe it.

Joe is the last to come in. He offers the formal, meaningless apology which guarantees entry and sits down next to Miles. A big smile spreads across his face. "Tom, what do you say to a Sandford teacher with a job?" He pauses for effect. "Over here please, waiter."

The laughter is initially muffled as no one knows yet whether this is a possible source of humour for the potential victims. But Joe's sheer, sincere naïveté makes it impossible even for Tom not to smile. "You'd better hope he keeps me on, because no one else will take you."

Joe was removed from one of his first-year classes for serial non-attendance, and his two passes at the end of the year meant he could only take two second-year courses. If he were removed from one of them, he would have to leave the college, and one of his English teachers already sent a letter home in the first week after each of his two mobile phones went off in the same class.

"All right, we spoke last time of how one acquires the moral virtues. Let us now take a specific example. Turn to your neighbour and ask how we should define courage."

Various mumbles. He overhears Joe discussing with Miles the benefits of strike action in terms of additional holiday. Joe sees the stare. "What are we supposed to be doing?"

"Ask Miles if he knows what courage is."

"No chance, Tom. He gets moist if the train is crowded."

Like many of the terms his students employ, Tom can only understand by assessing the context. He assumes 'moist' is this year's term for 'scared'.

Tom looks away in defeat. "Maya, what is courage?" Always most effective to start with the stronger students as they are most likely to have a response which will generate intelligent discussion. Equal opps training suggested he should not be selecting smart, white middle-class girls each time he starts a conversation, but given she is a nutter, then surely one could argue this is a form of being inclusive.

"Well, we thought it means acting in such a way that you overcome fear."

"Very good. So overcoming fear seems to be part of our understanding of courage. Now, is the person who runs into a burning building to save a child when there is no chance of success acting bravely?"

Miles looks at him. "If he's putting his life in danger, and he's scared, then it's brave but stupid."

"Aristotle argues it is stupid but not brave. Each virtue is what he calls a mean and falls between two vices. The person who acts without hope of success is not brave but rash. The person who runs away at the first sign of danger is a coward. The person who overcomes fear and acts in such a way that a good outcome is practically possible is truly courageous."

Now Maya raises her hand. "If these are called moral virtues, then does that mean that only morally good people could have them? Let's say someone is a powerful dictator, and he stands up to dangerous threats against his power when he could flee. Surely, that's courage, but the dictator isn't good."

"Ultimately, I think Aristotle must deny this is courage. He claims that the moral virtues are those capacities which help us to lead a flourishing life, and if we assume that the life of a dictator involves crushing others, then it cannot be a flourishing one. Such a life rules out fulfilling ourselves as social beings who need good relations with others. Genuine friendship, for example, is necessary for the best life, and the kind of people you're talking about must always live in suspicion and fear of those around them. He also argues that virtuous actions are those which a wise person would choose, and no wise person would choose to be a dictator."

Joe has been drawing for the duration of this conversation, but now looks up. "You said last time that in order to be virtuous you have to be brought up the right way. Does that mean that if you have the wrong upbringing, you will always be a coward?"

"Aristotle himself suggests this is the case, but most modern Aristotelians are unhappy with this claim. It would mean that we could not hold people responsible for their actions, as it is not ultimately their fault that they have been raised in such a way that they cannot understand the wrongness of what they do. If we take the example of the dictator, we hold him responsible, but we can do so only if we believe he is capable of somehow overcoming a poor upbringing. The best explanation of our intuitions on this would appear to be that, as we are all rational, we are all capable of recognising that certain forms of action are not acceptable and alter our behaviour despite our inclinations."

The third person in the female triumvirate, which includes Maya and Laura, is Amrit. She has moved to an expensive-looking hairstyle which may or may not have always been hidden beneath the veil she wore throughout her first year. Her concentration span is shorter than Joe's despite the absence of any obvious chemical explanation. She has made her way through her philosophical studies by copying, memorising, and reproducing effectively enough to secure a C. She now asks her first question of the year. "Why can't staff here spell?"

"What are you talking about?"

"Look at them posters."

In order to create a more philosophical atmosphere for the rooms in which most of their classes are taught, Tom and Mike asked the department's administrator to print off pictures of a series of philosophers and pin them to the wall. Rather annoyingly, she missed out the first 's' in 'Descartes', and Mike wrote it in by hand.

"It's a common error to misspell Descartes' name if you're not used to it."

"What about that other guy?"

She is pointing to the picture of John Stuart Mill, and Tom sees that the second 'l' has mutated into an 'f'.

The sniggering can only mean it is sexual, but Amrit persists heroically in pursuit of understanding. "Was 'Milf' his real name?"

More laughter, and it is Maya of all people who provides enlightenment. "'MILF' stands for 'mum I'd like to fuck'."

Any reference to sex makes it almost impossible to recover any focus for a class which still has five minutes to run. Tom considers briefly how he might bring the discussion back to courage but gives up. "We shall be covering the virtue of temperance in a later class. Prior to that you can demonstrate a more serious form of knowledge about the world by writing an essay on Aristotle's account of virtue, using the specific example of courage. To be submitted one week from today. Go."

CHAPTER FOUR

Tom and Barry know they will be kept waiting. They may even know before Dickie that this is what he is going to do. But the irritation brings with it a sense of satisfaction that his predictability gives them an advantage in a contest where he starts the stronger. They have already decided only to uncover as much detail as possible and to avoid getting into direct confrontation. Barry spent three hours on the phone the previous day with Colin Preston, the regional official who will now become increasingly involved. The strategy born out of years of such disputes is that they have to give the constant impression of wishing to work with management to overcome a shared problem. The general thinking seems to be that, if the managers feel you are cooperating, it makes it easier for them to back into the compromise you are offering. Antagonise them, and even good ideas will look unattractive. The cheap plastic clock shows two forty-five, meaning that one quarter of the time allotted for their meeting has already elapsed. They know that the meeting will not be extended.

They hear Sally's laughter from inside, and she then opens the door and says, "Sorry guys, Richard can see you now, do please come in."

Dickie looks at them and smiles weakly. "Had the Director of Sandford's Children Services on the phone," he lies. There is no question of an apology. They sit around what is possibly the one item of decent furniture in the building. The table is too big for the room, but it is a beautifully crafted walnut antique, polished to the point where it is almost mirror-like in the way it reflects. Tom always feels it has the reverse effect to the one intended because it serves to emphasise the cheap veneer glued onto the chipboard of everything else around it.

Dickie draws a deep breath. "This is a desperately trying time for all of us. Let me set out where we are and the journey we have taken to reach our destination. I then wish to outline how I propose to move the college forward so that we arrive at a point where we have the foundations in place to withstand whatever the winds of change and government cuts may throw at us.

"Last year, we had a full structural survey carried out of the premises. This revealed what we already suspected, which is that a building constructed in the nineteen seventies is not one which can meet the needs of an ambitious college of the twenty-first century. The cost of repairs is likely to exceed any reasonable sum, and we can no longer rely on funding from central government for a new Sandford College. The governors and I have therefore taken the decision that our only way forward is to dramatically modernise the existing site. Existing annual surpluses are insufficient to pay for the type of loan we shall require, so we must cut staff costs. No one regrets more than I the pain this will cause, but I am left with no choice, and I hope you will acknowledge the inescapable logic which has led me to this conclusion."

Barry is first to respond. "How many staff are you thinking of culling?"

"It's not a cull, Barry." Part of Dickie's quest to elevate himself is a habit of correcting others' English, substituting one word for another which he judges fractionally more precise. He doubtlessly thinks this creates the impression of a masterful command of the language, but even his senior managers complain of his annoying pedantry. "It will be a careful process in which we shall seek to make only those changes which we deem absolutely necessary to create the financial wiggle-room needed for this project."

"How many?"

"The precise numbers will be the subject of a paper which I shall be circulating to all staff within the next ten days. The final details are still under discussion, but the broad outline is now finalised."

"In broad outline, how many staff are you thinking of culling, uh, removing?"

"I regret that I cannot divulge this until the governing body has seen the final document on Thursday evening. I wrote to all staff as soon as it was clear that major changes were afoot, but it may cause undue worry to start issuing figures now which may be amended in the very near future."

"Can you say if we are talking in terms of single figures or dozens?"

"Barry, let's not get into numbers which are likely to mislead."

"Your email spoke of being unable to retain our 'generous' rates of pay. This college pays the nationally agreed pay scales. You want to breach that agreement?"

Dickie stiffens in his chair, and his tone sharpens. "It is going to be of no help to anyone if we start talking in terms of breaching agreements. I am working under enormous pressure to move Sandford forward at a time when much of the world seems to be in reverse. All of us need to accept that this cannot be achieved without difficulty."

Tom agreed with Barry beforehand that he would intervene if Barry looked as if he were straining to draw blood. It is clear Dickie has no intention of revealing any details, so

Tom decides to try another route. "I assume you have fairly detailed costings for this modernisation."

"The figures are mouth-watering, Tom. Fourteen million pounds over ten years just to maintain the bare necessities if we are to stay as we are. We propose the bolder move of aiming high and creating a site for us all to take pride in. We are therefore looking at expenditure of around twenty-two million over the next twelve years. But the savings are so vast when one has a state of the art erection that we shall recoup our costs in a remarkably short time."

If the subject weren't so critical, it would be tempting to ask Sally about state of the art erections at Sandford College, but no one even comes close to smiling. "How is it that you already have such detailed and costed plans?"

"Hard work over the summer and lots of major builders who are eager to get on board. We shall be circulating the architects' plans so that everyone can see …"

Barry can no longer hold back. "Did it ever occur to you to consult with your staff before settling on a policy in which their jobs go in order to pay for this madness? Half these projects go fifty percent over budget. You've already got staff talking about leaving, and if you keep to this plan, you'll have no one left to teach in your half-built glass-and-steel ego trip."

Dickie leans forward, places his right elbow on the gleaming table, beating out each word of his low, growling reply with his wagging finger. "Now you listen to me, Barry. This college needs modernising, and my way forward is the only way to do it. The sooner you grasp this the better, and I tell you now there's no point in stirring things up." He maintains his glare, but sits back in the chair.

Tom is unsure whether to let loose in support of Barry or to try desperately to restore the official strategy of being non-confrontational.

In the event, it is Sally who breaks the silence. "Barry, managers have to manage, and this is what Richard and I are trying to do. You have to let us do our job, and childish insults will not help matters. Now please help all of us in this very difficult situation by helping to maintain good relations in these meetings and by speaking responsibly with your members."

Until that moment, Tom has never truly resented Sally's rise through the organisation. She has struck him as a comical, harmless figure, appearing so ridiculous for having succumbed to Dickie that her humour value has exceeded the obvious injustice of her promotion. But he has never heard her speak like this. It is clear that she is centrally involved in the scheme which will result in God only knows what damage, yet she can do no more than trot out one cliché after another without any understanding of how revealing it is of her own vacuous stupidity and her readiness to take seriously a role she acquired by gripping those taps just a few feet away.

As Tom and Barry rise to leave, Dickie addresses them once more. "This is going ahead. Better get used to the idea."

Barry turns round, leans on the table, and looks down on him. "We shall see, Dickie. We shall see."

When they arrive back in the union office, Barry is still struggling to compose himself. "This is one last, big fuckin' ego trip for him before he goes into retirement. He could not give a shit about the staff and students of this college, he just wants a monument to himself. I tell you something now, it's bollocks to think in terms of compromises. Either we break him, or he breaks us."

"There are a couple of things he said which I don't get. The governing body has over twenty people from all over the borough. Most of them work full-time. I thought they only met up as a full group about once every couple of months, yet he's talking as if they meet almost weekly."

Barry nods. "We need some sort of information about what is going on there. I want you to see Deirdre Platts, the clerk to the corporation. She has to be present at every meeting, and the minutes should be available. That should give us some sort of insight into what they've all been saying."

"Isn't there anyone we can actually speak to? What about the staff governors?"

When colleges were liberated from local authorities in the nineties, certain laws were set down determining how their governing bodies should be composed. The majority of members are intended to be worthies from the local community. In practice, there is a search committee chaired by Dickie which selects candidates likely to have the searing business insights which will place them at one with the other visionaries they are joining. At the heart of this group is a selection of around half a dozen businessmen to whom Dickie distributes most of the tickets to the big rugby internationals which the college receives because it lets the RFU use its car park on match days. He lays on a lunch and champagne in the college restaurant before a semi-drunk stroll over the couple of hundred yards to the stadium. He also ensures that those who chair the most important committees within the college are recruited from this group, and newcomers quickly come to understand that here is the beating heart of this particular body.

This system has proved highly effective in ensuring that Dickie retain a firm grip on those above him. Dissenters are at best in a small minority and usually find themselves bullied into submission. There is the occasional resignation in protest over the undemocratic atmosphere which prevails, but for anyone outside the college the unimaginably trivial nature of someone resigning from a governing body means this can easily be ignored. The one constant irritant for this group is that the law requires there to be two staff governors, both of whom are elected. As no one ever wants to do it, the union has never tried to run official candidates, and this in turn means that neither of the present incumbents is one of their people.

"Who are they?" Tom asks.

"Richard Tomlinson is the academic one. Little point in approaching him." He is head of business studies. Whilst he has the salary of a teacher, he carries himself like a corporate raider, wearing well-pressed suits and expensive looking designer glasses. At staff meetings, he gives carefully prepared PowerPoint presentations instead of rushing through the tedious admin as others do. He is known to get on well with the principal, and in order to distinguish them he has been nicknamed 'Little Dick', while his boss got 'Big Dick'. If he knows what is going on, he probably supports it.

"The other one is Tony Coyle. He's head of IT support. Never met him, but I want you to try and talk to him. You've got more of a chance than I have of getting through to him. He'd probably think I'm some sort of raving Marxist."

"You used to be a member of the Socialist Workers Party."

"All right, but I'm not raving. Anyway, see if you can speak to him. Now the key is giving out as much information as we can to the members on Thursday and getting them fired up."

Tom starts by going to see Deirdre. He wonders if he should try some sort of subterfuge, but can't come up with anything appropriate, so he knocks on the door, walks in when prompted, and asks her for copies of the minutes of all governing body meetings for the last six months. She looks at him, smiles, and says, "Sub-committees as well, or just meetings of the full corporation?"

He sighs in anticipation of what this might mean. "Could I see everything please?"

When he gets home, Sofia tells him to sit outside in the small garden. There are a bottle of Rioja and a couple of wine glasses on the white plastic table on the crumbling patio. He goes to pour himself a glass but decides to wait for her. She comes out with some plates and cutlery and asks him about the pile of papers he has left in the lounge.

"Homework."

"For tonight?"

"I'll read it later. Sit down."

"In a minute." And she goes back inside to re-emerge after a few minutes carrying a bubbling pot of Spanish stew with the aromatic smell of cured meat.

When they first moved in together, cuisine was an integral part of their life. They started downloading recipes from the BBC food website, and even when they were short at the beginning of life in London, they would buy vegetables cheaply from market stalls and improvise dishes which theoretically required greater investment. On anniversaries, or even just on a whim, they would sometimes spend the day putting together a menu for a three-course meal and eating it with semi-expensive wines on discount. Somewhat perversely, these rituals have gradually been eroded as they've acquired the money to fund more extravagant efforts. This has partly been the inevitable effect of full-time employment in jobs where they are expected to work ever longer hours. The opportunity to have others cook and wash up for them has also meant more time in restaurants. But Tom has always felt personally responsible for much of the decline of this institution. Given his constant preference for the lightest option, they've established an impressive list of local home delivery outlets. Whereas they once cooked four or five times a week, they are now reduced to one or two major efforts a month. Sofia's mother gave them a set of sixteen carving knives when they moved to London. They now see their best service in the precise division of the pizzas they order in from an excellent little Italian in Balham High Street.

"When I'm made redundant, I promise I'll cook like this for you every night."

"This is what I was hoping for. Any progress at work?"

"Given the fact that I'm going to be boring you with this for the next six months, can we at least have a night off?"

"Ok. There is something else I want to discuss. I know we can't buy any place until all this is sorted out at your work, but I want us to start planning for when you win. I want to start looking for stuff that we can put in a new home."

"Does it make sense to start buying up stuff when we don't know where we'll be financially?"

"No, but can't we start getting stuff which doesn't cost anything? Even if we don't move, it will make life here more comfortable."

"I'm happy to think in terms of murder as a solution to issues at Sandford, but theft strikes me as too physically demanding."

"Come with me." She takes him by the hand and leads him into the kitchen. In what used to be a gap probably occupied by a tumble drier at some distant point in the past, there now stands a butcher's block.

"How much did we pay for this?"

"Nothing. Found it on Freecycle yesterday, and Lisa and I picked it up in her car this morning. I'm a bit worried that the shelf might be unstable, but my mother could fix it next time she visits." There is never any question of Tom engaging in DIY more advanced than the changing of light bulbs. This means that even the jobs which most children might attempt sometimes wait for months before he finds the energy to complete them. Anything more complex requires professional help.

He looks at Sofia and smiles. Two of the many differences between them are her relentlessly-positive approach and her supreme skills of organisation. She has no doubt that Tom will win his dispute and they will move into a flat in Streatham Hill which will be fit for *Grand Designs* by the time she has finished with it. She will be analysing every offer for furniture which might bring them closer to furnishing their new place before they have even found it. Everything she does is done with the same degree of conviction that everything she wants to achieve can be done, and as it can be done, it has to be done efficiently. After Mike explained to Tom how to go about downloading films, Sofia insisted that they needed to create a library. She would print off colour copies of the artwork she found on a site specially for such OCD types and made neat little inserts for the cases, which are now lined up in perfect alphabetical order. In order to maintain neat lines, they had to keep their rare bought DVDs separately, although Tom put his foot down when she suggested buying a machine she found online for printing the labels onto the discs they had burned. When they visited her brother in Oviedo, she was delighted by the traditional wooden dollhouse he had found for his daughter. When Tom went into the bedroom to tell Sofia to come down for dinner, she was arranging all the furniture in the appropriate rooms while her niece entertained herself with a jigsaw. He asked her later if this wasn't a little over the top, and she was bemused. "It didn't make sense. She had the dining room table in the attic."

Drinking good wine on a warm, laidback late September evening temporarily obscures the wider problems which have occupied him unceasingly for only four days, and which now seem to divide everything into periods of before and after in the way people with children often speak. They talk about Sofia's plan to do doctoral research. She wished to go back to the study of literature but is now considering a Spanish focus because this corresponds more closely to her current work and will therefore make finding an academic post marginally less impossible.

As a language coordinator, she has advantages which many dream of. She is one of twenty-three full-timers who teach all those who take language courses either for general interest or as part of a degree course. She teaches sixteen hours a week and works an academic year of only twenty-eight weeks. Yet unlike the lecturers, she has no requirement to carry out research, so time off teaching is time off. From mid-June to late September, her only professional commitment is to ensure that she remain abreast of current methodology and retain her skill levels in her teaching area. The latter means she needs to maintain her Spanish, and the former is a task she has approached with the energy worthy of Tom. And although she has enjoyed teaching her own language and loved summers of working her way through entire reading lists from options on the Victorian studies MA she completed several years ago, she has had a sense of stagnating. She has also been missing the intellectual stimulation of formal study, and she would be entitled to a reduction in tuition fees as a member of staff at Birkbeck. She has already spoken to one of the lit specialists in the Spanish department, and now wants to start auditing her seminars on Lorca with a view to enrolling the next year.

Tom wants her to do it because he would like her to achieve what he has not. He took six years to complete a respectable thesis on the role of emotion in Aristotle, and it was during this time that he started working at Sandford, first part-time and then full-time. By the time he finished, he was thirty-eight, and if he wanted to make a career as an academic he would have to give up his permanent contract at Sandford and enter the more dangerous waters of taking temporary contracts wherever they might come up. This would mean applying for everything and taking anything, perhaps accepting outrageous commutes or renting a room during term times before signing on for unemployment benefit over the summer. An even greater hurdle is his impoverished list of publications. He has published two articles in graduate journals, but only one in the type of peer-reviewed journal which will be taken seriously on a job application. One article. If he starts applying, he will not even be shortlisted for the jobs he doesn't want.

He is convinced that Sofia will be more successful. It seems she does everything with such efficiency that she will inevitably complete an excellent thesis and be able to slave through hot Spanish summers, out of which good research will emerge. Given her contacts at Birkbeck, she may even be able to combine her language courses with at least part-time academic teaching while studying and perhaps evolve into the academic which Tom would have wished to become. He is sometimes concerned that he really just wants Sofia to succeed on his behalf, but then he sees her devouring book after book by Meredith or James, and he realises that her success will be far beyond what would be required to achieve something on his behalf.

By the time she goes to bed, they have already discussed in detail the kind of theme she might explore. Tom clears up, finishes his third glass of wine, and then pulls out the papers he has brought home with him.

The first issue he has to confront is what he is supposed to be looking for. He decides it will make sense to try and acquire some sort of historical perspective on the events which led up to the decision to adopt the current policy. This may not reveal any glaring oversights, but it will at least give some clues about the governors' frame of mind. He also wants to look for any details of what might be contained in their plan for redundancies and cuts in pay. This will surely have been developed over a period of several months, and it will be useful to have some specifics prior to the branch meeting on Thursday.

Full meetings are scheduled once a month, and he decides to start with these. Sub-committee meetings are around once a fortnight and involve a small group of governors and managers who focus on specific functions such as employment, curriculum, or finance. He assumes that most of these are irrelevant but will come back to them if nothing turns up in the initial documents. He starts with the meeting held on the seventh of February. There are seven agenda items, the fourth of which is accommodation. This refers to a survey carried out last year, suggesting millions of pounds of essential repairs would be required simply to keep the building in a state which would allow the college to remain open under health and safety legislation. The minutes record a series of general concerns registered by many members, but they also indicate that management has been charged with developing a series of alternatives for addressing the financial challenges this would involve, and is required to report back at the next full meeting scheduled for March ninth.

The meeting has under item two the initial report produced by management on options for moving forward. There is a lengthy discussion, at the end of which the governing body has voted to accept the recommendations listed at the end of the report. Tom looks for the report, but it is not attached to the minutes. He then moves to the April minutes. No entry under accommodation. He skims the content of each of the items, but no reference to the building or to staff changes. He tries May and June, but still no references. July is the most recent meeting for which minutes are available. The first item is the governance committee's report and recommendations for accommodation and staffing changes at the college. Tom highlights this reference. There follow three pages of exchanges between different members, none of whom are named. From what Tom can gather, the chair of the governing body, the chair of the finance committee, and the chair of the curriculum committee are defending the proposals in the face of a series of questions from other members. At the end of the discussion, there is a vote in favour of the recommendations. As with the previous vote, the numbers are not recorded.

Tom sifts through the mountain of papers for the minutes of the governance sub-committee meetings. He misses them. Wine kicking in. He starts again, this time concentrating intensely. He misses them again, curses himself, and searches a third time. He realises they aren't there and looks for them among the papers for the full governing body meetings. Not there. He rubs his eyes and looks at the clock. Twelve-forty-five. He will be up in less than six hours, teaching in just over eight. Probably, an oversight on the part of Deirdre. But why would all the minutes of just one sub-committee be missing? Why are the reports on matters such as curriculum development attached to all the minutes but not those on the building? He wishes to avoid slipping into conspiracy theories as this would doubtless be little more than an entertaining distraction. He writes a list of documents he wants and decides to email Deirdre tomorrow. Fuck it, he thinks, do it now and maybe have them to look at first thing if she replies early in the morning. He asks for the report appended to the July governors' meeting and all the minutes of the governance subcommittee meetings from March onwards.

CHAPTER FIVE

He can't quite believe what he is reading on the screen.

```
Dear Tom,

I regret to say that I do not hold the min-
utes of the governance sub-committee meet-
ings, and I am not at liberty to send you
a copy of the report tabled at the govern-
ing body meeting of July 5th.

Regards,
Deirdre
```

He considers this for a moment, then beats a response out on his keyboard.

```
Dear Deirdre,

Many thanks for your swift reply. I wonder
if you could tell me where I might find the
minutes of the governance sub-committee
meetings and a copy of the July 5th report.

I would also be curious to know why you are
not at liberty to release it to me.

Many thanks,
Tom
```

The last couple of lines are a little unfair. Deirdre has been decent enough, and if she isn't able to send him the report, then it is clear who is behind this. She is obviously sitting in front of her monitor because the reply comes back immediately.

```
Dear Tom,

I am forwarding your previous email to
Sally Field, as she has responsibility for
all matters relating to the governance sub-
committee, including the list of people to
whom the July 5th report may be released.

Regards,
Deirdre
```

Tom now begins reviewing his scepticism about conspiracy theories. Deirdre is clerk to the corporation, which means she has a legal obligation to maintain full and accurate records of all meetings which relate to the running of the college. Has she been excluded from these meetings? Why would the head of personnel be organising a sub-committee of governors? A "list of people to whom the July 5th report may be released." Is Deirdre deliberately sending him a discreet message that this report is something he should continue to hunt for? He reflects for a moment and then types out a message to Sally.

```
Dear Sally,

I understand that you are the person to
contact about getting the minutes of the
governance sub-committee meetings and the
report submitted to the full governing body
on July 5th. As I am sure you will under-
stand, many of our members have asked about
the background to current developments, and
it would be very useful for us in piecing
together a full picture for them if we
could see this information. I would there-
fore be very grateful if you could send me
copies of these documents.
```

```
Thank you in advance for your assistance,
Tom
```

He sends it with a 'high urgency' status, meaning that he will receive an email back as soon as she opens it. He also blind copies it to Barry. Several seconds later, he receives confirmation that she's got it. Tom has the second lesson free and does some marking in the hope that Sally can email him back the documents immediately. It takes an hour for her to respond.

```
Dear Tom,

Thank you for your message of earlier this
morning. I fully understand the need for
you and your members to achieve a full and
detailed picture of why the proposals we
are setting out are the right ones. We
shall be issuing regular updates to all
staff, with the intention that they have
all necessary facts at their disposal. I
do not believe that the minutes of meetings
are a suitable means of conveying this in-
formation as they may well give a mislead-
ing account when taken out of the context
in which comments were made.

Regards,
Sally Field
Personnel Director
Sandford College
```

Tom forwards her reply to Barry, commenting that she won't give up the minutes and doesn't even refer to his request for the report. Twenty minutes later he is copied into an email sent from Barry.

```
Dear Sally,

I am formally requesting under the 2000
```

```
Freedom of Information Act that you provide
me with copies of the minutes of all gov-
ernance sub-committee meetings from Febru-
ary of this year up to now. I also wish to
receive a copy of the report on accommoda-
tion and staffing discussed at the govern-
ing body meeting of July 5th. You have
twenty days to comply with this request,
and should you fail to do so, I will con-
tact the Information Commissioner to re-
quest that she compel you to release this
information. Should you fail to release the
information at that point, you would be in
contempt of court and may face criminal
prosecution.

Best wishes,
Barry
```

Tom has been struggling with the aim of acting in such a way that management feels he is trying to work with them. Barry has clearly lost this fight in the early rounds. Sally's inarticulate prevarication was not something he was going to waste time on. And he has probably calculated that she will go straight to Dickie, who will be incandescent – always an attractive result in itself.

They also have to begin the tiresome process of balloting the membership for possible strike action. When Barry started as a trade unionist with the National Union of Journalists in the nineteen seventies, there would be a show of hands at a branch meeting followed by a swift walk to the gate to set up a picket line. Then came the laws on secret ballots, and after that came British Airways. The first meant that even a quick ballot would guarantee a month between declaring a dispute and walking out. Then, faced with strike action, the world's favourite airline went to court because there were a couple of dead souls on the list of union members, and the court made them ballot all over again. Now even tiny branches with a couple of volunteers have to crawl over membership lists, calling anyone they don't know to make sure they still work there. Tom and Barry have to submit a list of all members who are to vote to the union's national office, who will then send it to Sally with a letter checked by their lawyer. If Sally turns up the name of one person who has resigned or died or left the union, the college can ask a court to invalidate the ballot. If the letter fails to include the precise form of words demanded by the law, same result. At the branch meeting tomorrow, they will vote on having a vote for strike action. Both results will be a formality – but, my God, the time it takes.

He is still thinking about the papers that Sally will not give them, when Tili Kruk walks in. Although a psychologist, she shares the team room with Tom, Mike, and Alan Frost because the school can't fit her in with the rest of her kind. She works only four days a week, spending the fifth and most of her weekend on her more cosmic concerns. She is the secretary of a far-out group of Trekkies called LLAP ("Live Long and Prosper"), which refuses to acknowledge as valid any of the series or films which do not include the original crew captained by Bill Shatner. They find a purity in the early work which has been diluted into a more shallow, commercial form in the later efforts, and go as far as picketing the conventions held in London in protest at the inclusion of those pale imitations of the true heroes of the Enterprise.

Even her name confirms her commitment to the cause. She started life as Janice Corker, but when she decided to tie the stellar knot with a fellow Llappie, they each changed their names by deed poll to something more suitable. The correct pronunciation of her new name was something like Tssssh Krrrlllk, with her husband transforming from Colin Foreman into Plk Krrrlllkon, the suffix 'on' apparently indicating masculinity. Both names were selected from a list compiled by another member with a BSc in linguistics from Wolverhampton Poly. She had analysed half a dozen books from a spin-off of the original series called *Klingon Quest*, each of which set out a prequel to one of the confrontations between the Enterprise and a Klingon battle cruiser. From this she was able to put together the rudiments of a particular Klingon dialect, including a series of common names which one would expect to find given the general grammatical and phonemic structure. For the marriage ceremony, they commissioned a translation of their vows and decided to have the civil ceremony simultaneously in order to cut down on time and costs. So after the well-trained registrar asked, "Do you, Tssssh, take Plk to be your husband?" he stood sympathetically as the pair issued a series of clicks, squeals, and simpering sounds, at the end of which the Llappie-dominated guests offered the Klingon sign of approval by craning their necks and making a sort of goose-like baying sound.

On her return to work, she asked Tom if he thought it strange that they had been speaking Klingon despite being human. He found himself unable to answer, and she clarified the question by explaining that this white girl from Slough had been dressed and styled as Lieutenant Uhura, while her six-foot-four-inch pot-bellied beau from Croydon was decked out as Mr Sulu. Tom was still unable to speak.

Poor Tili had campaigned for several weeks to have colleagues and students pronounce her new name correctly. But aside from the infinite time she found herself spending on making people repeat it until they got somewhere close, it also made it almost impossible for her to be located within the organisation. Parents would phone up asking for Tilly Crook, only to be told that Tssssh Krrrlllk wasn't there.

"Who's not there?"

"Tssssh Krrrlllk."

"No, not Tasha Cripp, Tilly Crook. "

"Tilly is Tssssh."

"Her name is Tssssh? It says Tilly on this letter. Do you mind if I ask where the name comes from? Is it foreign?"

"Yes it is."

When she finally sent an email to all members of the department suggesting that everyone now pronounce her name phonetically, she told Jim Hollander at The Garden the following Friday that she hadn't felt so low since Spock died at the end of *Star Trek II*.

The fact Tom finds most bizarre about Tili, and there is plenty of competition, is that she gets on so well with her students. They know about her background, and the law of systematic exaggeration of all stories about teachers has her firing her specially made phaser at guests who didn't chant the special Klingon drinking song at the wedding reception. But she knows the theories she teaches inside out and has an expert knowledge of IT. This has been partly developed in pursuit of her dream to make a low-budget film about a group of radical Trekkies who live together in a south London housing estate and have to battle for their existence against a gang of local drug dealers. She has been hoping for crossover appeal from sci-fi and action movie fans, but no studio has yet picked it up. Her skills have been more useful in editing together YouTube clips of experiments carried out by Milgram and Zimbardo, followed by impressive PowerPoint presentations which are all available on her website. Students start by laughing at her, but soon realise that they are on to a good thing, and they don't laugh long. Neither does Tom whenever he leaves the team room hauling his portable overhead projector while she carries her memory stick.

She sits down and shakes her mouse to bring the monitor to life. Her screensaver is a rotating series of twelve classic shots of the bridge of the Enterprise. She checks her college emails before turning to Tom.

"Do you want to see some interesting research?"

This can only refer to some obscure aspect of Leonard Nimoy's early acting career, or something of equal importance.

"Look, please don't think this is rude, but I'm desperately trying to prepare something before tomorrow's meeting."

"I know, but I think this may be of interest. You said this morning that you were finding it difficult to uncover information about what this governance committee is doing. I emailed Plk to see if he had time to do some digging around, and he's just emailed me back. The college website has information about the governing body and all the committees. It doesn't contain details about their meetings, but it gives the names of all members, and he has done some searches on them. There are only three governors on that committee. One of them turns up nothing, but the other two."

She swivels her monitor so that Tom can see it. Staring back at him is a smiling woman with steel-grey hair and enormous plastic-rimmed glasses. Under the caption is an article taken from the *Sandford Gazette* about her reasons for stepping down as chair of governors at one of the local secondary schools. He skips down, and it turns out that the school had to go into special measures. So she left there and joined the governing body of the college almost immediately.

"What about the other one?"

"Even more interesting."

She clicks on the link to a Google search, and up comes over thirty hits about the same story. "Take a look at this one." She opens the link to a *Financial Times* article from early two thousand and ten. The headline is "Liefwint goes in Disgrace." The man who now chairs their finance committee was the president of an organisation called UK AdVENTURE, which represented British venture capitalists. In the dying days of the Brown government, the GMB ran a campaign about a group of them who were taking advantage of tax breaks for small start-ups. Instead of setting up ordinary businesses, they were borrowing money to set up new companies which would buy existing ones, selling the viable parts and closing down the remaining parts of any given company, with all employees losing their jobs. Once the sales and shutdowns were completed, the company was wound up, and all the profits were going into those adventurous pockets at a fraction of the normal rate of corporation tax. Even the cost of shutting down loss-making operations was being written off. Liefwint appeared before a group of MPs who were looking into it. He turned up ready to defend the divine authority of the free market but found himself answering questions on specific, high-profile cases of once-profitable companies which had been closed down, with the profits apparently going offshore. The *Financial Times* quoted the Labour MP who chaired the committee asking Liefwint why he could not explain the benefits of such major events when he had been told in advance that this was to be one focus of their enquiry. He was met with silence. One report after another described Liefwint as "arrogant," "out of his depth," "ill-prepared." Even the right-wing business reporters were infuriated that he had prolonged the impression that those he represented were little more than a bunch of crooks.

Tom turns to Tili. "Thanks. Sorry, if I was a bit sharp earlier. Just … you know."

"No problem."

He goes back into his email account to forward the *Financial Times* link to Barry and then opens a new email from Dickie, for which he is a copy recipient.

```
Dear Barry,

I understand that you are interested in
some of the recent discussions of the Gov-
ernance Committee. For the eminently sen-
sible reasons already provided by Sally, I
suggest that the minutes of meetings are
not the most effective way of transmitting
the depth and complexity of the relevant
discussions. As an alternative, I believe
it may be more appropriate if I could
arrange a time when you and Tom may meet
with representatives of senior management
and the members of this committee. Their
next scheduled meeting is for Wednesday of
next week, and I shall write again to con-
firm your invitation.

Kind regards,
Richard
```

He leans back in his chair, cups his hands behind his head, and tries to make sense of it. Barry walks in five minutes later.

"Have you read Dickie's latest email?" He then sees it open on the monitor. "So we're supposed to meet with some half-wit who led another school in the borough into special measures, and her support act is a disgraced financier. All we need now is a former *News of the World* editor for the full set."

"Still nothing about the July fifth report."

"Exactly. They reckon they're going to fob us off with some charming explanation of what they're up to, and hope we don't find out what's going on. I'm going to write back thanking him for the invitation and tell him we still want the report. Have you spoken to this staff governor yet?"

"He hasn't responded to my email."

"Get down there and find him. If he says he doesn't want to speak to you, tell him he has to as he's on the governing body to represent your views. Find out how much the other governors know about all this. If they're as much in the dark as we are, then we might be able to drive a wedge between them."

"In practice, how much of this could have been done without all governors knowing about it?"

"Look, Dickie runs this college like it's his own personal empire. He can get away with it because his mates like to drink his red wine and watch England stuff Italy. If the top ones are on board, then the others won't want to lose their match-day seats. Just find this guy and ask him what he knows." He turns and walks out. He sees Tili curiously following the conversation and says, "Bye Trisha," as he leaves.

Tom stands up and walks downstairs to the IT support centre on the ground floor. He enters and is suddenly reminded of the bizarre physical aspect of its inhabitants. Three of the technicians are shaped like enormous footballs with smaller balls sitting on top. The fourth is a bearded, long-haired, stick-like creature who looks as if he has arrived on twenty-first century Earth from *Planet of the Apes* to find himself in a Texan fat camp. At the far end sits Tony, roundest of them all. He looks up when Tom comes in, then looks down again without acknowledging him. Not a promising start. Tom approaches him. "I wonder if I could have a word."

Tony is reading from some sort of report and speaks without looking up. "Terribly sorry, but you need first to speak to my colleague on the help-desk by the door."

"It's not an IT question I have." The others are tapping away with such conspicuous concentration that they can only be focusing with absolute attention on the conversation now taking place. They know who Tom is, and they have a pretty clear idea why he would want to speak to Tony. He continues reading until Tom speaks again.

"I have some questions for you as my representative on the governing body. It shouldn't take too long." He pauses. "I'd be happy to ask them here and now if you like." He says this with as much politeness as he can. The gamble is that however little he likes the idea of speaking to Tom, Tony might feel even less attracted to the idea of publicly fielding some of the questions which might be coming his way.

He looks up and smiles broadly. "Perhaps your representative could buy you a coffee." They walk out of the room, but before they reach the canteen, Tony grabs his arm. "No, not in there. I can't be seen with you. Take me to your office." Tom starts back towards the staircase, but Tony pulls him back again. "No, I mean your union office. No one must see us together."

Tom unlocks the door and kicks aside last year's placards demanding a twelve percent pay rise for teachers. Fortunately, this only resulted in one day's loss of pay for strike action. It has always struck him as unrealistic to take action for any sort of pay increase, but as the extreme left dominates the national executive, reality has never been an obstacle when formulating policy. Many of them view even Barry as a weak, unreliable moderate.

He pushes a heap of flyers off a chair and beckons Tony to sit down. Tom opens his mouth to speak but is immediately silenced with a raised hand. Tony leans forward and motions for Tom to do the same, until their faces are no more than a foot apart. He begins speaking in a low, nervous whisper. "I am in great danger. You don't know how much of a risk I am taking even agreeing to talk to you here. If it gets back to them that I have revealed anything to you I am finished." He looks from side to side, sits back, and looks up at the ceiling. Tom sits back, but as soon as he does so Tony leans forward again, and Tom does the same. "They laugh at me. They fucking laugh at me. In my face. They think I am some sort of idiot, but they know nothing about me. I used to run my own company. Yeah. That surprises you, doesn't it? Ran a consultancy, and only do this so I can be closer to the family home and see my wife and kids. Didn't want to be one of these absentee fathers who see their children only at weekends and think expensive holidays and lots of designer goods are some sort of substitute for being with them as they grow up. And now this?" He leans back again and shakes his head.

Tom's first thought is one of concern at just how many hours he will have to sit for in order to obtain what might be relatively low-grade information. He opens his mouth to speak, but Tony silences him once again with a raised hand. "Don't talk. Just listen. You are doing all right. They are nervous. Follow the money. This is where their weakness lies. They think that I have no understanding of what they are doing, but I have run my own company. I know about finance and how major deals work. They have screwed up before, and it is essential to prevent this from going through."

Tom ponders what on earth he can do to get some sense out of him. After a moment he leans forward and ushers Tony towards him. He speaks in a barely audible whisper. "We all know what enormous courage it takes for you to have to work the way you do. I can't imagine what it must be like on that governing body with people like Kilman and Liefwint a constant threat. But I need certain information which I think you can help me get." Tom looks slowly from side to side to make sure that no one could possibly have sneaked within earshot and then brings his face to within a couple of inches of Tony's left ear. "I need to know how big your cock is," he wants to say but settles instead for, "We know about the July fifth report – we need to see a copy."

They both lean slowly back in their chairs, looking at each other as they go, potential double-agent and would-be controller. Tony breathes deeply. "I have to think about it. I have been turned down for promotion twice in the last three years. Dickie knows I am not one of his supporters, and who knows what he would do to me if he found out I had leaked this. I have to think of my wife and children. It's easy for you to make this sort of request, but you don't understand how much you're asking."

"Just place a copy in a blank envelope, put my name on it, and send it by internal mail. No one will know it was you."

"I have said I will think about it. Now I need to go. I have already stuck my neck out just being here. Please check outside the door to make sure no one is walking by."

Tom opens up, sticks his head out, only to see a steady stream of people coming in and out of the canteen. "Quick, it's clear!" Tony barrels forward and out. Tom closes the door and sits down in disbelief. He knows from one of the Unify reps who works alongside Tony in IT that his biggest business deals as chief exec of his own company were ordering spare parts for the damaged PCs which came into his computer repair shop in Peckham High Road. When that went bust, he was the only applicant for an IT post at Sandford paying a fraction of what he would pick up in any tenth-rate private-sector operation. The difficulty is knowing if there is anything of substance here, or whether the role of secret agent working fearlessly behind enemy lines is just a replacement opportunity for this former high-flying captain of industry to spin a few more fantasies. Seeing the report sooner rather than later might make it worth a little more time with him. Does "follow the money" mean he knows something about the financing of the deal, or is it simply that he has watched *The Wire?* When he said they were nervous, was this pure melodrama, or are the governors now being circulated with email updates on what the union is doing? This could cost a lot of time for absolutely nothing, and Tom starts wearily back up the stairs to his office. Time to finish preparing his contribution for the branch meeting to be held tomorrow.

CHAPTER SIX

Barry rises, and there is silence.

"This is a strong branch. There are people I see here who have worked at this college for the twenty years I have, and there are those who have been here longer than that. The people here have made this college a place where students will get up at six in the morning because they want to cross London to study here. The people in this room go into classrooms every day because they want to do something which has value, and this place is not going to be pulled down to satisfy the dreams of someone who does nothing for anyone but himself.

"Every month I attend meetings of our national executive, and every meeting has details of another college where the principal wants to get rid of staff, or cut their pay, or increase their teaching hours, or reduce their holiday. And every time this comes up, it's the same pattern. The colleges where the union is strong and where people stand together are the colleges where they protect their standard of living no matter how hard management comes at them. These are also the colleges where they have the best standards because the people who work there have a sense of their own dignity, and management haven't demoralised them to the point where they don't see any reason for what they do. This is one of the colleges which will fight against the injustice of an aggressive management, and this is one of the colleges where we'll win because we're strong, and we're committed, and we're right."

He stops as the enthusiastic clapping of a few provokes the entire room. They are used to meetings in the canteen where thirty attend. This time there are two hundred hemmed into corners, squeezed two at a time onto chairs. For many it is the first time they have attended a union meeting, the first time they have done more than skim the newsletters on their screens, the first time anyone has told them they may no longer work. The union used to be a dull necessity. But now!

"Kilman thinks that he can push through his reforms because a few nodding dogs on the governing body have told him he's a hero of change. He thinks he can sit in his office all day and work out what's best for a college where he never teaches, never talks to his staff, never sees his students, and where a good day for education is when classes end early so he can get pissed on red wine and watch rugby. We are the ones who care about this college and the students who come here, and we need to make it clear that no one is going to destroy our staff to pay for changes we can't afford and don't need."

More applause. Barry shuffles some papers on the table in front of him, puts on his glasses, and holds up a piece of paper.

"Can everyone see a copy of the resolution?"

He looks up as everyone strains to find one of the copies which they have placed on chairs and tables prior to the meeting.

"I shall read it out and then ask for any amendments. 'This branch deplores management's decision to cut jobs and pay among staff at Sandford College. It is outrageous to be destroying jobs in an institution which helps to create them, and we call on management to withdraw their plans for their unaffordable building programme and to engage with staff unions in proper negotiations concerning the future direction of this college. We further deplore the decision to devise plans of such enormous importance without full and proper consultation with staff, as well as the decision to push these plans forward without first discussing them fully and openly. We call on the union leadership to organise action up to and including strike action in opposition to these changes'."

He takes off his glasses and looks up. "Any suggested amendments?"

One of the chemistry teachers attending her first meeting raises a hand. "Do we know exactly what he is proposing?"

Barry looks down at Tom, whose slim knowledge extends further than most due to reading the minutes of the governors' meetings.

"We are meeting with the governance committee on Friday of next week. They have been responsible for coming up with most of the details, and we have requested a copy of the report which sets out all their current plans. So far, the minutes of the other governing body meetings only seem to suggest that they have been presented with a case about the absolute need for a massive programme of maintenance and repairs because the building is falling down. It looks as if they also wish to add some new offices and completely rework the college's IT network. They think they can pay for it by cutting the number of teaching posts, and then cutting the pay of the staff who remain."

The room dissolves into muttering and headshaking. Barry breaks in.

"Once we have the details, we will be able to show anyone who's interested the insanity of this. Until then, our best weapon is to show that we are not prepared to allow anyone to destroy our college. Any amendments?"

A hand is raised by another first-timer. "Is there any indication how much strike action there would have to be if it comes to that?"

"Judging by other colleges, it usually takes two or three days of action before management eventually come round and a sensible deal is worked out."

Same teacher again. "I understand there was a major dispute in Tower Hamlets, where it took longer."

"It did."

"How much longer?"

Barry pauses and draws a deep breath. "They started with a series of one- and two-day strikes, which didn't work. They then threatened unlimited action and management wouldn't back down. So they came out for eleven straight days and won. This is very rare, and chances are even a nutter like Dickie would never contemplate allowing things to get so bad."

There is a near-perfect silence which articulates with extraordinary precision the fear that this is exactly what Dickie would contemplate. Barry looks around. "All right, if there are no more questions, we shall move to a vote. All those in favour of the resolution."

A sea of hands rises. Out of two hundred and five, all vote in favour but for two who abstain. When the result is announced, there is a cheer, and Barry speaks again.

"Dickie will receive a copy of the resolution this evening, and he will know that, if he pushes ahead, he will meet a branch which is ready to fight him."

They cover some other more minor matters, and everyone files out. They will not only inform their principal but also their national officers. They will then receive ballot papers which they hope will result in a massive yes vote. In five weeks they will have selected their first date for strike action, and if there is no movement, they will give seven days' notice before doing all they can to shut the college down. If they must go out, then it will be solid for the two or three days they anticipate they will need. But the danger is so terribly straightforward. More strikes mean more financial problems for more members who may start to doubt the possibility of success. Most admire Barry, but many also fear that his devotion might be unrealistic. He knows this but is so utterly convinced of the justice of his cause and the power of the union that he is sure he will be vindicated.

As Tom travels home, he is conscious of an odd sense of invulnerability. Regardless of how determined Dickie is to pursue whatever changes he wants, there is an absolute and utter dependence on the lecturing staff to make the college function. Tom knows from previous exchanges with Dickie that he studies the motions they pass and the numbers who vote for them. He taunted them with comments about how unimpressed he was by the crushing majority of twenty-three votes to seven against the introduction of performance-related pay. Suddenly, he is going to see many times the usual number have turned up to a meeting, and there is absolute opposition to him. It is an odd feature of Dickie's psychology that he hates strikes, and his usual approach is to find some sort of deal which will avert a local dispute. The national ones he hasn't been able to do much about, but he has made sure to dock pay as early as possible, and the letters he has sent home to parents on each occasion make clear the betrayal of which he believes his staff to be guilty.

When Tom gets back, it is almost dark in the flat. He opens the door into the lounge to find candles lit and Sofia sitting on the sofa with a bottle of Rioja on the coffee table.

"Never a good idea to start a revolution on an empty stomach. Unless … Wait. The branch is against any action and has decided that cutting pay and jobs is the best way to take a college forward."

"You know you are really starting to understand the nature of British trade unionism."

She stands up and kisses him. "Sit down, I need to warm something up."

He pours himself a glass of wine, sits, and leans back on the sofa. "And so it begins," he thinks. Either Dickie will back down, or he will break them. Tonight he feels as if they cannot possibly lose.

Sofia comes back in carrying four plates of tapas. This is a powerful reminder of their early days in London, when they would shop with no money and buy enough to make the best meals they had ever tasted. Some of the dishes are simple ones, but he knows that some of the lamb and the squid took hours and that she must have planned this several days ago. He looks down at the food. "If the dispute lasts a year, can I expect this sort of spread every night?"

She laughs. "Oh, Mitch phoned. I told him I would play in the Centurion Cup final, and he wants us to come round for dinner the weekend after next."

Tom can only smile. "Would I be right in assuming that he invited us for dinner before he asked you to play?"

"What could I say?"

"I'm sure that was his thinking too."

Mitchell Murray is the president of the Griffin Club, where they play tennis. They found it by punching their address into

Google Earth, and up came a cluster of courts in Streatham. The Griffin was the closest, and when they first went there, Sofia was delighted when she saw what she believed were clay courts, but turned out to be shale of such inconsistent quality that two identical shots might finish around your ears or your ankles. Mitch was the sly, old devil who ran it. He had come over from St Lucia in sixty-five to live with an aunt while he trained to be an electrician at Lambeth College, and then did an apprenticeship with a white electrician who was prepared to hire a black teenager. When he qualified, he worked for the London Electricity Board before deciding he could make more on his own. He set up an office in his aunt's spare bedroom and made a good enough living to buy himself a flat in West Norwood, where he set up an office in his own spare bedroom.

Then, after years of getting by, came the nineteen eighties. Ted Knight was running Lambeth Council, and anti-racism was the new priority. Margaret made the councils seek at least three bids for all major jobs, and Ted made the departments look everywhere for equal opportunities. Mitch started getting work on rewiring council flats, and when this turned out well, he was offered schools and council offices. He took on four more electricians, leased a real office, and had to start sub-contracting to the white firms the council had stopped using. Then it just got better and better. As the City boomed, its people spread into Clapham South and Balham. Peeling three-storey Victorian wrecks now had character, and every time they gutted somewhere, every plug, wire, and light fitting had to be replaced. He renamed the company 'AAA Electrics' so it would appear first in the Yellow Pages and paid over the odds to hire a middle-class white girl to run the office. "Mr Murray is on a job at the moment, but he would be free to come round and give you an estimate on Friday morning. Would nine a.m. be convenient? Lovely, he'll see you then." He would walk through the door, and the City wife would blanche at the absence of the simple, honest, strike-a-light cockney she had been expecting. They were so overly polite, he knew they were unsure if he was going to mug them or just rewire the house. But my, how it paid! By the time of the housing crash in eighty-eight, it just meant he turned down less work. When he bought his five-bedroom Edwardian detached in Killieser Avenue, he didn't even sell his flat. Just rented it out and waited for the next boom.

His old man used to take him to the local club in Castries before he moved over, and by the time he saw Ashe beat Connors, he was earning enough to pay for lessons twice a week and got into a regular doubles with three of the Asian guys who played at the Griffin. When he was waiting to go on the court one day, the accountant who ran the club walked up to him, and he expected to be asked if he knew this was a private club for members only. Instead, he was invited to play in the upcoming one-day doubles tournament, and he could either find his own partner, or they would find one for him. When he played, he was surprised that people knew his name, and soon he was playing the regular social evenings and buying rounds of drinks on the terrace while they watched twilight doubles. The more he played, the more he liked it. He became third team captain and started driving his players up and down the A23 in his Espace on Sunday mornings to play Surrey league matches. He took over management of the internal leagues, had his secretary move everything onto spreadsheets, and started a ranking system. When the accountant stepped down, he couldn't wait to step up, and he started putting his own money in. They had four decent macadam courts and four unplayable shale ones. He converted the shale into artificial grass and turned some of the overgrowth into a lawn with deckchairs. He put the floodlights up himself.

By the time Tom turned up, the club was less of a poor relation to its neighbours, and when Sofia joined, Mitch already had plans to make it the strongest club in the area. He got in touch with some of the people he knew at Lambeth and cut a deal in which the club offered courts to the council's coaches to train local talent. Mitch then offered them free membership, and they started carving up the kids from other clubs back for the summer from boarding school. But what he wanted above all was to win the tournament played between the five local clubs each year. He had done well, but he was tired. He was tired of the looks he used to get when he went into those big houses. He was tired of Jamaicans calling him "small island." And he was tired of the exaggerated courtesy from the brigadier's-wife types who ran the other clubs with their curled hair and Laura Ashley dresses.

His problem was that he could field strong juniors, but he couldn't find adult players as good as the other clubs' top men and women for the key singles matches. When Sofia arrived, he almost made Tom pay the full fee and gave her free membership. She quickly stopped playing any of the club's internal tournaments because she found no competition. They wouldn't let her enter the men's singles, which at least spared Tom the horror of having to play her in another competitive match. She would train with the first-team men on Monday nights, but the two American guys who were capable of beating her didn't play the leagues either, and she soon grew bored of crushing the beta males. When Mitch asked her to play in the opening round of the Centurion Cup, she won the two sets in less than half an hour. Tom asked her afterwards if she had considered shipping a game out of compassion, and she shook her head in disbelief. "In two thousand and ten, Rafa won three majors. That's one boy from a tiny island winning more big tournaments in one season than your entire country has won in fifty years. You think he did it through showing pity to the weak?" The only challenge he could think of was suggesting that her description of Majorca as tiny reflected a general snobbery about any part of Spain not connected to the mainland. At any rate, even Mitch felt so uncomfortable that he didn't want to select her again unless they made the final. Now they were there, and he wanted her out to roll over the next victim. She could hardly say no, having accepted the dinner invitation.

"He wants me to play the women's singles and you to play the mixed doubles. At least you get to play your strongest format." She smiles.

The club has a board which records the names of all those who have won the club's summer tournaments going back to eighteen eighty-three. Tom talked Sofia into playing the mixed doubles with him in their first year at the club by telling her she could become the first woman to complete the treble of singles, doubles, and mixed in the same year since nineteen fifty-seven. She liked this and quickly smashed her way to the first two titles and to the final of the mixed. There they met one of the other men who had worked out that this was his only chance at Griffin immortality. He was playing with the woman who had preceded Sofia as the club's top female player. They hit everything at Tom on every point, and his falling confidence declined further when Sofia dropped her serve after Tom dumped three consecutive volleys into the net. When he apologised, she didn't look at him. Now he could barely hold the racket. At two all in the final set, the other man suffered the collapse Tom had prayed for, and they took four games with barely the loss of a point. He still had to pay for dinner, and she didn't play any mixed after that.

It is still a source of amusement for her that he takes such pride in his first and only conceivable title, despite it being the least prestigious available. He found a company online which made inscribed trophies, and at her next birthday he presented her with a six-inch cup with their names on it. This was the least embarrassing way he could find of permanently displaying his triumph.

After he pours the remainder of the Rioja into their glasses, he looks up at the trophy and then over at Sofia. "You were lucky I was there to pull you through that match."

"I know," she says. "I know."

When he wakes on Friday morning, he is instantly aware of having drunk too much wine the night before. His head is pounding and there is disbelief that he has to rise already. This is the worst state in which to cover what he must do today. He always finds it very difficult to teach Book V because the discussion tends to be so far at odds with the theories which dominate current thinking. It is also the messiest of the sections he has to teach, with some of the claims apparently unrelated to the preceding discussion.

"Would we agree that a just person obeys the laws of the state?"

Even Amrit looks unconvinced, but Miles is first to reply. "What if the state is unjust? Wouldn't a just person be under an obligation to disobey unjust laws?"

"Agreed, and perhaps the best way to understand Aristotle is to assume that he had in mind the idea that the just person is someone who obeys the laws of a just state. Can we agree on that?"

This elicits unconvinced nods. "All right, can we also agree that a just state is one which requires people to act the way virtuous people do?"

Now Maya is suspicious. "So the state must force us all to be brought up in the right way to ensure we are virtuous?"

"No. He doesn't think it's practically possible to make everyone virtuous, which would require everyone to be brought up in such a way that they enjoy doing the right thing. He makes the weaker claim that the state should ensure people perform only virtuous actions, but this would include people who dislike doing the right thing but do it anyway because they fear the alternative."

Maya is still unconvinced. "Doesn't he think being witty is a virtue?"

"That's right."

"So the state should compel people to be funny and punish them if they fail to tell good jokes?"

"Unfortunately, it seems to be the case that if just laws are ones which force us to act in accordance with the moral virtues, then this would follow."

"Does anyone believe this?"

"No, but there is another aspect of what he calls 'universal' justice which is of greater interest. He argues that one sense of justice is that it means having all of the virtues. So one meaning of calling someone a just person is that she treats all other persons in the right way, for example. It means that she is generous, honest, courageous, and so on. This seems a more plausible claim."

Miles raises a hand. "In the handout you gave us, he talks about different ideas of justice. What does he mean?"

"He contrasts universal justice with particular justice, which is a specific moral virtue. He explains that injustice in this sense is driven by people who are too grasping. They want more than they are entitled to, and this leads them to treat others unfairly."

"So every time someone is unjust it's because they are too greedy?"

"That is more or less what he says."

Maya once again looks unconvinced. "If I die and give all my money to my favourite child and leave nothing to the other, that's unjust, but it can't be because I'm greedy."

"I agree it's very difficult to defend this as an account of injustice in all cases, but there I think he is right in his explanation of what motivates injustice on many occasions. Surely, there are many cases where someone is greedy for more money or more property or more power or a higher status, and this leads them to ignore the interests of others."

There is a dissatisfied silence which indicates they accept the narrow defence he has offered. He completes the lesson by giving them an extract to read and goes through the answers to some questions he has set on it. As always, he leaves the room dissatisfied because much of what Aristotle has to say seems either part of the kind of dull, common-sense stuff which is done by courts, or else it is inexplicably poor theory. He empties his pigeonhole on the way back to the office, picking up a package of papers which includes copies of the union flyers which he must distribute, some late essays, and other random papers. He is about to sift them when he realises that Laura is standing beside him, and he starts in surprise.

"Sorry, I thought you knew I was here."

"No problem. What can I do for you?"

"I, uh … I was thinking of retaking one of the first-year units to improve my chances of increasing my overall grade. I just need advice on which unit to retake."

"Didn't you score an F in unit one and a C in the other?"

"Yes, so should I just re-sit unit one?"

"Yes," he says, trying not to make it sound as obvious as it is.

She looks down. "All right. Thanks. Bye."

He watches her in disbelief as she turns and leaves. What's wrong with that girl? He goes back to sifting the rubbish from his pigeonhole, coming finally to a re-used A4 envelope with his name irritatingly misspelled as Tom Phillips. He opens it and pulls out a forty-page document. It is dated July fifth.

CHAPTER SEVEN

"He's fuckin' mad."

"He's not. These calculations have been done very carefully, and there is a rationale to their thinking. This plan cannot be simply dismissed."

Colin Preston, the regional officer, is there for the day. He wishes to discuss both the report and the proposed strategy they must adopt at the meeting.

"Going in there and shouting abuse will not move them. They need to have the impression that we are all on the same side. That way they will find it easier to shift their ground."

Tom is never entirely comfortable with the full-time officers. On the one hand, they have seen the same picture a hundred times before and have a way of dealing with those principals who see butchering their staff as a personal privilege. But he also suspects a tendency to look for a compromise which is better than the worst case and then move on to the next dispute. He fears they will settle for a less awful outcome than the one Dickie is offering but will concede more than is necessary in order to avoid the uncertainty of a major dispute.

Barry will have none of it. "On the same side! Eighty staff is a quarter of the teaching force. We need to make it absolutely clear that we will not accept compulsory redundancies or pay cuts."

"You are missing the point, Barry. Of course, we won't accept his plan, but the issue is how to make him change it. If he thinks we are spoiling for a fight, he will respond in kind. If he thinks he is in a negotiation where both sides are giving ground, we are much more likely to get what we want."

Tom is instinctively loyal to Barry but is also concerned that a more aggressive approach will suit an opponent who wishes to destroy them.

"When you say that we have to give the impression that we are interested in genuine negotiation, which aspects of his plan are ones on which we can negotiate? We can't accept compulsory redundancies, and we can't recommend to our members that half of them have their salaries cut."

Colin sits forward in his chair and looks squarely at Tom. "The key proposals in this report revolve entirely around money. They're saying that they need to make savings to pay for the building, and staff costs are the only budget they can cut. You have to make them think that you recognise the need for savings but you have alternative ideas which will make it all possible. If they see that you have moved towards them by accepting the premise of their argument, then they are more likely to give up on the more extreme ideas. In the end, they will probably be able to make most of the savings they want because there will be a stampede to get out. They will probably offer some voluntary redundancies as well, and a bunch of staff who were going to retire anyway will take it. Then you will have other people who actually retire. They can avoid replacing almost any staff who leave and dress it up as a phased reduction, which circumvents the need for compulsory redundancies. Eighty-odd posts will dwindle to twenty, and they will find that they don't need to make quite the savings they thought they needed to. You'll end up with fewer teachers doing more work, and that is as good as it gets."

"The plan also states that they wish to create two levels of lecturers with differing pay scales."

"This is the sort of thing which principals come up with all the time. The report contains all the usual nonsense about challenging staff and introducing new motivational forces which will encourage them to strive for higher achievement. In the end, they will have to get used to the fact that no one likes their ideas, and if they are getting major savings which they agreed on with the unions, then they will just forget about their ingenious new plan in order to avoid a protracted dispute."

Barry draws a deep breath. "I'm not happy about this. If we go in and launch a charm offensive, it may look like weakness."

"They know you are balloting for strike action, and they won't forget it simply because you don't crack them over the head with it in this evening's meeting. I suspect it may require a couple of days' action to make the point, but you're in a much stronger position if it's easier for Kilman to approach you."

"You do realise he hates us."

"All the more reason for you to make it as easy as possible for him to speak with you. If he thinks you will treat any concession as a humiliating climb-down he is much less likely to offer one."

Barry looks over at Tom and then back at Colin. "All right, we'll try it your way for the time being. Probably better you do the speaking tonight. If I sound reasonable they'll think it's some sort of trap."

Colin is visibly relieved. "We need to find out certain details which aren't specified in the report. We know they want to make eighty posts redundant, but they don't specify the timing. They will probably be thinking in terms of May of next year, or even August if we're lucky. They also refer to some sort of selection process for creating the two tiers among the teaching staff. We need the details of that to see if we can nail them under equal opps legislation. I also want to understand better why they need to save so much money so quickly."

Barry does not teach on Fridays and will spend the day taking Colin to meet various teams in different parts of the college. Tom rises to return to his room to prepare for his classes later in the day and to look again at some of the details in the report. Before he leaves, Barry calls him back. "Have a word with your mate Tony before this evening. Might be he can tell us something about this before we see them. Makes us look stronger if they think we know what's going on inside the governing body."

Tom rolls his eyes at the thought of another meeting with Deep Throat and gloomily climbs the stairs back to his cupboard. When he checks his email, there is one from Sally Field to Alan Frost, with Tom as a copy recipient.

```
Dear Alan,

I would be grateful if you would come to my
office in 1B7 at midday today to discuss a
very serious allegation which has been made
against you by two students. Following our
earlier conversation, you have nominated
Tom Phelps as the union representative you
would like to be present, and I notice from
his timetable that he is free then. Unless
I hear differently, I shall expect you both
at that time.

I would like to emphasise that this is not
yet part of a formal disciplinary process,
but minutes will be taken and a formal
process may ensue depending on the outcome
of this informal investigation.
```

```
Regards,
Sally Field
Personnel Director
```

A series of trivial thoughts cross his mind before he begins to consider the more important content of the message. He notices that Sally has now taken to describing herself as a director rather than head of personnel. It also occurs to him that Alan has nominated him as his representative despite there being a caseworker who specialises in individual cases such as these. He wonders if he could palm Alan off to the English lit lecturer who does this, but quickly decides that this is personally impossible. Alan has nominated him because they have sat in the same room together for six years and have spent too many evenings at The Garden. Finally, he wonders what this psycho has done now.

Tom had been one of the staff on the interview panel when Alan was appointed. Like most RS teachers, he seemed almost self-consciously opposed to the stereotype of the kindly vicar. He turned up to the boiling mid-July interview in a woollen pinstripe suit and sat almost inhumanly erect as Tom and Mike leaned back in their chairs, sporting summer shirts and knee-length shorts. They weighed the problem of his being too much like a relic from the last days of the Raj to teach the dimwits who took the course because they interpreted their solitary B at GCSE as a sign of aptitude for the subject as against a reflection of the shockingly low standards required to pass an RS exam. But if they re-advertised, then there was no guarantee of a stronger candidate, and neither he nor Mike wanted to teach the subject themselves. So they took him because he knew his way around the ontological argument and because he was a more plausible candidate than his new-age rival with tats and a facial piercing.

From early on, Alan was happy to join them on Friday nights, and his pool was good enough to make him a satisfying victim. But when he drank, he revealed a set of views which were detached even by the bizarre standards within philosophy departments. He completed a BA and PhD at Durham, specialising in Nietzsche. Tom had attended a reading group on *Beyond Good and Evil*, and couldn't fathom how Alan found it possible to train for the priesthood whilst retaining sympathy for a philosopher who described himself as the Anti-Christ. Insofar as Tom could understand Alan's views, they seemed to be that the higher types depicted by Nietzsche represented the message of authority which was central to the New Testament. Christianity gave the best account available of the unfolding nature of human existence and provided the most effective framework for making sense of the human condition. After a couple of years, Tom decided that if any of this meant anything, it was nonsense, and more or less gave up discussing philosophy with Alan. Mike, who struggled to discuss any theory which could not be translated into formal logic, never really tried to get to grips with him.

Along with the idiosyncratic theories came an oddly misanthropic approach to most other people. Alan explained this as an acceptance of Nietzsche's claim that solitude was one feature of the life of the higher man. It has always struck Tom that it is more likely to have been the consequence of being a day boy on a scholarship at an expensive boarding school. Alan rejected the view that compassion was at the heart of Christianity and found suffering to be a positive feature of the world which generated stronger, better humans, and was therefore part of God's grace.

His relations with women were suitably entertaining, and he spoke of them with the openness of the true social misfit. His most transformative experience came when he took up briefly with a Japanese art history student at Durham, whom he had met at an aesthetics conference jointly organised by their respective departments. He had been intrigued by her paper on the expression of dominance in Roman Renaissance painting, and after a couple of conventional sessions, she asked him in an accent which he loved to mimic, "You rike to pray games?" He thought he had a pretty clear idea of what this meant, and although he considered himself a naturally superior type, he was also impressed with Nietzsche's view that the more perspectives one could occupy, the better one could understand the world. So he agreed to her request that he sit naked on the floor as she cuffed him to the leg of her bed in the graduate hall of residence. He waited curiously until she came out of the bathroom wearing a pair of high heels, set up her beautifully compact camcorder, and started walking back and forth across the room glaring at him and issuing what he took to be abuse in Japanese. From time to time, she would approach, put a painful heel on his chest and ask questions. When he failed to respond, this appeared to enrage her even more, and the abuse started again. After about twenty minutes of this, she asked her final question and flew into her final rage at his silence, pushing her face to within an inch of his as she bellowed at him. She then hooked the camcorder up to her laptop and played back the footage for them both to watch as she sat astride him.

He barred her calls to his mobile, listed her email address as spam and switched the focus for his thesis from perspectivism to the value of truth. He also became far less experimental and married a former Church of England missionary at St Martin in the Fields a couple of years after he started at Sandford. He now supports her and their two children on his lecturer's salary, so words like "serious incident" and "disciplinary" are not ones he must enjoy, especially from a slavish type like Sally.

After the first lesson, Tili comes back in with her mobile clamped to her cheek. "I'm out tonight, but I can have a look at it tomorrow ... Yeah, great ... OK ... Live long and prosper."

She looks down at Tom. "Plk is trying to organise a series of all-night screenings of the *Star Trek* movies at the Prince Charles," she explains. "He's put together a proposal for me to have a look at, and I just think this could be massive. We're hoping that if we can bring the films to a new audience, we can generate new interest in the original series."

He is relieved to see Alan follow her in and to be able to avoid another rehearsal of her arguments on the metaphysics of warp speed travel. He asks Alan if he has a moment, and they go into one of the interview rooms.

"I have an email from Sally Field which says there is an informal investigation into you."

"Ah, that. Yes. Well, just a combination of misunderstanding and people being too thin-skinned, really. Not sure there is any real need for any of this, but I suppose we have to go through with it if the forces that be say so."

"What happened?"

"Well, it really comes down to two students whom I have told before to arrive at my class on time after lunch and who refuse to do so. I made it clear this couldn't continue, and they have obviously tried to make me out to be the villain of the piece."

"What did you say to them?"

"It was clear I was being ironic."

"What did you say?"

"I just don't see why everyone has to be so humourless about this sort of thing. I was trying to exercise discipline in a light-hearted way which could have made the point without generating any ill-feeling."

Tom waits. Alan takes a deep breath, obviously feeling somewhat self-conscious about what he is about to reveal.

"They came in late, explained why, and I said …"

He delays again. Tom looks at him. He must once again look through a forty-page document, speak with Tony, and teach a class in the four hours between this meeting and that with the governors in the evening. In addition, he will now have to work out what Alan has done, think of some sort of defence, and try to get him off the hook before the matter becomes a formal disciplinary one. Such a turn of events would bring with it the risk of a note going on Alan's file, which will have to be included in any reference provided by the college. Tom is torn between grabbing him by the neck in order to demand that he turn back time to delete whatever has occurred and more practical measures aimed at uncovering the information he needs. Maybe he should just say that the union will not defend a Nietzschean and see if he can track down the footage from his Japanese lover to upload onto the college's learning resources portal for religious studies. At least it would attract more hits than the impenetrable personal reflections Alan posts there.

"Unless you tell me in your next sentence what you said, you will have to find someone else to represent you in the thirty minutes between now and your meeting with Sally."

"If you need to practise strapping on your suicide belts, then don't do it during my lesson."

Tom breathes deeply. "Would I be right in thinking these students are Muslims, and the reason they are late for this class is that they attend the Islamic Society during their lunch hour?"

"Not members exactly."

"Well, what were they doing there?"

"They organise it."

"Did you consider asking them to wear orange jumpsuits and leg irons during your class as well?"

"You see that's the sort of dark humour which I hoped they would respond to. Instead, we all have to act as if we are actors in the theatre of political correctness, and we all waste time pretending to take such comments more seriously than we ought to."

"Listen to me very carefully. The key is to get these students to drop any accusations before it reaches the formal stage. The alternative is slugging it out and defending your innocence. Given that you acknowledge you made the comment, it will come down to whether you have acted in a way consistent with the professional standards expected of a teacher or whether you have breached equal opportunities legislation by acting in an offensive manner. Even if you meant all this in jest, you can be judged to have behaved unprofessionally if they are legitimately offended. It may be difficult to avoid that outcome, so you just have to forget about your dark humour and eat some humble pie."

Alan sits in unhappy silence. Tom looks at him. "Well?" He nods reluctantly and agrees to say nothing in the upcoming meeting. Twenty minutes later, he has still barely spoken to Tom as he knocks on the door of the director of personnel.

"Come in."

There is a sharpness in Sally's tone which is already a bad sign. In the past, she seemed to go out of her way to appear friendly, perhaps because she often felt a residue of embarrassment at how she had acquired her post. She does not look at them. Tom sees the pages of a thick novel on the ledge of her window sill. "What's the book?" he asks, hoping to establish a slightly better atmosphere. The key is that they all feel they are trying to iron everything out together before it gets too serious.

"You're not the only one who reads, Tom." This is uttered in the same sharp tone and still without looking up, ostensibly because she is looking for a file, but more probably because she wishes to look busy and give an impression of serious efficiency.

"It's Danielle Steel's latest."

Before Tom can feign interest by nodding, Alan says, "My goodness, you call that reading?" He laughs and looks at Tom and Sally in anticipation that they will all share in the insightful humour of his latest joke. Tom wishes to drive his colleague's head through the cheap double glazing but smiles politely. Sally looks up for the first time and stops pretending to work.

"We have received a report from two students who have suggested you offended them on religious grounds. At this stage, we are only at the informal stage, and it is hoped that it need go no further. To begin with, we need to see if we can agree on the facts. They claim you accused them of being suicide bombers. Is this true?"

"No. I suggested that they may be using their lunch hours to practise putting on suicide belts, but I said nothing to indicate I thought they would ever use them."

Like all continental philosophers, Alan would argue that logic is ultimately groundless but finds good use for it when not setting out any philosophical views. Before Sally can compose herself in order to register her irritation at this response, Tom breaks in.

"Look, I think there's a danger that we start turning this into something more serious than it is. Alan regrets what he said, and he realises that it could be seen as inappropriate.

But it wasn't meant to be, and it doesn't make sense to make this into a full-blown disciplinary case."

Sally is not placated. "Both students were deeply offended, and this is not the sort of comment which promotes the atmosphere of universal respect we aim at here."

"They weren't so offended that they felt unable to enter the class. They stayed for the whole lesson and apparently answered questions and raised some of their own. This doesn't suggest they were too wounded to carry on. It also has to be set in the context of someone who teaches students from all backgrounds every day and has organised debates between different faith groups in order to promote greater understanding."

"Be that as it may, we can't just ignore this sort of comment."

"He was being facetious, and they know it. There is also the issue of their consistent lateness for his lessons. Given that Alan is prepared not to press the issue of their being disruptive every time they walk in at ten past the hour, they can surely exhibit a touch of discretion. Will they accept an apology?"

She considers this. "I can ask them if they will accept a written apology for any offence."

"The apology will be for any unintended offence, and it will emphasise that Alan has a long history of commitment to the college's policy of equal opportunities."

"I'll see what they say."

Her silence makes it clear that the meeting is over. There is no verbal communication of this and no artificial courtesy when they leave. As they walk down the corridor, it is clear that Alan is not yet ready to accept Tom's proposed solution.

"What if I apologise and then they decide they won't accept it. Doesn't that mean I have acknowledged my guilt before the trial has even begun?"

"You said it in front of twenty students. If this becomes a formal case, management may feel they have to take a hard line for fear of bad publicity. Half of our students are black or Asian, and Dickie can't afford for them to go anywhere else because they think we're not serious about racism. The two students are probably shitting themselves about this already, so you'll be off the hook, and all you have to do is stop making bad jokes."

"I'm not happy about this. Why is it that I can't bring a case against students who ask if my training for the priesthood involves forcing the choir to blow me before Easter service? Why is it that when one of the students in the Christian Union said in jest that he wanted to organise a debate called 'Was the death of Bin Laden the end for Islam?' no one is allowed to laugh?"

"Because Christians have been sticking it to the rest of the world for centuries, and the price you have to pay is being more aware of Muslim sensitivities while you flatten their countries. Think of it as your own little Sandford version of Christ suffering on the cross."

"This is exactly what I'm talking about. Why do you get to make jokes about my religion, but I can't make them about anyone else's?"

"Oh, for fuck's sake, because that's the way it is. Anti-Christian jokes are funny, and anti-Muslim ones aren't, and I don't know why, but please don't press the issue by making any more."

Alan shakes his head in disappointment but is mercifully ready not to pursue it any longer. "All right, and … thank you."

Tom smiles at him. "By the way, your line about suicide

belts is funnier than the one about the choir, and your Christian student should be writing for *Have I Got News for You*. Maybe in a decade or two the world will be ready for your line of humour."

He is relieved at the thought that this should bring Alan's case to a close, but now he must somehow try to extract some items of sanity from Tony Coyle. He leaves Alan by the staff canteen. He decides that the most effective way forward is to try and focus on a single issue and to bring Tony back whenever he begins to wander. In this way, he hopes to restrict the scope of the discussion in terms of both time and subject matter. He knocks and enters the IT support room. The Munsters are apparently enjoying some anecdotes about tricks they have played with printer cables, but Tony's face ices over when he sees Tom, and the others look down. He feels like Michael Corleone walking in on Carlo toward the end of *The Godfather*.

"Do you have a moment?"

Tony rises and leads him out. They walk towards the union office again, but Tony stops just before they reach the door. "No! I can't go in there with you. It's too risky."

So they remain in the corridor with staff passing them on coffee runs.

"I received my copy of the July report. Thank you for that, it was very brave of you."

Tony's eyes widen, his lips tighten, and he looks from side to side. "Listen to me very carefully. You did not receive that report from me. You understand? You did not receive it from me. If they think I am passing stuff to you, then I am finished, and I will be unable to guide you against them."

"I understand exactly what you're saying. We all recognise the difficulty of your situation."

"'All'! 'All'! What do you mean 'all'? Who have you told this to?"

Tom realises his error too late, and he must now find some means of reassuring him in order to see if he has anything to say which is open to rational interpretation. "There is an elite group of leaders within the union which orchestrates our actions. We have to share information in order to decide the best way forward, but I have concealed your identity. We refer to you only using your code name."

"What is my code name?"

"Mr X," he replies lamely, unable to come up with anything more plausible at such short notice. But Mr X nods in quiet satisfaction. Having warmed him up, Tom now hopes he can extract some sort of semi-useful material from this giant ball of madness.

"One of the things you said last time is that we should follow the money. What did you mean?"

"Why do you think they're getting rid of all these people?"

"They've told us they need it for repairs."

"Fourteen million for essential repairs over ten years and another ten million on top for bells and whistles. This college runs an annual surplus of eight hundred thousand pounds a year, and we have reserves of four million. Even in big business, we would find these numbers pretty good. All they would have to do to save the extra amount is not replace a few staff who leave."

"So why the changes?"

"What happened to recruitment last year?"

"We dropped by a few hundred students."

"Why?"

"Competition from other colleges. Some new sixth forms."

"Numbers of students rose across the whole of London,

but ours went down. Students are desperate to come here because they can't get jobs, so why did we lose numbers?"

"What are you getting at?"

Tony breathes deeply and looks around once more. "The funding agency stopped funding a series of IT courses. They wrote to all colleges in the autumn of last year telling them that there would be no more government money, but someone fucked up. We carried on recruiting for those courses and ended up taking in four hundred students for courses which bring in no money. And it gets worse. Now they are here, we have to offer the courses, so we are teaching students who bring in no money and who are taking up the spaces which we needed to offer students the government would fund."

"So why not just pay for the loss out of reserves."

"The funding agency tells you the maximum number of students you can take in. They base it on the previous year's numbers. That means that because we are down by four hundred students on funded courses this year, we will have our maximum reduced by four hundred from now on. That's two million pounds a year. Paying for repairs wouldn't have been a problem, but now we can't afford it."

"So what have the governors said to all this?"

"We only found out in July, and it was all rolled up in talk of the need for a more efficient staffing structure. It got overshadowed by all the stuff about pay."

"There's a public sector pay freeze across the whole country. Dickie gave us nothing."

"Not your pay, his. The remuneration committee decided on some kind of new arrangement for him and the other senior managers, and even some of his mates weren't happy."

"What's he on?"

"No one knows outside the remuneration committee. They claimed that, because it's related to the pay of individuals, it's not appropriate that people like the staff and student governors should know the details."

He is about to continue, but then his eyes bulge out. "Fuck me." And he turns to face the door of the union office, through which he had earlier refused to walk. He desperately yanks the handle of the locked door up and down but soon gives up and turns to face his fears. Dan Corporal, the vice principal is standing beside them. "Hello Tom. Uh, Tony, the sound on my PC has disappeared again. Any chance someone could come and have a look at it?"

"Of course. I will take care of it personally this afternoon. I was just answering a desperate call from the union to look at the computer in their office, but Tom has forgotten the key."

Dan looks at Tom. "Is it the universal key?"

"I believe so."

"No problem, I have one." He pulls out an expensive-looking leather key purse and hunts through the selection, finding the right one with his second attempt. He opens the door and smiles sympathetically. "There you go. Now you can tell them how to hack into the management's emails."

Tony is stone-faced. "Sorry, no time now." And he strides off.

Dan turns to Tom. "I thought he was going to fix your computer."

"I think he's forgotten his repair kit."

Dan looks down the corridor after him. "You know, I sometimes think that man is a little odd."

Tom waits for Dan to disappear and then makes his way back up to his office. When he gets there, he opens an email from Sally Field which is addressed to Alan and copied to Tom.

```
Dear Alan and Tom,

I have spoken to the two students who is-
sued the complaint concerning comments made
in your religious studies class earlier
this week. When I informed them you were
prepared to apologise, they were satisfied
and do not require this in writing.

I wish to emphasise that this college
places a strong emphasis on equal opportu-
nities, and we will take very seriously any
further episodes in which you apparently
fail to reach the high standards that Sand-
ford's management expect.

Regards,
Sally Field
Personnel Director
```

There is a moment's relief that one blaze has been extinguished, but this is quickly subsumed by his unease at the thought that he must see Sally again in two hours. The difference this time is that he must meet all of those from whom he has most to fear. He texts Alan to congratulate him and suggests meeting at The Garden in the evening. He also texts Mike, who will offer better competition on the pool table. He hopes this will provide a release after what now stands before him.

CHAPTER EIGHT

Liefwint enters, and there is silence. It is absurdly dramatic. Sally is making small talk with the other two governors, and the artificiality of her greeting reveals an extreme nervousness. The governors offer equally forced smiles of welcome. This discomfort transmits itself to the union members, all of whom shift in their seats as Liefwint walks, straight-backed, to an unoccupied part of the square of tables, nodding only to the governors and managers. His hair is greying but so perfectly styled that he looks as if readied for entry onto a film set. His clothes, glasses, watch, everything about him suggests a careful and refined selection which blends oddly well into the overarching impression of coldness. Tom is reminded of *Revelation*. "And I looked, and behold a pale horse: and his name that sat on him was Death, and Hell followed with him." Actually, this isn't quite accurate. He is reminded of *Pale Rider*, which he watched on E4 after coming home drunk from The Garden last Friday, and the next day he googled the biblical passage from the scene where Clint enters the prospectors' camp.

Bella follows Liefwint in with a tray of drinks. She moves initially towards Barry, whose seat is closest to the door. Sally sighs in irritation and motions to her to serve the governors first.

The meeting is to be led by Jeremy Morgan, who chairs the governing body, and Jennifer Unwin, the vice chair, who sits beside him. Dickie has brought only Sally Field. This gives Tom and Barry the answer to one of their questions. There have been rumours that the vice principal, Dan Corporal, has been largely excluded from drawing up these plans. Now they know it is true. They are with Colin Preston, and they have agreed that he would take the lead. Morgan opens the meeting.

"Right, what I suggest is that we divide our time into roughly two parts. We feel that it would be helpful for you to understand why the governing body and management wish to take the college forward in the way we have set out. We feel you will be more sympathetic to what we're doing if you understand the background circumstances. We also want to give a clearer picture of our vision for Sandford. But in advance of this, we feel that certain basic points need to be made as clear as possible."

He breathes deeply, as if preparing himself for an extended underwater dive.

"We, that is to say, both governors and managers, have obligations. We all have. You will be aware of this as teachers. But our obligations as governors and managers, our obligations as custodians of this college, they, well, they must be met in ways which sometimes give the illusion of toughness. What I'm getting at ... What I think you must make every effort to understand, to grasp, to come to terms with, is that ... Well ... Let me think how best to express this ... We have obligations to ensure that this college's finances are stable, sensible, rational ... that they make sense. We must under no circumstances allow instability or short-term thinking to undermine what we are all working together to achieve here. We, and how shall I put this? We ..."

Liefwint shuffles some of his papers. "I think the union understands the key point, Jeremy."

"Yes, of course. In which case, I shall be asking Piers to explain in the first instance why it is we are where we are. Why it is we need to think in terms of …well …" He turns to Liefwint.

"It is easiest to think in terms of the several distinct causal factors which require the action we are taking. First, the college suffered an unexpected shortfall in student recruitment at the start of the last academic year. This requires a budgetary adjustment. Second, we must meet essential costs for building repairs in a climate of economic austerity. Third, we need a staffing structure which incentivises all staff to perform with maximum efficiency. Taken together, this requires changes to both staffing numbers and salary arrangements to generate greater efficiency at a lower cost. These measures are painful but necessary."

He stops abruptly, and Colin nods. "Thank you for that. I think we can understand the basic logic of your argument. Can you explain why the college suffered a drop in student numbers?"

"Grades fell, so fewer students were recruited into the second year."

"And is that the only reason?"

There is a flicker of unease, but his tone remains robotic. "I suggest we focus on where we are, and how we move forward."

"All right. You state that jobs must go because income has fallen. If it emerges that income has fallen because senior managers have recruited students for courses which aren't funded, then surely you need to look at removing inefficient managers who have failed to meet their obligations."

Liefwint rolls his eyes, leans forward with nostrils flaring, and bellows his reply. "So that's your response. Hang a few senior managers from the college gates to satisfy your members. Does it not occur to you that will do nothing to help your people? Does it register that a college cannot exist with deficits and a building falling apart?"

Morgan and Unwin break in to try and restrain him, but he continues, now in a low, rhythmic tone.

"This organisation requires a staffing structure within which it can make ends meet. It also requires a modern building which will attract clients. The cost of this means fewer jobs. Now live with it."

Barry leans forward, but Colin places an arm on his. He is still remarkably controlled, even amiable. "I think you are missing my point. I am not suggesting any job losses, but if you are genuinely committed to efficiency, then this can only be achieved if you have managers who are as astute as possible with the money we have. I'm just curious why you are looking only at job losses among staff who bear no responsibility for the college's financial problems, and not considering the current performance of the senior managers who have cost the college two million pounds a year in lost revenue?"

Dickie now stirs, realising not only that he is the obvious target but that information he did not really wish to be discussed is now likely to be broadcast across the entire college by Barry.

"Gentlemen, the intricacies and complexities of running a college with such a myriad of courses and dealing with such a confusing and ever-changing mix of funding bodies means that all colleges must forever perform a series of manoeuvres to extract whatever money is available from bodies who often seem reluctant to give it. On occasion, we have missed opportunities, but I can assure you that we have also seized many that less effective managers would have let slip by. I can say with hand on heart that I and my close colleagues have brought in many more pounds to Sandford through ingenuity and hard work than the occasional lapse may have cost."

"Can we assume that the new arrangements you wish to introduce will include a bonus scheme for you which will reward your ingenuity?"

Liefwint now intervenes once more. "I have already stated that we must improve efficiency through a more effective salary scheme. The arrangements for individuals are confidential. All of your members will be better off with managers who are maximally motivated to run the organisation in the most efficient way."

"Forgive me, but you seem to be saying that making our members redundant and cutting the pay of those who remain is a benefit."

"These are the necessary measures which are required to secure the future of those who remain."

"If these measures are as rational as you say, why did you not consult over them with your staff? It seems unfortunate to many of our members that they have to find out the details of this through a copy of your July fifth report being leaked to us."

For the first time they are obviously thrown off guard. Morgan is the first to respond, directing his question at Sally.

"I had the impression we agreed to release a copy of the report to the union leadership."

Sally shrinks back in her chair as everyone focuses on her. "I … I … don't understand. I gave the clearest possible instructions that a copy was to be sent. I am so sorry, and I … I can assure you all that I will look into it. But as far as consultation is concerned, we did invite the union representatives to the meeting where the final report was to be discussed and they declined the invitation."

Barry and Tom look at one another, and it is Tom who understands first. "We were told that the subject of the meeting was to be maintenance. No one said anything about redundancies or restructuring."

Liefwint has now recovered his composure. "So you were invited to the meeting and refused to attend. As for the subject matter, it is entirely accurate to say that maintenance was what was discussed. I am afraid I cannot account for why you did not receive the July fifth report, but you shall have a copy tomorrow."

It is extraordinary how something could be so clear and yet missed by everyone. Tom's irritation at the deception for which he and Barry have fallen as well as his satisfaction at Sally's discomfort almost cause him to overlook the obvious explanation that the copy of the report they have received came from management and that Tony Coyle was telling the truth when he said it hadn't come from him. Difficult to say if the nut was too paranoid to send it or too much in love with his shrewd-secret-agent-in-danger fantasy to give up on it that easily. At least now they need not waste any more time on him. Colin continues to press for the many details they are missing.

"The report speaks of eighty jobs going, which is a quarter of the teaching force. When do you plan to start the redundancy process?"

It is Liefwint who once again assumes control of the distribution of information. "It is most effective to move quickly and clearly in this sort of situation. The longer it drags on, the more the organisation risks falling into demoralisation and postpones the moment when it grasps the future. The criteria for the selection of staff who are to be released will be set out next week. Those selected will receive notice of redundancy in two weeks."

"And when do you plan to make the first redundancy?"
"Half-term."

Barry reacts quickest. "That's five weeks away."

"The statutory minimum period is thirty days. The final day of the half-term holiday will be the thirtieth day."

Barry leans forward, but Colin restrains him once again and continues to address Liefwint exclusively.

"You speak of the statutory minimum …"

Sally now intervenes, enthusiastically demonstrating her mastery of the topic. "Yes, Colin. The minimum period required for up to one hundred staff is thirty days, and we will of course comply fully with the law. And can I just add that we appreciate what a difficult time this will be for many of your members, and we shall be offering counselling services and advice on job-seeking in the sincere hope that not one lecturer will be out of work for a moment longer than is necessary. We take very seriously our duty of care towards our staff."

"Just to be clear, are you talking of reducing the college by eighty posts or eighty staff?"

Liefwint looks genuinely curious. "Why should it matter?"

"Your report speaks of reducing the staff by eighty full-time equivalent posts. The law sets minimum requirements for the number of persons to be made redundant, not the number of posts. Given that many staff are part-time, eighty full-time posts would require over one hundred people to go, and this means the minimum period of consultation is ninety days. Should you fail to offer such a period, then anyone made redundant by the college would be entitled to compensation to be determined by an employment tribunal. Should you try to select only full-time employees, then you would be in breach of equal opportunities legislation and the same outcome would follow. You are, moreover, required to take seriously the proposals put forward during any period of consultation, and I can assure you that we shall indeed be putting forward alternative proposals."

Everyone in the room looks from Colin to Liefwint, whose extended, expressionless silence is sublime, and it is Morgan who must eventually break the spell.

"Can I suggest that it is in all of our interests, and above all in the interests of Sandford College and the many fine students who come here to study, that this should not descend into a legal contest. Can we not agree on a sensible way forward which will meet the needs of this college that all of us wish to protect and see prosper?"

Colin nods sympathetically. "I think that is an ideal way of approaching the issues. Perhaps I could suggest that there be regular meetings between senior management and union representatives, say weekly, in which they explore the financial issues facing the college and ideas for taking it forward. There is no reason why reductions in staff numbers need be controversial, as I am sure that the numbers of staff who leave each year will allow management room for manoeuvre."

Dickie is mortified. "Weekly! Surely ... surely, Barry and Tom are far too busy for that."

Barry shakes his head. "Richard, we will make the time, and we will all sit down and work this through together." He then turns to Morgan. "Jeremy, let me thank you on behalf of your lecturing staff for helping us find a route out of this."

Morgan is delighted at this. "Splendid, splendid. Well, I think we can bring things to a close, and we will look forward to receiving updates from Richard and Sally regarding progress in your talks."

Barry buys bitter for Colin and himself and a small glass of Chilean Merlot for Tom. Colin says nothing while they wait for Barry to return and appears unconsoled by his apparent victory. "I recommend that you continue with the ballot in any case."

Barry is surprised. "I thought you were against unnecessary acts of aggression. They'll think we're still getting ready for a fight after they've raised the white flag."

"All they've agreed to do is talk and obey the law. If they think we can reach a compromise on staff reductions, then that may be enough for them, but I am nervous about this Liefwint character. It's very unusual to see people like him on a governing body. You tend to get do-gooding old farts like Morgan, who turn up and say what the principal tells them to. Did you see the way all the others kept their mouths shut when he spoke? He's not here to pad out his CV, he wants to serve the common good by turning the place into a model of private sector efficiency."

"So we ballot and hope for the best."

"No. You ballot and plan for the worst. Ninety days means everyone is safe until Christmas. If they are so ignorant of the law and so unconcerned about the impact of what they do that they try this in September, then they're not going to let up because it's the season of good will. Better be ready."

"Can you believe Sally's bullshit about how much concern they have for the welfare of the staff?"

"I've heard that speech a hundred times before from a hundred different managers. Their training manuals tell them the importance of being sensitive to the reactions of staff in these situations, so they use the right language, and it doesn't occur to them that they lack any of the right feelings. The odd thing is that it makes them look worse rather than better. At least Liefwint is honest."

The conversation begins to drift into wider issues of what is going on elsewhere in London. Tom sees his chance and rises, but Barry looks at him in disbelief. "Off already?"

"That RS teacher who had a personal case is on the other side of the bar. I just want to have a word with him to make sure he's all right with the outcome." This is a lie. Tom has had enough for one day. Too many meetings where absurdly uncooperative characters must be painfully manipulated into the right position. Too much obsequious diplomacy and second guessing where a rational exchange should have led to a resolution. Now he wishes only the violent release of cracking a pool ball with the distinctive feeling of oncoming drunkenness.

He makes his way around to the pool tables, where Alan sees him first. "How was the meeting?"

"Explosive."

"Fuck off."

"Such language from a man of the cloth. How badly are you losing?"

"I took the first frame but none of the last eight."

Mike has grown up with a snooker table in the conversion built over the garage. The transition from the larger to the smaller baize was enforced by the difficulty of playing regularly even in halls at Cambridge. When he plays he marches round the table, cracking the white with ferocious power, and always playing for perfect position on the following ball. This means that when he is playing well, matches last a few moments. Tom breaks, but no ball drops, and Mike clears the table. Mike breaks, and a stripe rolls to the brim of the pocket before a painfully slow descent into the pocket, and he clears the table again. Tom looks around and sees a man sitting on his own, reading. He beckons Mike over and whispers into his ear. "Who's that strange guy who keeps looking over at you? You see? That one reading the book in Cyrillic."

To any ordinary person this would be so transparent an attempt to disconcert Mike, it would be embarrassing. But there is a near-perfect consistency to the paranoid mind, which makes even the most innocent events seem like evidence of a real threat. Mike looks over, but his glasses will not allow him to decipher the language on the cover of the book. With divine luck, the man looks up, sees Mike staring at him, holds his stare for a moment, and looks down at his book again. An hour later, Tom takes the train with Mike to Clapham Junction, pretending to check incessantly in order to reassure him that a man who was reading a novel in a pub is not in fact a Russian assassin and is not following them. Tom also generously consoles Mike in light of his collapse into easy misses and air shots. Well, given that Mike grew up with a snooker table, this was really just levelling things up. But through the amusement, there is another thought which troubles Tom after they part. Suddenly, winning feels more important, and he cares less about how he achieves it.

CHAPTER NINE

When she steps on the court, he assumes this is a question of formality. The format of the encounter is that there are nine matches, each of which is the best of three sets. The team winning the greater number of matches wins the final and, therefore, the tournament. Griffin trail three four, but the final match will see Mitch play an opposing captain against whom he has always triumphed with crushing ease. This means the straightforward victory expected from Sofia will deliver all. Dulford have three times the number of members, many of whom have contributed the funds which have gone into the ultra-modern artificial clay courts and the huge clubhouse. They have heard of Sofia and also field their top woman. Michelle 'Mitzi' Thornton is a south London beast to make a heavyweight quiver in his sleep. She is higher, wider, and deeper than Sofia. A wall of muscle which has grown and grown through the years of her twenties and early thirties, long after the optimism of her junior national ranking had faded into the career of the trainer who was never quite a player. She bounces up and down on the court as Sofia removes her tracksuit, and one fears the surface may crumble. Tom is reminded of *Predator*.

Even when they warm up, Mitzi strikes the ball with hideous force. The whole, exaggerated body is thrown forward to impart the maximum power for each blow. This need mean little on a tennis court, where control and patience are often more effective than strength. Sofia has spent ten years playing the club's top men, allowing them to hit shot after shot as hard as they can while she sends it back deep to a corner again and again until they overhit. Mitzi opens, tossing the ball high and propelling her body forward to thunder down a first serve which far exceeds the pace of anything Tom can generate. She holds easily, and Sofia responds by kicking high serves into the corners of the service box, making the ball spin wildly away from the receiver on landing. She also holds. Mitzi misses her first serve on each of the next two points, but Sofia's returns are five feet short of the baseline, and Mitzi steps forward to drive ferocious winners into each corner. Sofia serves again, but Mitzi is now standing back further to give herself time to adjust to the spin of the ball as it leaps off the court. She plays controlled returns deep to bring herself into the point. Sofia tries to move her from side to side, but sooner or later Mitzi is able to get to a shot early and hit with greater power. In doing so, it is she who begins to move her opponent around the court, and once she elicits a weaker shot, she moves forward to smash the ball down a line. After twenty-five minutes, Sofia hits a return into the net and loses her first set to a British woman. Mitzi turns to her teammates, who are gathered on the deckchairs near one corner of the court. She points to them as if to cue their response, and they clap and cheer furiously in their *Downton Abbey* accents. "Good girl, Mitzi. One more set. Come on now." As they change ends, Sofia looks over at Tom and smiles faintly. She is being destroyed. Now he doesn't care about the Centurion Cup, or any other tennis match. He just wants this to end. He just wants to hold her.

Sofia must open the second set, and she does so by hitting a harder, flatter serve. It is short and right at the edge of the service box, so Mitzi must stretch. She reaches it easily but cannot generate the usual pace, so Sofia is able to strike the ball early to the other corner and come in to the net. Mitzi runs with inhuman strides to make a return, but Sofia volleys comfortably into an empty court. She now aims at a sideline with every serve and every ground stroke. More go in than out. Her opponent can no longer reach as many shots with the time and ease she needs to power the ball back. Now she is running more, and her muscle becomes a burden she must carry as she pounds from side to side. She must pause between points to recover. The monstrous serve remains invulnerable, with shot after shot hammered down. But when momentum shifts in a tennis match, it is never a matter of someone just playing better. When you have been crushing an opponent, and you suddenly find yourself in an even contest, it is a curious fact of sporting psychology that you begin contemplating defeat. It is as if the move from dominance to parity is part of an organised motion towards your opponent dominating you, and the fear of this possibility plays a large part in its coming to pass.

When the score reaches four-five, with Mitzi now serving to stay in the set, her earlier destructiveness is diminished. Now the plummy voices which cheer her do no more than betray the doubts which everyone knows she is also feeling. Her first serve is long, and her second strikes the net cord and falls back on her own side. Her first serve in the second point is also long, and her second serve is hit so nervously short that Sofia is able to play a comfortable winner down the line. She serves an ace, then another double fault gives Sofia two set points. She hits a powerless first serve to ensure she gets it in, and both players play controlled shots from the baseline hoping that the other will gift them the point. Mitzi hits a short ball. Sofia runs in but hits it wide. Mitzi then strikes a monstrous first serve, but Sofia leans into it and smashes the ball cross court for a winner to make it one set all. She turns to the Griffin players, raises a clenched fist and shouts, "Vamos!" The crowd goes wild.

Sofia must now serve to open the final set. She continues to hit every shot as near to a sideline as she can, with Mitzi hoping for something closer to her. Sofia takes the first two points with ease. On the third, they exchange twenty-two blows, with Mitzi racing from side to side, before Sofia plays a drop shot. Mitzi rumbles in and strikes a beautifully controlled slice to within a foot of the baseline, but even as she is recovering position the lob is looping back over her. The immense thighs propel her to an improbable height from which she smashes the ball out. In a poor imitation of the upper-class voice from earlier, Griffin's junior girl, a lippy kid from one of the Streatham estates, shouts, "Good girl, Mitzi." Even Mitch has to suppress a laugh as he tells her to belt up.

On the next point, Sofia plays the drop shot once more, and Mitzi doesn't run for it. Now comes the colossal serve again. But the balls have been used for an hour by now and are softer. Sofia has seen the serve for an hour and is able to pick it up more easily. Mitzi has served and run for an hour and is able to hit the ball less powerfully. Yet towering over all these factors is the fundamental shift in the sense of who is the better player. Mitzi begins with two first serves. The first swings wide, and Sofia cannot return it. The second is directly at her, and she steps to one side, pushes a return into the corner, then follows it in to volley away the weak response. Mitzi's second serve is now cracked back down the line for a clean winner, after which she is once again caught by a drop shot. She then double faults going for a huge second serve. Tom wishes to stand up and give the Dulford members the wanker sign but manages to restrain himself and just laps up the remaining twenty minutes of Sofia moving her opponent around like a child pulling on the string of a yoyo. Six–two. Forty-five minutes later, Tom is taking pictures of Mitch holding the glass trophy, smile like a kid's.

Mitch puts two hundred pounds behind the bar to pay for everyone's drinks and speaks to all those who have turned up to play or watch. After an hour, he sits down next to Tom.

"You need to stop forcing so many home deliveries down her. She had me worried for a set. Thank God she turned it round in the end."

"I like to think that my straight sets win in the mixed doubles made it all possible."

"I bet you do. Tell me, how do you come to terms with being a radical and playing your mixed doubles with someone who works on the international desk at Goldman Sachs?"

"I'm hoping my fine play will let her see the attractions of being poor and on the verge of losing your job and pension."

"I saw some reference to your dispute on the BBC website. Didn't sound too good. Something about a quarter of the teachers losing their jobs."

Tom sighs. One curious aspect of his life is a deep discrepancy between the depressing reality of his work and the merciful release of his time with Sofia and on the tennis court. He resents it whenever thoughts of Dickie Kilman and Sally begin to poison areas which he wants to be immune from them.

"One of the sociology lecturers lives next door to a woman who writes for the website. The journalist was interested because the local MP is a former education minister, and she liked the angle that a minister is making public speeches about the need for a high-skilled economy just as his local college is closing courses which are supposed to give us precisely those skills he is telling us we all need. They ran the story after there was a huge vote for strike action and it looked as if it was all going to blow up."

"So is he stepping in to save you?"

"Some public words about the need for staff and management to come together for the sake of the students, but a Tory can't side with a union, and he doesn't want to be associated with a management which is destroying education, so he'll just sit it out and tell everyone afterwards that he had always spoken of the need for compromise. The principal put a halt to all meetings for two weeks after the piece appeared and the local press picked it up."

"But now he's talking to you again."

"We've had seven weeks of talks. We're arguing that he can just wait till the end of the year and not replace the staff who leave. He claims he may need to cut jobs sooner, and more of them."

"And you?"

"Difficult to know. He hates the union, but it's risky getting rid of union reps in case it looks like victimisation. He's more likely to go for people who teach expensive courses like engineering or science."

"Good idea. That way we can have philosophers build bridges and carry out surgery. It's odd that you haven't even been on strike yet. When I think of disputes I think of miners living on two pounds a day for a year."

"So do I, but the truth is that virtually the whole of any dispute is talk. You talk to managers, to journalists, to lawyers, to members. The rest of the time you just work normally and occasionally have to come out."

"Your Goldman Sachs girl over there was telling me that they released forty traders after two thousand and eight. They just gave them a year's pay, and they left without a whimper."

"That's what the smart colleges do too. It's expensive, but it's very easy to get rid of people if you pay them enough to go. Our guy is offering a couple of months' pay for people to go voluntarily, and all they can see is a short delay before unemployment. Offer them a year and they can think in terms of six months' holiday before they come back to find another job."

Mitch pauses. "Listen, I hope you won't feel patronised, but if things don't go well, then speak to me, and I may be able to help out if you're in a pinch."

"That's very good of you. I'm pleased my local tennis club is going to take good care of me."

"Oh, I just want to make sure you can keep Sofia happy."

"You know I can see why you've done so well Mitch."

Tom appreciates an offer which he knows to be genuine. Yet this also lays bare the crude simplicity of Mitch's financial security. He has done so well that he need never work again and is never prey to the unfortunate tendency of the wealthy to worry endlessly about their money. The upshot is a man at ease with himself, relaxed in a life of family and friends, distantly supervising a company ticking over with effortless efficiency, and worrying about nothing more than his second serve. For Tom, life seems to have arced in the opposite direction. The years of penury after returning to London were relieved when they found their safe public-sector posts, but money is now pressing down on them again as it had before. Public-sector pay freezes means inflation cuts their salaries by five per cent a year. Were Tom to lose his job, it would not simply return them to where they had been before. He is past forty, owns no property and teaches a subject viewed by many as decadent at a time when even teachers are considered a necessary sacrifice in the struggle for national stability. He is not at an age when talk of pensions is abstract any more.

Years of play in Valencia means he must now cling to a job in which he must work longer for less money to secure a lower pension, and this seems dramatically more attractive than returning to unemployment. Even if he were to find work again, he knows that it may well be one short-term contract after another so that it is easier to get rid of him. And there are aspects of this which begin to damage him with increasing force. Part of the internal disruption is the breaking of two associations which have hitherto seemed well-drawn. The first is that if you work in education, you will have a job which is underpaid but safe. Now he would be underpaid and unsafe. The second is the relationship between aging and security. He imagined that the moment of his signing a permanent contract at Sandford constituted an irreversible step towards a life standing upon a materially solid foundation, which has seemed like compensation for the physical decline of which he is has increasingly been aware. Twelve years ago, Sofia used to tell him how well he ran as she manipulated him from side to side on court. Now his receding hairline contrasts badly with an ever-expanding midriff, pushing out like a super slo-mo from *Alien*. This sense of simultaneous physical and material decline imposes a sense of anxiety which rarely leaves him. It also fills him with near pathological levels of disdain for Dickie, whom he now sees as the cause of everything in his life which refuses to go well. If he hits a backhand wide, it is all down to work-related pressure.

CHAPTER TEN

The meetings are so painful there are times when redundancy seem preferable. By the time they reach mid-November, they have progressed only in the sense that no one has lost their job and there hasn't been a strike. The regulars are Dickie and Sally for management, with occasional guest appearances from curriculum or finance specialists. Tom and Barry are accompanied by Colin Preston, and sometimes bring with them an accounts lecturer when a financial document is tabled. The same argument is repeated in fractionally different forms at each meeting. Dickie might claim that the college needs financial stability, or that any healthy organisation must generate a surplus, or that the community cannot risk the loss of its only major sixth form provider through bankruptcy. Colin continues to take the lead in negotiations, emphasising how much the union wishes to work with management. Tom finds himself having to crawl over accounts and financial projections in order to detect ways in which the numbers have either been exaggerated, or else come up with some means of reducing losses without redundancies. In the face of every suggestion, Dickie's response is that he needs to be absolutely convinced that the proposal doesn't endanger the college and that he hasn't reached that point yet. Dipping into the four million pounds in reserves will diminish the college's ability to respond to any financial emergency. Raising money from other sources sounds good but is impractical in this general climate. No other costs can be cut because everything except salaries goes only toward essential works. Nietzsche argued that one test of whether you truly had the resilience to be a higher type was whether you would accept living every moment of your life over and over again. It occurs to Tom that one ultimate means of failing this test would be if there were single moments which you would never agree to live through again under any circumstances. Every one of these meetings is such a moment.

The only redeeming interludes come when Barry can no longer restrain himself. At one point, he suggests that, if Dickie were to give up his bonus and accept a cut in salary, then this would be evidence of the commitment to his staff which he claims to have. Dickie's eyes bulge, and his face reddens as he stands up to lean across the table and wag his finger, bellowing back, "You can have no idea of the responsibility of leadership – I have made this college what it is, and I deserve every penny of the money I earn!"

"You've lost us millions and you want to pay yourself a bonus to sort out the mess you created. What's your plan? Are you hoping the Royal Bank of Scotland will make you chief executive once you've wrecked this place?"

"Get out! This meeting is over, and there will be no more until I receive an unreserved apology for this outrageous slight."

The union side leaves, and they can only reconvene thirty minutes later when Colin manages to convince Dickie that Barry has expressed genuine contrition as against the unbroken stream of bile which he had released in the union office. The meeting then returns to its relentlessly dull beat.

By early December, they have met twelve times and have inched towards an agreement which will at least delay any further disagreement. Dickie has at last relented and agreed that the college's reserves might be tapped for a one-off expense. This doesn't imply running the permanent deficits which no one is suggesting. The money will go towards an enhanced package of voluntary redundancy which will be offered to all teaching staff at around five months' gross salary. Management will also put in place a redeployment policy which means that where staff leaves in areas where they are needed, staff at risk will be moved into those jobs and given training to do them. The idea of two different levels of lectureship with differing pay scales is dropped. Staff will leave at the summer half-term, which means their teaching will be finished and the payoff will see them through to the following autumn, by when they will hopefully have found a new post. The unspoken premise to all this is that so many people are so unsettled that there will be a race to get out, and this will remove the need for any compulsory redundancies. Dickie has agreed to present this to the governing body, where it should be formally endorsed next week. It is left open as to what will happen if too few staff leave, and the fear is that talk of compulsory redundancies will return. The hope is that this might be conveniently forgotten in order to avoid a damaging fight, and the staff may enjoy a rather more relaxed Christmas.

In the days after Tom trudges out of the office with the deal done, he feels no satisfaction. There is only a curious relief that the sort of deal which should have been hammered out to begin with is now in place. If anything, he still feels a sense of extreme irritation that it has taken three months of Sisyphean struggle to achieve what could have been done in a few hours of rational discussion. Colin Preston was right that the major obstacles had nothing to do with practical reality. It has simply been a question of Dickie's enormous ego satisfying itself it has exerted sufficient power to allow some scraps to fall the way of its enemy. They know that he will be feeling he has demonstrated breathtaking skill in balancing the financial needs of the college against the potential damage of a strike and shown great humanity into the bargain.

Having spent years thinking of the classroom as a source of nervous exhaustion, it has now become a merciful escape for Tom. You can step outside the atmosphere of anger and demoralisation which has settled over the staff and enter into a sphere where the people you deal with are only vaguely conscious of what dominates the thoughts of their teachers. Whereas any conversation with colleagues is either about losing your job or a temporary distraction from that topic, each class allows you to re-engage with the same material which has existed prior to the September announcement that jobs would be going. It's like watching a slideshow of shots from a happier time, which makes you momentarily recall what this place used to be.

Tom enters the classroom, and only Laura is there. He smiles at her, and she looks down at first but then looks back at him.

"Could I speak with you after the class?"

"Sure. Something up?"

"I just need to discuss something."

Before they can continue, Amrit and Maya come in. Miles follows two minutes later. Tom is about to begin when Joe enters and walks straight past him. Tom rolls his eyes. "Come here."

"What's up?"

"Come here."

Joe stands his ground and kisses his teeth. This means 'arsehole', but it is almost involuntary on the part of many students, and Tom chooses to let it pass.

"Why are you late?"

"Trains."

"It's one-twenty. Why are you late?"

"Had to see a teacher."

"Who?"

"Photography teacher."

"Which one?"

"Jeff Thomas."

"You were booted out of photography last year, and Jeff Thomas left this college in the summer. Why are you late?"

"Don't know."

Tom sighs deeply. "I've already told you it is not acceptable to turn up late. Next time you won't be allowed in."

Joe turns to walk to his seat, but Tom isn't finished. "If you arrive late to any class, you apologise, and you don't kiss your teeth."

"Sorry," he says with obvious irritation. Tom watches him with rising anger as he makes his way to his seat.

"All right. Aristotle provides a theory of action which many feel is a perfect common-sense account of the way in which we all think on these matters. What is the relationship between the following concepts: voluntary action, responsibility, praise, and blame?"

Miles looks up at him. "Is it the obvious?"

"Yes, so state it."

"If we do something voluntarily, then we are responsible for the action, so we can be praised if it's good and blamed if it's bad."

"Exactly ..." He is about to continue when he hears Joe mumble something. "You have a question?" He then realises Joe is whispering into his mobile. "Are you fucking kidding me?"

Absolute silence.

"Sorry, important call," he says to Tom before speedily

concluding, "I'll call you later," and placing the phone on the table.

"Put it in your bag."

He puts it on the lip of his rucksack.

"Put it inside the bag."

He pushes it fractionally further down.

"Attendance in this course is purely voluntary. Feel free to leave if you're unhappy with the rules which apply here."

No response.

"All right. Now if we hold people responsible for voluntary actions, this means there is an obvious relationship between Aristotle's theory of virtue and his theory of action. If morally good actions are voluntary ones, then we need to know what is meant by the terms 'voluntary' and 'involuntary'. How might we define an involuntary action, Joe?"

"Dunno."

"Maya?"

"One where you're forced to do it?"

"Good. So it could be when you are physically forced to do it, for example when you are dragged into a room. But Aristotle also thinks that involuntary actions could be ones where you are ignorant of certain key facts. Let us say for example that Joe is not someone who has been at this college for over a year and knows the rules governing the use of mobile phones. Let us say instead that he is new at the college and is ignorant of the fact that one may not text people when your teacher is addressing the class. Is this act of undermining my authority voluntary or involuntary?"

Joe looks up as Tom glares at him. "Last chance today."

"Aw'right."

Amrit raises a hand. "If Joe is genuinely ignorant, and he's not intending to challenge your authority, then it might be involuntary?"

Joe grimaces at the reference to his ignorance.

"Very good. Involuntary actions are ones performed through compulsion or in ignorance. Voluntary ones are those we choose to do in possession of the relevant information. Aristotle has a third category for people such as Joe. Let us say that Joe started off as ignorantly as you suggest, sincerely unaware that there is a rule he is breaking. The question is what happens when he finds out he has done something wrong. Aristotle claims it cannot be a voluntary act because he didn't know he was going to irritate me. If he finds out he has done something wrong and then issues a sincere apology, we can say it is involuntary because it looks as if he would not have done it had he known. But if he finds out he is in the wrong and clearly doesn't care, then Aristotle describes this as nonvoluntary. The point would be that, even if he had known it was wrong, he may well still have done it."

Joe considers this. "So am I in the wrong or not?"

"You have arrived late. You were reluctant to apologise, and two minutes into the class you broke a rule about which you have been told a hundred times. You tell me."

Maya now raises a hand. "So we blame people for their voluntary actions, and these actions are a result of character?"

"Correct."

"But doesn't he think that character is a result of upbringing?"

"Also correct."

"So if we are not responsible for our upbringing, then we're not responsible for our character, then we're not responsible for our actions, so you can't blame Joe."

"This is one popular line of criticism of Aristotle's position. It would mean that whenever we find someone to be despicable, we would be unable to blame them because it is all a result of poor upbringing. But it looks as if the theory of action makes it clear that Aristotle does believe in what we would now call freedom of the will as against determinism. So it looks as if there may be a contradiction between his theory of virtue and his theory of action."

"Are you saying I'm despicable?" Big smile brightens Joe's face. Legs move in and out at terrifying speed.

"Your addiction to your stupid machines puts you in that category at times."

"You didn't say that when I showed you how to change the date on your phone last year."

"I'm not denying you can be useful on occasion."

Maya interrupts them. "Can we finish what we were talking about? Does he think we are free or determined?"

"The best reading of the text is that he thinks we are free. In another section, he suggests that those who repeatedly perform evil actions made certain key choices when they were younger, and they can be held responsible because of those choices. The best explanation may be that he thinks a good upbringing makes it possible to be fully virtuous, but even those with a poor upbringing will have had sufficient input in the form of good examples to have some grip on virtue, as well as having enough reason to work out that there will be consequences if they continue to act non-virtuously. This makes it possible to explain why we can legitimately blame even those who appear incapable of much concern for others. Even if they don't feel it, they should be smart enough to realise that if you keep stepping over others, there is a limit to how long they will allow it to continue."

He finishes the class early, and four of the five students file out. Joe has already resumed his earlier mobile conversation before he reaches the door. Tom looks at him and says, "No use of mobile phones inside the classroom."

"Sorry mate, shit upbringing." And he carries on.

Tom is about to leave when he realises Laura is still sitting there and recalls that she wanted to speak to him. "So, what's up?"

"Can we talk somewhere more discreet? There's a class in here next."

His irritation rises on understanding that this is likely to take more than the ten minutes between classes. Mike is working in their office, and the meeting room is being used by Jim Hollander, who is talking with the parents of one of Tom's first-year students who is being expelled because his forty-five percent attendance is forty percent below the minimum acceptable standard. The only place he can think of is the union office, and he guides her down there. She sits in exactly the spot which Tony Coyle had at their first meeting.

"Thank you for seeing me. I was told by my tutor that I should speak with someone about why I'm not doing better."

"Why not speak with your tutor about it?"

"My tutor is Alan Frost, and I don't feel terribly comfortable with him. He suggested I could speak to one of my teachers if I preferred, and as you've taught me for two years, I thought I could see you."

"Of course. So, what makes you say things are going badly? Your work in philosophy seems all right." He is lying. In fact, she has submitted only two pieces of work to him and none to Mike. Each essay is half the length it should be and was obviously completed in haste the night before or even earlier in the day.

"My parents expect very high grades, and they believe I'm not going to achieve them. My sister's now at Manchester, and they want me to go to a top university as well. They say they won't support me if I only get the grades for an average one. I just feel under a lot of pressure."

"Have you tried speaking to your parents about this?"

"It's impossible. They just expect me to work hard and achieve what my sister has."

Tom is starting to sense that this might go on for some time and doesn't want to end up spending hours with her. "Look, I think you need to try speaking to them again. Put them in touch with me if you like, and I'll try to explain how good the supposedly average universities are. You probably don't realise how much they care for you, and they will be mortified if they realise how you feel."

"I cut myself."

Silence. He inhales deeply. Still silence. "Look, you need to see a counsellor. I'm not qualified to offer advice on this sort of thing. Both the college's counsellors are excellent, and they will be able to offer the kind of guidance which I can't." He has never even seen them.

"They're both women. I can't talk to women."

"They can probably arrange for you to see a male counsellor."

"It's getting worse. I now keep a knife under my pillow, and I used to do it only once or twice a week. Now it's every day. I just want to speak to someone about it."

He is caught between the knowledge of his own ignorance on this and the feeling that he cannot just send her off somewhere else.

"Why do you do it?" he fumbles.

"I don't know. One of my friends spoke to me about it, and I tried it and liked it. It made me feel better."

"You understand you may cause serious harm to yourself."

"No. There are sites where people tell you how to do it and how to avoid any major harm. I just don't see what's wrong with it if it makes me feel better."

"Firstly, I doubt if the information you're getting is completely reliable, and you may well end up hurting yourself very badly. I assume that this is a result of some deeper problem, and you can't treat cutting yourself as some sort of solution. Look, you have to speak to someone more qualified about this, and there is a danger anything I say will not be the best advice." He is desperate to end the conversation and looks at his watch to indicate he is under time pressure.

"I think I do have some deeper problems." Having sat in more or less unbroken silence through eighteen months of his teaching, her first major contribution could not be more removed from the value of art, the nature of goodness, or Aristotle's *Ethics*. Instead, she talks him through a world of tortuous relationships with family, friends, and lovers. Each time he tries to convince her to see a specialist she brings up another issue which she desperately needs to air with someone who can listen to her sympathetically. He finds himself no longer confronted with the slightly annoying and uncommunicative teenager of the past two years but with a bag of hang-ups and twisted responses to a world entirely unwelcoming of her. After two hours, Tom has to stop because he is going to miss his next class but is completely at a loss as to what to say to her.

"Look, I'm going to speak with one of the counsellors myself and ask for the kind of advice they would give to someone in your situation. I can meet you after classes finish tomorrow. Find me in my office, and I'll speak to you then." He pauses. "If I ask you to remove the knife from your room, will you do it?"

She looks down, and then back up at him. "Yes, but …" She looks nervously away and then fixes him firmly with a stare. "I'll do it if you slap me."

What he later recalls most clearly is not his sense of absolute shock so much as a single symptom of it. He feels his heart is beating with such extraordinary force that it must be externally audible. What he also comes to realise is how completely child-like he is in the face of this. All the years of experience in the classroom and the piles of intellectual endeavour just melt away in terms of giving him any sort of preparation for such an encounter.

"That's out of the question," he bumbles.

"Of course, I'm sorry, I shouldn't have asked," she says in a remarkably conventional application of good manners given the nature of her request. "Can I still speak with you tomorrow?"

"Yes. See me at four-thirty." He knows what an error this is but feels so out of his depth that he no longer dares to try anything assertive on the grounds that he has no idea what he should be saying. The full extent of his predicament is revealed when he manages to see one of the college counsellors after his final class.

"How long did you spend with her?"

"Two hours."

She sighs. "Even those trained in the profession would never spend more than forty minutes with someone. It develops a level of dependence that is unhelpful. Insofar as you can say, did you keep asking her stuff, or was she just giving you more and more information?"

"Every time I tried to bring things to a close another nightmare emerged, and I didn't feel I could just boot her out."

"One thing to understand is that whatever lies at the heart of this, there is a tendency in such people to bring others round to their way of doing things in order to survive. Rather than just giving up, they work out ways of going on, and this often involves making the world conform to their outlook rather than acting in ways which we would consider more normal."

"You sound very critical."

"Look, she's a victim, but that doesn't mean she's harmless. Did she talk of her family relations?"

"Mother, passive. Father, old-fashioned values, distant, and very strict. Please don't tell me she sees me as some sort of replacement for her father."

"More likely a cross between father and lover. Did she indicate any sort of attraction towards you?"

"What? She asked me to slap her."

"And you refused, which suggests the care she craves and fails to receive from either her father or her boyfriends. The obvious contradiction between seeking both affection and violence is essentially what she needs to sort out."

"So how the hell do I get rid of ... how do I convince her to see someone who is better placed to help?"

The counsellor is stony-faced. "When you see her tomorrow, just tell her you have been advised you are unable to help her. If she doesn't want to see a woman, then tell her to make an appointment with the male counsellor who comes in on Thursdays and Fridays."

"You don't seem too shocked by any of this."

"Anywhere between ten and twenty percent of young women are thought to be self-harming. No one knows the full extent because they are so discreet. Add in those with eating disorders, abusive boyfriends or parents, and a range of other nightmares, and you have the people I see six hours a day. Laura is not unusual and probably more typical of your own students than you will ever know. Come and see me again if you need to."

He picks up a coffee from the canteen and works his way back up to his office to collect his things. He has a court booked for eight-thirty and wants to grab a slice of pizza on the way home so he can digest it before playing. When he gets to the office, Barry is sitting in his chair.

"Where have you been?"

He doesn't want to say he was seeing a counsellor. "Had to meet a student."

"Better read this. He's come for us again."

CHAPTER ELEVEN

Dear Colleague,

As you are probably aware, our college faces a series of financial challenges in the years to come and we are in a position of having to make essential changes in order that we may meet those challenges. I have been engaged in detailed talks with union representatives over recent months. They have spoken, and I have listened. We reached a point where I felt there was an alternative to the proposals I published in September which was sufficiently realistic to bring before the governing body for consideration. These ideas were received very sympathetically, but I regret to say that in the final analysis neither I nor the governing body found them robust enough to address our college's need for a firm financial foundation on which to build an education for a difficult present and a hopeful future.

We have nevertheless decided to take certain steps which reflect our concern for our staff. The number of full-time equivalent posts to be deleted will fall from eighty to forty-seven. The plan to introduce the posts of junior and senior lectureships is to be postponed, and we will countenance a budget deficit in the current year. We also feel that it does great damage to the individuals concerned if they are required to work knowing that they will be leaving the college in the months to come. Letters of redundancy will therefore be issued on Monday, December 1st, and staff in receipt of these letters may leave on January 1st despite being paid for the three months following that date. We shall also be engaging the services of a specialist firm which offers counselling and employment advice for anyone affected. Once again, the college will pay for this.

Finally, let me say that this is a difficult time for all of us, and I think it is incumbent on all those with a genuine commitment to Sandford to pull together and take our college forward to a great future.

Regards,
Richard Kilman BA
Principal and Chief Executive
Sandford College

When he has finished reading, Tom continues looking at the monitor. "'Chief Executive'. It's like some dictator adding titles to increase his status."

Barry shakes his head. "So he strings us along during the formal consultation period and now hopes to get rid of everyone so fast that we can't do anything about it. We have to give seven days' notice of strike action, and Colin will have it go out tomorrow, informing him the first day will be next week."

"Make it for the Thursday. It's a parents' evening. That will generate more embarrassment."

"Good idea. Get down and see your mate Tony first thing tomorrow morning to see what happened in the governors' meeting. Also, get the draft minutes from Deirdre to see if he lied about anything he agreed to in the meetings with us. We'll have an emergency branch meeting for the day after tomorrow. It's important that anyone who's got one of these letters feels supported."

"I assume his reasoning is that, if he gets rid of staff very quickly, we won't have time to put together the kind of prolonged campaign which might wear him down. How practical is it to have strike action after January first if he has already got rid of people?"

"He's still paying them till the end of March, and he's got to sort out all the classes which will be closing down in the next four weeks. He couldn't have had it planned already, or else we would have heard. Difficult to do that if there's no good will from your staff, and there'll be fuck all of that now."

Tom leans back in his chair and looks up at Barry. "I think we should get something out now. Give members the impression that we are responding quickly."

"You're starting to get the hang of this. A couple more rounds of redundancies and you'll be ready to replace me."

Barry sits down, and they work through what they need to say. They start initially on a direct message to the membership, but decide in the end that there may be a better way.

```
Dear UCL Member,

You will by now have read the message from
the principal informing us that he plans
to make redundancies on January 1st. Below
is a copy of the reply we sent earlier
today. We urge you to attend the emergency
branch meeting on Thursday at 4:30 p.m.

Barry Egham (Branch Chair)
Tom Phelps (Branch Secretary)
```

Dear Richard,

You wrote earlier to inform your teaching staff that you hope to make one fifth of them redundant. This comes after three months of talks in which you have spoken of "the enormous value that Sandford's lecturers have brought to our college" and "the great provision only made possible by such a professional workforce." You also made it clear that you believed the proposals to go before the governing body were ones you found acceptable. Now you choose to ignore the people who have made this college what it is in order to sort out a financial mess of your own creation. Your bad faith in our recent meetings is trivial in comparison to your betrayal of your staff.

There will be an emergency branch meeting Thursday evening, at which we will be recommending industrial action and where we are confident of overwhelming support. Within forty-eight hours, you will receive formal notice of the first strike days, and this action will continue until you withdraw the letters of redundancy you plan to issue. We urge you to avoid a long and damaging dispute by changing course, and we remain ready to re-enter genuine negotiations over how best to move the college forward in ways which ensure stability both financially and in terms of industrial relations.

Regards,
Barry Egham and Tom Phelps

Barry nods and hits the 'send' button. "Colin would be proud. We talk about how desperate we are to negotiate even as we threaten him with the kicking he deserves."

Tom is less confident. "A little risky to presuppose that the membership will definitely support this."

"There's plenty who've criticised me for not taking action earlier. If you allow management to make threats and do nothing, it makes people feel weak. Trust me, this is what the members want to hear, and they'll be pleased that we've responded quickly."

Tom draws a deep breath. "So this is it. No way back now."

"Don't be so sure. He's made some important concessions, and it's surprising how much time you can spend with people without understanding what they're like. I bet Dickie managed to convince himself and the governors that they could do this quickly, get all the pain out of the way fast, and the staff would soon get over it. Now they're looking down the barrel of a local dispute just when half the continent looks like it's ready to blow. Helps to focus minds when you move from peace to the verge of war."

"He can't back down twice, Barry. He's too vain."

"Probably not. My guess is that we come out two or three times, and then he caves in but makes it look like a compromise. Anyway, get home and get yourself psyched up to speak to Mr X tomorrow morning."

He is at work by eight-fifteen. Bizarrely, he must copy and prepare materials for a nine o'clock lesson on Plato's critique of art, just as he would if dozens of his colleagues were not within a few days of knowing that they are going to lose their jobs. Once he makes the copies and extracts from the plastic wallet the overhead transparencies which he has used for the past four years, he emails Tony Coyle to ask him if he has time for a coffee later that morning. He considers trying to work in terms such as 'mole', 'dead drop', and 'sleeper' but fears that Tony will either have no clue what the message means or else detect the irony and refuse to divulge whatever useful information might otherwise leak out of his very own *Tinker, Tailor* world. Tom is relieved when he receives an out-of-office reply telling him Tony is on a training course.

He completes his class, and Mike is sitting opposite him when he returns. "Good note to Dickie. No response yet, I assume."

"Not yet. He'll probably have to inform some of the governors before he comes back to us."

"Look, I'm sending you something which I went through this morning. Might be of some interest."

Tom picks out Mike's email from the dozens which have hit his inbox since Dickie's message from last night. He reads with increasing disbelief. "Are you sure about this?"

"I've checked twice, but it doesn't seem that surprising really."

Tom lifts the phone and dials Barry's number. "You'd better get up here. Something's come up … Yes now … Yes right now."

Barry comes through the door a minute later, and Tom points to the email. Barry reads it, then looks up at Mike. "Are you sure about this?"

"I've checked twice, but it doesn't seem that surprising really."

"It's obviously going to be a surprise for someone."

Tom looks at the email again for fear the calculations may change. "Do we send this to Dickie or go straight to the governors?"

"Neither. Are you teaching last lesson?"

"No."

"Good. Find half a dozen others from here and tell them to meet me in the canteen at four-twenty. Also, I want to meet with your mate who works in IT."

There are fifteen of them in total, mostly from Humanities and English, the departments which provide the most impassioned union support. It has always been a frustration for Dickie that they also attract the most qualified staff and the most flattering inspection reports. He has never acknowledged any relationship between the first proposition and the other two. Barry takes nine of them to the main gate, while Tom stands at the side gate with the others. They are grouped in an arc around the gate, and the students begin to emerge from their final classes in a trickle which soon turns into a flood. They hope to give every student one, but they know that even if only a quarter make it home, it should be enough. They aim to be as friendly as they can in order to maximise the chances that the message will reach home. Once it reaches home, they have a chance. They wince as they see copy after copy discarded just yards from where they stand. Most are curious, and some are overtly sympathetic. Others walk past in irritation and refuse to make eye contact. "No fangks. Don't collect junk mail." Big smile to the mates.

The exodus lasts for only twenty minutes, but they stay until the flood becomes a trickle again. When they finish, Tom thanks the others who have stood with him. He then walks down the road and picks up all the copies which have become litter already. As he heads back through the gate, he sees the security guard is speaking with someone, but only when he comes through the gate does he realise it is Sally.

"How dare you organise a demonstration without informing management? Do you understand that this is illegal and that you are breaking health and safety guidelines by acting in this way?"

It shames him afterwards that he is scared. He hopes she hasn't noticed, but he knows that he fears her because his may be one of the names selected for redundancy, and she has the power to do this to him. He once found her amusing, and now he must compose himself to be able to respond.

"It's not a demonstration. I don't believe leafleting outside the college requires any special permissions." The poor language is nervousness.

"So now you stoop to frightening the students. Perhaps you might have the courtesy to show me a copy of what you have been giving them."

"Given that you have told them nothing of what is about to happen to their education, you should be grateful that someone is informing them." This feels like a better reply.

She snatches a copy from his hand, shakes her head in melodramatic outrage and marches back into the college. Her face is frozen in anger as she makes her way up to the first floor and into the outer office where she started as a secretary. She looks at Bella, who is putting on her coat. "Is Richard with someone?"

"Uh, just a sec, uh …"

"Oh my God. Is the principal with someone?"

"No, but …"

"Thank you." She knocks on the door and opens it before she hears him say anything. "I need a word." She walks in and passes over one of the crumpled letters which Tom had picked up off the pavement. Dickie looks at the dirty, ripped sheet without comprehension. Sally's rage is undiminished. "The bloody union has been distributing letters to the students. This is scandalous. They dare to lecture us on respect for students. They dare …" Dickie raises a hand to stop her as his focus shifts to the letter. He reads it, places it on the table in front of him and looks up at the ceiling as he draws in a deep breath. He then looks down at the paper. "Fuck."

CHAPTER TWELVE

Dear Parent or Guardian,

You may be aware that the principal of Sandford College wishes to make around fifty members of the teaching staff redundant on January 1st. We have been engaged in negotiations to avoid such an outcome for several months, and we reached an agreement two weeks ago which Mr Kilman has now chosen to ignore. We would, however, like to make clear what the implications are for your son or daughter if these changes go ahead.

A lecturer at Sandford typically teaches eight different classes, with around twenty students in each class. The college will have to close every class taught by every lecturer who is made redundant. This will mean terminating a student's course on just under eight thousand occasions, with most students being affected more than once. Your son or daughter will almost certainly have at least one or two of their courses close and may be one of the unlucky few to have all of them go. We are unaware of any detailed plans for dealing with this, and it will be a practical impossibility to transfer students into classes which remain open. Even where there is space and the other course happens to fall where a student is free, unless the other class has been taught the same course options in the same sequence, your children will either repeat what they have already done, or else miss out on key material in options their new teacher is not delivering. For students in their final year at the college, this will also mean an end to any university application.

We see this as a fundamental betrayal of students, parents, and staff. There has been no consultation on the specific details of this latest plan, and had our views been sought, we would have pointed out the impracticality of such an idea. Your concerns will naturally lie with your child's education, and it may be that there is a detailed strategy of which we know nothing. We therefore urge you to contact the principal for an assurance that your child's education will not suffer as a result of these changes. You can contact Mr Kilman directly by emailing him at rkilman@sandford.ac.uk, and we advise you to copy your message to the chair of the governing body, Jeremy Morgan (jmorgan@sandford.ac.uk). Should you be interested in the background to current events at the college, you can find all the information you require at www.savesandfordcollege.co.uk.

Regards,
Barry Egham
UCL Branch Chair, Sandford College

CC Jeremy Morgan, Sandford UCL Members, The Sandford Gazette

"A fuckin' masterpiece," whispers Barry after rereading it for the fortieth time. "Makes management look vicious and stupid, makes us look like brave defenders of the students. Makes the governing body aware of what a prat Dickie is."

Bella walks over to them. "Richard and Sally are having a pre-meeting. Can I get you something to drink while you're waiting?"

Barry looks up. "Maybe some tea now, and put some champagne on ice for when we come out." He then lowers his voice. "Any emails from parents?"

Bella looks around furtively. "Three hundred sent last night and this morning. Over a hundred parents have demanded a meeting."

"Excuse me, but perhaps you would not discuss confidential matters like that!" Sally is standing in the doorway and ushers them in, her glare fixed on Bella as she does so. They enter to find Dickie sitting, looking down at the tattered copy of the letter which Sally handed him yesterday. Barry sees it. "We can run off a clean copy if you like. Might look better in case you want to frame it."

Dickie's face remains completely unchanged, making the remark that much more satisfying. When he begins, he issues each word like a drumbeat, giving the impression of an enormous effort of self-restraint.

"I have spoken with the governance committee. We have decided that the provisional plan of releasing some members of the teaching force on January first is not one which is in the best overall interests of Sandford."

Tom is also feeling more confident. "Can we now discuss alternatives to compulsory redundancies?"

"I will return to that, but let me come to another issue first. I …"

Barry starts. "Hang on. Surely we have to deal with redundancies before we can move on to anything else. Without agreement on …"

"Do not interrupt me! How dare you release such information to the press? Do you have any idea what will happen if the college attracts adverse publicity? It takes decades to build a reputation, and you seek to destroy it in moments."

"Adverse publicity? So your vanity concerns you, not your staff or your students. And you expect us to take that seriously?"

"If we lose more students because of your scurrilous accusations and irresponsible threats of strike action, even more jobs will go because income will decline further. Do you understand this?"

"Every crap manager in history has always told the union that if they resist they'll do more harm than good. The truth is that you're responsible for any money problems this college has, and if we hadn't stopped you, half of us would be gone already."

Dickie stands and jabs his index finger in Barry's direction. "My changes will go through in order to save this college, and I will not allow you to stop me."

Barry is also out of his chair, clenched fists pressed against the beautiful table to support him. "Your changes will wreck this college, not save it. And remember this. You've come for us twice, and we've beaten you without a single day of action. Come for us again, and next week will just be the start. You can withdraw your threats, or we come out."

"Get out. There will be no more meetings until you desist from your outrageous guerrilla actions."

Tom smiles at the oddity of the language, and Dickie's head revolves slowly in his direction whilst maintaining the look of uncontrollable anger. Tom is momentarily frozen but then stands and places a hand on Barry's shoulder. "Come on. We've made our point."

They walk slowly down to the union office without speaking. The silence reflects the fact that they both know Barry has made a tactical error. Having forced Dickie to back down, they needed to sit in complete calm while he ranted at them to give himself a sense of vindication and power. After that he may have been ready to cut a deal. The humiliation of sitting there while Dickie vented would have been the price of minimising the danger. They will never know, but the chance has gone, and now they face the much more uncertain path of striking.

When they reach the office, Barry turns to Tom. "Get the coffees in while I clear some space for us."

By the time Tom sits down, Barry has already emailed Colin Preston to inform him of the news that there will be no redundancies before Christmas but that they are still under threat. He looks at Tom.

"Would be good to know whose names are on the list of those he wants to get rid of. Wonder if we can request it under FOI."

"We can't get confidential information relating to individuals. It's the same reason we can't find out how much Dickie will get if he makes all the redundancies he wants to."

Barry tilts his head back. Tom knows that he is distracted by the thought of his earlier reaction. Barry eventually lowers his head and looks at Tom once more. "We cannot shift our ground on next Thursday's action whilst he is still threatening jobs. We need a general email to go round now so we are the ones giving the good news about our victory in saving everyone's job but warning the members that he still wants us out the door. Shift the emergency meeting to Monday evening so we can arrange picketing. I'll write to Dickie now asking him to suspend the threat of redundancies in favour of negotiations. He won't agree, but it makes us look reasonable." He then hesitates and half-smiles. "Better late than never."

Tom opens Outlook in order to send around the news to the membership, but he stops when he sees in his inbox a message from 'sexybanana' under the title 'Meeting Up'. He assumes it is junkmail from Russia but opens it to find it is disappointment from Laura. He realises that he had been distributing the letters at the college gate at the time when he was due to see her.

```
Dear Tom,

I waited half an hour for you the other
night, but Mike said you were busy doing
union work. I understand how important this
is, but I really need your help. I haven't
been able to do what you ask. Please, can
we meet?

Laura
```

He puts his head in his hands and sighs. He is aware that of all the issues this raises the one which concerns him least is that she may still be cutting herself, and he is unsure how to understand his own response. He knows that his primary reaction to being told that Laura must see someone else was relief that he would no longer need to deal with her. This is partly because he fears her but mostly because he sees her as a much lower priority than his responsibility within the union. He doesn't know if he can rationally defend being less concerned by a girl mutilating herself than by dozens of people losing their jobs, and he refuses to consider the matter. He is also uncomfortable with the thought that he is now at the disadvantage of having to pursue her to organise a meeting and having to apologise for missing the previous one. His being in the wrong creates a feeling of obligation that he must compensate for the error by helping her. He doesn't want to do this and decides that he will apologise but nevertheless say what he would have if he had seen her as planned.

He first thinks of finding her timetable on the system and putting his head round the door during her next class. This looks rather desperate, and he decides instead to find her mobile number and call her. He is also unhappy with a course of action which will reveal he has access to such personal information as it suggests a proximity which he wishes to avoid. His way forward emerges when he realises the email has been sent from a Blackberry. He emails back asking her to find him in his office when she is free. Seven minutes later, she is standing in the doorway, and he is so nervous he is unsure if he can speak coherently.

"Let's find … One of the other staff may come back, so … Let's see if there's an empty classroom." He walks past her, and she follows him without saying anything. They pass one room after another which is full, with the journey of just a few steps between each room increasing his sense of unease. Finally, they come to one of the history rooms where the usual class has been cancelled because the teacher is at a job interview. He enters to find six black girls testing each other on material for a mock exam. Probably from the south London estates. People who fought their way through GCSEs at a tough inner London comp and now travel to the suburbs for a better sixth form. He must choose between asking them to leave and continuing what may be a fruitless search for another room. One of the girls sighs. "Are you teaching in here now?"

"I'm really sorry, but I need the room."

They are good-humoured about leaving. He sits at the teacher's desk at the front of the room and asks Laura to pull up a chair on the opposite side.

"Firstly, I'm very sorry about missing our meeting the other day." He has been unable to find a suitable lie and so opts for the truth. "I'm afraid I simply forgot because of all union work I've been doing."

"Please don't worry about it. I know how busy you must be. Must be a lot of pressure for you, and then I come along." Her tone is jokey, relaxed, intimate.

He speaks in a manner which he judges to be as coldly formal as he can be without appearing machine-like. "I spoke with one of the college counsellors. She has said that it is a grave error on my part to have spent so much time with you last week. She is clear that I am not in a position to help you. I've got some material that she gave me, and I've arranged for you to meet a male counsellor on Friday."

Her initial reaction is impassive. She slowly reaches forward to take the flyers from him and places them in her expensive handbag. After a few more seconds, she places her face in her hands and begins sobbing. He wants to hold her but knows he cannot. He sits there and waits for what feels like the days she takes to recompose herself and look up.

"I'm very sorry," he says. "I'm afraid that I am simply not the person you need." He instantly realises this is a mistake. Too much compassion, and so too much encouragement. She rises slowly and leaves the room without speaking. He feels none of the relief he has hoped for and only an unanticipated sense of absolute betrayal. He wonders how he can possibly teach her for the remainder of the year.

CHAPTER THIRTEEN

When the alarm goes off, he has the thought that he must have set it wrongly as it is too early to wake. This idea is made so inarticulate by the cloud of sleep out of which it emerges that it is more like a sensation than an organised sequence of words. At the last branch meeting he had offered to organise the schedule for picketing. This is usually done in ninety-minute stints, with members of the branch executive doing all or most of it. They will stop at midday as anyone who comes into a college will be there by twelve. Since Tom was in charge of allocating a time for each picket, he had anticipated being able to delegate the early slots to others so that he could arrive for the rush hour at eight-thirty, when those ignoring the strike would begin entering. This made it more difficult to nod enthusiastically when Barry roused the troops with lines such as, "Tom and I will be at the gates by seven, and we're asking all of you to join us at some point to make sure management understands the strength of feeling and the unity and the commitment of the members of this branch."

Tom's Thursdays usually begin with a ten-twenty class, which means he can rise at nine. He teaches only three lessons, finishing at three-twenty, and then plays doubles followed by poker at the Griffin. Now he must rise at five-thirty to stand outside the gates for five hours on a December morning. He felt like crying as he energetically clapped at the end of Barry's oration.

When he switches off the alarm, he remains still for a few moments in search of the psychological force required to make it out of bed. This quest is made more difficult by the soft, continuous breathing of Sofia, who stirred only momentarily when the alarm sounded. He swings out of bed, pulls on his thick dressing gown and walks down the freezing corridor to the bathroom. There is no heating in it, so they have a fan heater whose cable stretches out into the hallway and must be switched on for four minutes in order to make the small room ready for humans to shower in winter. He takes his clothes with him in order to be able to dress in the relative warmth of the bathroom before returning to the coldness of the hallway. He decides to buy breakfast at Clapham Junction but is then unsure if the franchises will be open before six-thirty and opts for toast and coffee instead. He will have no access to a toilet for the five hours of picketing and must therefore time it so that he can use the one at Sandford Station when he arrives.

He goes back into the bedroom to kiss Sofia before leaving, a ritual which is observed even if they have argued. She barely opens her eyes but smiles and wishes him good luck. As soon as he steps outside, he appreciates the relative warmth of the flat. He walks quickly and listens to The Strokes. At this time of morning, the 319 runs only once every twenty minutes, and he would rather walk to the train station than stand and wait for it. He will be standing for five hours. He goes down Webbs Road to avoid the irritating possibility of seeing a bus pass him. He is surprised at how many others he finds at the Junction, and he realises that there are those who must be here at six-fifteen every morning. Few of them are dressed in suits, and he suspects that whatever they do pays a fraction of what he earns.

Even now the trains are frequent, and he takes the slower one so he can spend more time in it and still arrive before seven. On ordinary teaching days, he takes the same train ninety minutes later and either reads in order to calm himself before the storm or chats with Jim Hollander, one of the senior tutors, who gets on at Putney. Today, he must read and spends the eighteen minutes buried in *Transition*.

He is walking up the road to the college at six-fifty, and it is not until he is within a hundred yards that he can clearly make out the two figures at the main gate. Barry and Colin are already there, having arrived ahead of time to catch those who had hoped to enter unopposed by rising two hours earlier than they would normally. They wish to avoid the shame of being seen, whilst feeling none when sitting at their desks for five empty hours knowing that those outside may be saving the jobs of those inside. Even now Barry's smile lifts him.

"Welcome, Mr Branch Secretary."

"Has anyone gone in yet?"

"Some have probably come by car and gone in through the back entrance, but only a couple through the front. Richard Tomlinson drove right past us, and one of the IT lecturers said he felt bad but he couldn't afford it. Otherwise, quiet as the grave."

"Must be annoying for those who want to go in that they have to get up so early on a day like this."

Over the next twenty minutes, they are joined by two others who have agreed to do the early shift at the front gate, with three of the art lecturers covering the back gate from seven till eight-thirty. Even the picketing is done by departments, with office buddies continuing ordinary work-related banter on the line. For the first ninety minutes, they all stand on an empty street with the temperature around five degrees. They talk of this dispute and others, of Dickie and Sally, of what they can expect after the first strike, of anything. By seven-thirty, Tom can feel his toes beginning to go numb. He has a pair of tennis socks under his thick woollen ones and a pair of thick winter boots bought cheaply on Amazon, yet still he freezes in the cold, empty darkness. At seven-forty-five, he sees someone approaching, and he prepares to challenge the first teacher who has come to pass him on the line. It is only at the last moment that he recognises Alan Frost.

"I thought you had signed up to start at eight-thirty."

"I did, but I just had to get out of the house."

"Some sort of theological dispute with Mary?"

"Much more serious than anything to do with God. Mary took Benedict to a children's birthday party on Sunday afternoon. I got lost in this article I'm trying to write on truth and decided to take a break and pop up to Starbucks. I forgot that Anselm was asleep upstairs, and when he started crying the neighbours thought something serious must be up, so they pushed open the back door, and the alarm went off. When I got back, they had called Mary, and she was explaining to the police that this wasn't a burglary. The police told her that if either of our children were left alone again, they would inform Children's Services. She hasn't spoken to me since."

"You forgot your ten-month-old son but remembered to set the alarm?"

"You can't be too careful, Tom. Sandford isn't as safe as you'd think."

By eight-thirty, the second shift is beginning to arrive, and those who have accepted the early start are rewarded with the early trip home to a day off work in the middle of the week. Tom must stand for another three-and-a-half hours. Mike is in this group and brings him an Americano from the station. The warmth of the cup and the kick of caffeine revive him so that he is more alert when the first of the teachers who will cross the line begin to arrive. Strategy is to engage them in reasonable conversation with the aim of convincing them to change their minds. No one ever does. If they have decided to come this far, they are ready for the discomfort of being made to feel they are betraying their colleagues, including those they count as friends. Success would mean that they don't cross the next time.

As they prepare to meet what they hope will be a small number of non-conformists, they are approached by Andy Fortnum, the security guard, who has remained within his warm little hut until now. Here is a man with the heart of an SAS warrior but a day job in a cheap uniform inspecting the ID cards of those who enter a sixth form college. His six-foot-seven-inch frame makes it easier for him to swagger in a manner which he believes suitable for someone who protects thousands from external threats. He plays *Call of Duty* each night against online gamers from Germany and Japan, and queued to buy *Black Ops* at midnight when it came out. Yet the one impression of him which is more powerful than any other is that he would just love to feel he could brutalise someone in a way which would seem justified. Here is a man who wants to perform his acts of violence with a sense of justice on his side.

He strides over. "Right, listen up. Picketing's your right, and you can do it. But there's certain rules. I don't want any intimidation, and I don't want any insults. Be polite, and there'll be no problem. If anyone has any issues with that, then you'll have me to deal with."

Barry is about to respond, but Colin precedes him. "Fine." Fortnum looks over the group, nods and returns to his hut. Barry is incensed. "Why did you let the fuckin' Nazi get away with that? He needs to know that no one's scared of him."

"He's not to be taken seriously. We don't want to give

management any excuse to call the police and generate bad publicity. He's just some mindless git who wants to make himself feel big. Who cares?"

As they are speaking, a car approaches the gate. Kate Hilton shares an office with thirty other English teachers, including Barry. She stops and winds down the window with obvious irritation as Tom waves to her. "Good morning, Kate. You know we're on strike today?"

"Obviously. And I know all the arguments. I can't afford to lose a day's pay, and it's all going to happen anyway, so what's the point?"

"If yours is one of the names on his list, then you'll lose a lot more than a day's pay."

"Then I'd be a fool to throw more money away now."

"There's no reason to think that this cannot be stopped. There are …"

But she is already winding up the window and pulling away in the neat little MX5. Tom had thought of buying one but has decided the combination of not needing a car and middle age made this unwise. Possible redundancy makes this decision seem even better. Barry walks up to him. "Silly cow. She joins the union to make sure she can have representation if she needs it but crosses every picket line. If she is one of those who might be out the door, you can be sure she'll be shouting louder than anyone that we need to be protecting her. Dickie can have her for all I care."

At ten to nine, Dickie drives up in his Porsche Cayenne and swings in past them, barely slowing to take the bend. He and Barry exchange a brief look, cold as the weather. The low temperature makes the picketing physically demanding but also easier. Staff of two minds are more likely to stay at home, and students of two minds would not even consider getting up. The result is that by nine-fifteen they have seen only a dozen teachers come past them and perhaps fewer students. Barry receives a text from a geographer at the back gate to say that twenty-two have come through. This means that almost their entire membership has come out, with those going in mostly the non-unionised. They will circulate this first thing the next day, knowing that they are more likely to retain support for any further action if everyone has a sense that others are supporting it. If ninety percent come out, they are safe. If it begins to slip lower, then the statistical decline creates an impression of moving towards defeat, and this becomes self-fulfilling. To bring this many out on the first day is a victory, and the pressure now falls on management and governors, who must confront the reality of their opponents' success and the prospect of more action.

Tom sees Barry and Colin in conversation, and the two then walk over to the rest. "Right. Enough's enough. Let's get down to Paolo's for breakfast."

Tom looks at his watch, not wishing to believe they could be finished for the day and then be disappointed. "It's ten-fifteen."

"Even Wakefield wasn't this cold. Anyone who's coming in is already here, and any stragglers can have a free pass for today. Let's get going."

Banners and leaflets are put in the boot of Barry's 1991 BMW estate, and they walk to the Italian near the station. Entry into the warm interior feels like deliverance, and Tom drinks the best coffee of his life. Those from the back gate arrive five minutes later, and Mike Flight, the college's only geologist, pulls out a letter he has received. "As my daughter studies here, I also receive stuff sent out to all parents."

```
Dear Parent or Guardian,
It is with enormous regret that I must in-
```

form you that members of the Union of College Lecturers have decided to take strike action on December 8th. This action is unwelcome, unnecessary, and unforgiveable. It will result in damage to your child's education and reflects an unthinking radicalism which flies in the face of the economic reality of the world in which our college must operate. I have personally conducted negotiations with union representatives for many months, and it is a betrayal of both your children and of the collegial atmosphere of this institution that this action should have been decided upon. For my part, I assure you that I will continue to strive for a consensual approach based in rational dialogue in order to resolve the differences which exist between management and some staff. It saddens me that the forty-four percent of teachers (only one quarter of the entire staff) who voted for this action should compel the college to close, but I am sure you will understand there is little option.

Richard Kilman BA
Principal and Chief Executive
Sandford College

Tom looks up first. "So the idiot tells everyone that the college is closed and does our job for us. No wonder there were no students. At this rate, we can just announce a strike and not bother picketing at all."

Colin is less sanguine. "Better get something out to do with these numbers. Most people won't know that postal ballots always have a lower turnout. Stick to the figure that eighty-five percent voted for strike action. Also, he's trying to pass this off as an inevitable consequence of general funding cuts. Make sure everyone knows that this is about purely local issues. That way he looks incompetent and a liar into the bargain."

Before he can continue, Barry's mobile goes off. He listens for a few moments. "All right, ten minutes." He then looks up at everyone else in the café. "Right, let's go. Back to the picket line." He is met with incomprehension. "The press is here. I told them we'd be around till midday, and they want to know where everyone is. Come on, you can come back later. Let's go."

Tom sighs as he puts his coat back on. Having only just had feeling revive in his lower body, he is now reluctant to return. He takes a bite of his bacon sandwich and then trudges back with the others. Barry raps on the window of the car containing the *Sandford Gazette*'s reporter and photographer. When they get out, Tom recognises the former student who is carrying the notepad. He walks up to her. "Jenny?"

"Hi." The smile means they are guaranteed good coverage. He can't remember if she got an A or a D and realises he must steer the discussion away from her grades, just in case it was the lower of the two. Tom is able to run the line that it is Dickie who has screwed up the college's finances and is now trying to pass it off as part of a national problem. He is also able to speak of how the principal will receive a bonus if he can get rid of his teachers and how he had planned to close hundreds of classes in January. To make such claims means that they have given up on creating an atmosphere in which they can find a compromise and plan on generating so much pressure that the governors will force Dickie to back down. Given his vanity, they already know how he will react when he reads this, but that is now beside the point. The subtlety of Colin's psychological approach has been replaced by outright confrontation.

Jenny stamps her feet to keep warm as she scribbles some quotes. "Good job you are out today, or else we might not have been able to cover it."

"How come?"

"Only two of us to cover everything, and the editor decided we had to cover the release of one of the London rioters on Monday and the local demonstrations against closing the drop-in centre and a hospital ward. If you'd come out earlier in the week, we wouldn't have been here."

"The *Gazette* only has two journalists?"

"When I started eight years ago, we were twelve. Now we're down to two, and the parent company wants to merge three of its locals."

"Sounds like you'd be covering the whole of London."

"I'll be happy if I get one of the jobs. There'll be three full-time staffers to cover the whole of west London and then some graduates to cut and paste press releases and agency articles."

"Thank God a free press will be keeping a close eye on events."

"Seriously, though, if you want good coverage, then try to be as offensive as possible so that the editor thinks there's a good headline in it. Otherwise it's just some twenty-two-year-old media studies graduate who lifts a paragraph from your press release and a paragraph from Dickie's and copies them into a template. Anyway, today's strike."

When they finish the interview, they take Jenny and the photographer back to Paolo's for a local branch's version of wining and dining the press. By eleven-thirty, their first strike is complete. They anticipate two more days at most. They will come out for twelve.

He texts Sofia from the train, knowing she finishes at eleven on Thursdays. She replies instantly, and they arrange to meet at one of the small, independent cafes at the top of Northcote Road. This will give him a chance to browse at Waterstone's. The whole area has now been returned to its appearance from before the two-thousand-and-eleven summer riots, and he recalls how watching what was happening so near to him contrasted with an odd sense of satisfaction the next day. It was as if the rioters had inadvertently produced an intellectual utopia in which all brash consumer outlets have been destroyed and only bookshops remain in the world. He is almost nostalgic for this as he picks up a couple of tennis shirts he doesn't need from TK Maxx.

He still manages to find a seat in the café before she arrives, and he must ask twice for the woman seated nearest the door to move slightly so he can make his way to a free table. A Clapham mum. Tom sees them as little more than conventional snobs, but Sofia found in them a new sociological category. Aged thirty to fifty, their employment seems to be selecting expensive yum-yum clothes for themselves and much more expensive objects for the extended and converted Victorian piles around Wandsworth Common and Clapham Common West Side. They are married to City types who travel up the Northern Line each day, and how they bathe in that money. The children go to the local day schools, which were cheaper and allowed the semblance of conventional family life, which would be impossible if they were boarding on a frozen moor. Yet there is one feature which makes them more noticeable than any other. Sofia once took their neighbour Lisa's son to a play group in one of the churches on Trinity Road. On arriving, she opened the door for someone wheeling a pram up the ramp behind her. When she looked at her and smiled, the woman gave a forced smile and a formal thank you. At the end of the session, the woman and her friends circled their chairs to chat with one another while Sofia watched in isolation as all the children played together. Tom recalls stepping into the road as a four-by-four rolled round the bend and he had to reel back when the woman failed even to consider the possibility of braking. Whenever you come across them, you have the impression that, as they make their way around the world, the visual perception of the human form is only ever converted into that of a person if they recognise something close to themselves. Most humans are either invisible or else obstacles which have to be circumnavigated rather like furniture. What gives Sofia the impression they are distinct is their apparent pleasure in living among those they largely ignore. They relish public display rather than withdrawal into isolated private homes buried in the country. They appear unaware of any sense of wider decline.

When Tom sits down, he is already irritated by the woman's failure to apologise or even to look at him as she moves her chair to let him pass. He pulls out his book, but the raised, plummy voice means he cannot avoid listening.

"I offered her nine pounds an hour, which I thought was reasonable, but she said that twelve-fifty was the standard rate in London and that she had a copy of her diploma with her. I thought, 'You cheeky little cow, just look at the kind of place you're going to be living in'. Anyway, we compromised on eleven, but when Greg got back from Zurich, he was livid, so we told her we'd decided to go for an English nanny in the end because of the language issue. Phoned up the agency again and got a lovely Romanian girl."

"How much?"

"Eight-fifty!"

"Oh, that's much better."

Tom stands and makes his way out, deliberately knocking the corner of her chair as he passes her. She tuts, but he leaves without looking at her. He is frustrated that she will be unaware of the meaning of his last gesture, and even more frustrated that she will irritate him for hours whilst he will be forgotten in moments. She will remain wholly untouched by anything economic.

He calls Sofia and tells her to meet him at Buena Sera instead. When she arrives, he tells her of the earlier incident, aware that they must resist a rehearsal of the similar events they have seen over the years, which would ruin their lunch. She shakes her head. "The standard rate for a cleaner in London is ten pounds an hour, and they probably don't pay that either." She says this without any of the usual fire.

"What's up?"

She smiles. "All language classes were cancelled today, and the head of the centre called an emergency meeting for all teachers. We're being restructured."

"Christ! This is never-ending. How badly?"

"They're cutting four posts."

"What about you?"

"They're getting rid of Czech, Polish, and one of the Russians."

"Thank God." The words are out before he realises what he has said. He is suddenly aware of having been reduced to relief at others losing out instead of Sofia.

She looks at him. "I'd be disgusted if I hadn't had the same reaction."

"Will they get a decent payoff?"

"They're all on sessional contracts. They work until the courses finish at the end of March, and that's it." She hesitates. "They're also cutting one post from Spanish."

"But not you?"

"The six of us met after the announcement. Five of us will go down to four days a week from next year. Saves someone actually losing their job."

He recognises the anomaly, and she tells him before he asks.

"Lara."

"She's married to one of the professors, and she won't take a pay cut?"

"She says she doesn't want to be financially dependent."

"She doesn't want to be dependent? Didn't the union help her with a grievance last year? Now she's going to share an office with five people who've taken a twenty per cent pay cut when she refused."

"Look, given what's going on at your place and what they're doing to the Slavs, I'm just relieved it's not worse. Everyone suspected this sort of day was coming, and at least it's quick." She smiles at him. "Not a great time for making plans, is it?"

This is an aspect of their current situation he has sublimated because of its enormity. Both want children together, and the plans to which Sofia is referring are that buying somewhere seems a sensible precursor to parenthood. They can't have a child in the ruin in which they now live, and she had carefully sought out ground floor flats with a garden which would fall within their means. Then they are supposed to marry, which neither particularly cares about but which is unavoidable given the sheer weight of Catholics on Sofia's side. The family likes her Spanish-speaking Englishman and is quietly tolerant of their living together, but an illegitimate child would be an act of such anti-clerical force that they may never be able to set foot in Valencia again.

They have compromised on the idea that a small civil wedding would at least be more appropriate than two atheists accepting God's blessing in one of the city's many glorious cathedrals.

Now their means will contract with Sofia's cut in salary and will disintegrate if Tom's name is on the list that Dickie is drawing up. There is a sense of everything they have settled on slipping away, and with this comes a sense of extreme impotence. They simply can't do anything, as all the decisions being taken are outside their control and all the obvious options are also being closed down.

He sighs. "Depending on how things work out at Sandford, we could think about going back to Spain."

"I had the same thought, but starting again in a country with rising unemployment and no jobs? We'd probably be even worse off there. Difficult to see how we could buy a house."

"Maybe we should try Greece. With one job we could probably buy an island these days."

She laughs, and he is pleased that the kind of dark humour which has shaped the jokes at work is something which can appeal to her even on a day like this. When he arrived at his desk last Friday and switched on his computer, he realised that someone in IT Support had altered all the start-up screens so that instead of going to the college's homepage they went directly into the *TES* jobs section. By ten-thirty, an apology went around from Dan Corporal, and images of joyous students were restored. Senior management never identified which of the five possible candidates had done it and couldn't work out that they had probably all colluded.

She looks across at him as their meals arrive. "Look, I think we just need to wait until the summer before we decide anything. Maybe someone else in my department will leave, and I won't have to drop down. Even if they make redundancies at your place, you might be safe. I think there's a good chance we can still do what we wanted, but there'll just be less eating in places like this."

So many different pieces in play. So many ways in which their situation seems ever more precarious.

CHAPTER FOURTEEN

When he wakes, he lightly touches the digital clock. Five-seventeen. He knows he will not return to sleep. His first thought is of Dickie passing him in the Cayenne. He recalls the deliberate way in which the head was held very high and the excessive speed as he passed through the gates. Tom replays the image over and over again. It captures all he despises, but he cannot stop replaying it. He imagines Dickie being fired and having to walk out the gates, passing them as they look at him in silence. He looks down, defeated and unable to meet their eyes. Tom now replays this image repeatedly, but its sheer improbability limits any satisfaction. He finds images of defeat more realistic, and for reasons he cannot fathom he therefore finds himself constantly returning to fantasies of Dickie smiling down at them as they crawl back into the college.

After a while, he turns to a series of calculations he and Barry have been considering over the last three weeks. They had been included among the copy recipients for the monthly printout of the college's accounts. They wrote directly to Jeremy Morgan when they came back in January, requesting to be added. Whether Morgan decided it was a reasonable request or whether he knew from Dickie that they would have to send it anyway if a further FOI request went in, they don't know. But they do have all the key documents, and they have had two of the accounts lecturers run through them. They are now in a position to put together a financial case for no redundancies. By making some conservative assumptions about the likely numbers of staff who will be leaving in the summer through retirement or resignation, it is possible to work out how much money can be saved simply by not replacing them. Work on the building can be restricted to maintenance and repairs. Given the college's cash reserves, voluntary redundancy packages could be offered which would be attractive enough to tempt further staff to leave and which the union could back. This means that staff numbers could be reduced without anyone being sacked. The college cannot cut student numbers without losing income, so fewer lecturers will have to teach to larger classes. This is a policy the union has spent years opposing, but Tom and Barry believe they can sell it to their members as the cost of a deal, and they must sell something.

After the first strike day, Dickie sent around an email thanking the forty-five lecturers who had come into work. The second time, he sent no email, and they assume at least the same numbers had been out. This meant that two hundred and forty-one of their two hundred and eighty-six members were striking. Dickie's response after the third day was to increase the rate at which he docked pay. He had started off by taking one three-hundred-and-sixty-fifth but moved to taking one two-hundred-and-second. He claimed that teachers were only paid for the days on which they taught as against each day of the calendar year. He could do anything he wanted, and they simply had to take it. He wrote to all lecturers in advance of the fourth strike to inform them, and the first message in everyone's inbox the following morning thanked the one hundred and two brave souls who had crossed the picket line to teach. He had peeled off fifty-seven people. Only around three quarters of the union's members were now on strike, and coupled with the non-unionised staff it meant that a third of the whole teaching force was at work. Students were told that they must assume that their classes were running and come in as usual, using empty classrooms for independent study if necessary. Most ignored this, but many were beginning to lose sympathy with their teachers and starting to worry about how much work they were missing. This meant that, whereas on the first day they saw only a handful of staff and almost as few students, over a thousand people now walked past them at the gates.

Barry's response was twofold. They had to try and reverse the decline in numbers coming out. The national union started offering strike pay of fifty pounds a day, which was less than half of what most people were losing. Tom and Barry also started visiting team rooms each day to try and encourage everyone, but they were aware of a perceptible shift in the attitudes they found. In many they saw only unenthusiastic support, and some began questioning directly whether there was still any point. Bizarrely, the fact that no one yet knew who was set to lose their job started to work against them on the grounds that most felt they had no more than a one-in-six chance of being among the victims. This meant that they might be weakened still further when the names were released.

The second strand of what they were trying came after pressure from Colin Preston. The union had to find some alternative to put to the governors in the hope that they might step in to end the dispute. However much the union was hated, the strikes were creating an obvious and deep unease with the endless, bad publicity they generated. Jenny's articles were not only sympathetic, they were everywhere. She wrote directly for the *Sandford Gazette*, but she also started writing stuff which was syndicated and was turning up in all the other locals. The fact that the *Gazette* had only two journalists left meant that you only needed one on your side to guarantee that anyone in London who found an article about the college was reading the same person's take on it every time. The dispute attracted wider attention, with the coverage creating an image of principled teachers fighting a greedy, vicious management. This made an approach to the governors more realistic, but each claim had to be indisputable, and the overall strategy had to be one which was financially plausible.

Tom now runs through each aspect of what they are proposing again, and still it adds up. He checks the time again. Six-eleven. He rises as quietly as he can to make himself breakfast and read over the draft one more time on his computer before leaving for work. He was doing the same thing until midnight last night, and even if he won't need to look at it tonight, he knows he will not be able to get to sleep before midnight again and will wake before six tomorrow.

When he leaves the flat, he is already weighed down by the tiredness which is now with him always. This comes with a near-permanent sense of irritation, which generates in him a curious new psychological activity. He finds himself selecting people from his past or present who have acted in ways he dislikes and repeatedly runs through what they have done. He then embellishes this with further fictional events which allow him to make the original crime so much worse. Dickie and Sally provide endless opportunity for this, but he also selects those close to him. He takes arguments with Sofia from years ago, which he felt were never resolved as they should have been, and develops them into much more serious issues revealing an imagined selfishness on her part. He must struggle to rationalise this, bringing to the forefront of his mind moments when he has seen her acting in the ways that have made him love her. When he comes home and she smiles at him, he feels guilt at the venom and injustice of his earlier thoughts. His relief at her being there with him stands in painful contrast to the anger he feels towards her during these searing fantasies, yet he goes on doing it. The capacity to analyse these moments as a consequence of the pressure at work does nothing to alleviate them, and he has concluded that they will continue for as long as the dispute. He fears that, if the union loses, these moments may become embedded, corrupting even those areas of his life which have value and lie ostensibly outside the realm of work. His sense is that the union is beginning to lose, and this makes the need for some sort of deal all the more imperative.

When he arrives in the union office, Barry is already there battering away at the keyboard. Four other members of their executive committee enter over the next few minutes. The others have faded away. They run through the details of the plan, but it is Tom who raises the first objection to the document he has drafted himself.

"If all our projections are correct, this means the college will move back into surplus in two years. By any normal standard this should be acceptable, but it's at odds with what the governors have said Dickie needs to do. They've demanded a return to surplus by the end of this year."

Barry is puzzled. "We know that, but any deal means everyone has to compromise. We'll be teaching bigger classes, and they have to go slower on saving money. We can't drop these proposals now."

"I'm not suggesting dropping them, but if we make them more attractive, it increases the chances of acceptance."

"How do we make them more attractive?"

Tom sighs, knowing that Barry won't want to hear what

he is about to say. "I read an article about a midlands manufacturer of aircraft parts where the whole staff, including management, took a pay cut."

Barry's eyes bulge. "Ask members who've been out on strike to have their pay cut? And we suggest it? You'd have the cleaners paying the college instead of the other way round. Why not just give in?"

"Just a second. We could make it progressive so that low-paid staff lose nothing, main grade lecturers lose, say, two percent, and so on up the line until you get to the senior managers who take the biggest cut."

"Listen to me. You cannot say to your members one day that you want them out on strike and tell them the next that they earn too much money."

"No one is saying that. I'm talking about undermining the argument that we know will come out, which is that our ideas are unaffordable. Everybody taking a pay cut has to be balanced against dozens of people losing their jobs. If you spread the pain more evenly, it's better than a minority bearing all the pain."

"Bollocks. Absolute bollocks. Stop trying to be clever by doing management's job for them. Our job is to organise and to defend people. This isn't some abstract, philosophical discussion."

There is a general, uncomfortable silence, eventually broken by Barry. "Unless there's any other comments, I suggest this plan goes forward as it is."

No one speaks. There is some further discussion about deadlines for the next newsletter and the next branch meeting. Tom goes up to his office and pulls out his materials for his class. He says nothing to Tili or Mike, and they choose not to bother him, a practice they have adopted increasingly over recent weeks as his mood has been declining. He is relieved to walk into the classroom where the focus he must retain to deliver the material is such that even the dispute is shut out. Only three of the five students are there, with Maya and Miles missing. Since they are the two strongest, it makes the possibility of any decent exchanges more remote.

"All right, we've already seen that Aristotle claims that we all aim for a flourishing life and that such a life is broadly similar for everyone. One of the strongest arguments in support of this claim is that all humans are social beings and that friendship is therefore essential for a good life. He claims that we just couldn't be happy if we lived in isolation. Amrit, would you agree?"

"S'ppose so."

"Joe?"

"Couldn't some people be happy just on their own? There are people who just don't get on well with anyone."

"Aristotle would claim that, although some struggle to get on well with others, that will probably mean they cannot flourish because they can never be fulfilled in this key aspect of their lives."

Silence. All he can do is carry on. "One significant feature in his discussion of friendship is that he thinks we understand it in terms of three different levels. There are those friends who are useful to us, such as effective work colleagues. There are those with whom we experience pleasure, such as someone who is good fun when you go out. And there is the highest level of friendship, which is when each of the friends admire one another. Does this seem accurate?"

Laura looks down, and he doesn't wish to engage her if he can avoid it. Amrit raises her hand. "If someone said she was my friend because I was useful to her, I wouldn't really think of that as friendship."

"Very good point. Perhaps the best way to understand this

issue is to consider the problem of translation. 'Friendship' is the most commonly used term for the ancient Greek word 'philia'. But 'philia' seems to take in a much broader range of relationships. It means something closer to getting on well with someone. What about the second two levels of friendship, those based in pleasure and admiration? Are these typical of what we think of as a basis for friendship?"

Laura looks up for the first time. "So if you experience pleasure with someone, you can't admire them?"

Joe smiles at the obvious sexual connotation, and Tom replies quickly in order to steer the discussion back to philosophy. "The most complete friendship will involve elements of all three levels. This means the highest form of friendship will be one where you admire the person, you have fun together, and there is also a degree of mutual advantage because you help each other out when necessary."

Amrit raises her hand again. "So you have to admire someone if it is the best form of friendship?"

"Yes. You must find the person to be someone of good character, and you must wish them to be successful."

Joe interrupts. "You said you liked *The Sopranos*. They admire each other, but they don't have good character."

"*The Sopranos* is a perfect example of what Aristotle is talking about. There is clearly a basis for friendship in mutual advantage in that they work together to steal money. There is also pleasure they derive when they are successful in pulling off some job, or when they are eating good Italian food together. But each of them is in constant competition with the others for status, and they deeply mistrust one another. They may recognise the success of the others, but the fact that they lack qualities such as honesty and loyalty means it is impossible to admire them for their character. Tony kills many of those close to him, and he is in therapy precisely because he has such tortuous relationships with all those around him."

Joe again. "So you can only have this highest level of friendship between morally good people?"

"Morally good people have the qualities of character which are ultimately necessary for friendship. It is when we recognise such qualities that we are likely to be drawn to someone in the appropriate manner. This also provides a basis for a more stable relationship which will endure when our taste for certain pleasures changes and when things become difficult."

More silence. He cannot be bothered to try and extract anything more from them, so he distributes a passage from the text and sits down to think about what occurred earlier with Barry. When he sits at his desk after the lesson, he checks his voicemail and there is a message from Colin Preston asking him to call back urgently. He finds a meeting room to ensure privacy.

"Tom, yes, thanks for calling back. A couple of things. I've just sent something through to Barry which you need to look at. Should help with at least one of your major issues. I've seen the latest draft of the proposals to the governors, and I think they should go forward as they stand. Barry said you'd suggested something about accepting pay cuts, but I don't think we're there yet."

"I thought Barry was going to rip my head off when I raised it."

"This is the other thing I need to talk to you about. Barry tends to take on an awful lot. He always has done, but there's something else now. His father is ill, and he's been travelling up to see him every other weekend. On top of everything else, it means he's starting to get even more irascible than he usually is, and he's refused to consider taking time off work. What we cannot allow is that he starts making bad decisions or pissing off other members of the local leadership because he's under so much pressure. I want you to have a word with him about this, and you also need to cut him some slack when he flies off the handle."

"I'm seeing him at the end of the day. I'll try and discuss it with him then."

He goes back to his office and deletes as many of the emails as he possibly can without reading them. These are generally ones telling the stories of meltdown from other colleges which he receives as a result of Barry adding his address to a list of local activists from other London colleges. Others are junk from elsewhere in the college concerning the leaving party of people he's never met or events he will never attend. Two are from Barry, and one is from Laura. He has taught her only twenty minutes earlier, and in the time between the end of the class and now she has sent him a message from her Blackberry. He is already concerned that this may mean the end of their implicit understanding. Since their meetings before Christmas, they have adopted a quintessentially English manner of confronting what occurred, which is to say they have carried on as if nothing had ever happened. He has been slightly more restrained in the comments he makes on her mediocre written work and less impatient when she walks in late. He is convinced that even she may be unaware of any change in his behaviour and is sure that no one else is. Her own conduct is also indistinguishable from what he saw before their little meetings. He takes a deep breath before opening the message.

```
Hi Tom,

I am sorry to bother you again, but I need
to. I have tried seeing the counsellor as
you suggested. But it's a disaster. He is
not helping me, and he keeps staring at my
```

```
breasts. Things seem to be getting worse,
and you are the only person I can turn to.
Please help me.

Laura
```

Five lines of text, yet he has the impression that there are novels with slimmer content, and he finds many reasons for being uncomfortable with this. Perversely, it is the clichéd attempt to single him out as the only one who can possibly help which does most to limit any concern. He recalls the comments of the counsellor he had spoken to about the dangers of people like Laura, and he finds the cliché and much of the rest to be crudely manipulative. He is also uncomfortable with the sexual reference.

But there is something else which now begins to worry him. If he fails to respond in the way she wants, he fears she may become more difficult. How would it be viewed if it came out he has spent two hours with a female student in an office with no one else present? She has now written to him accusing a counsellor of some sort of sexual impropriety. What if she brings the same accusation against him? If such a claim were to get back to Dickie, then he might intervene to suspend Tom on grounds of breaching regulations on safeguarding.

He saves the email to a folder he creates under the title 'special cases'. What to reply? He ponders this for a moment, then decides.

```
Dear Laura,

I am very sorry to hear that things are not
going well with the counsellor. I am afraid
that I am simply not capable of offering
you the support you need, and I genuinely
fear I may make matters worse. I can only
```

```
suggest that you try to see one of the oth-
er counsellors.

Best wishes,
Tom
```

When he sends this, he again hopes that this will deter her. He is unsure what to make of his own reaction. He knows that talk of his own inability to help is mere convenience. Is he simply too exhausted to care any more about someone in such obvious need? Has the dispute damaged his capacity to show concern for her? He considers this for a while, but the weight of what lies before him is so great that he soon leaves it and turns to prepare for his next class.

When Tom walks into the union office, Barry looks up with a smile as broad as his face. "Take a look at this." Tom takes the copy of a letter which Colin has sent to Dickie.

```
Dear Richard,

I understand that you have increased the
deductions from staff who have taken in-
dustrial action from 1/365th of annual
salary to 1/202nd. It is the view of the
UCL's solicitor that this action is ille-
gal. The 1998 Employment Act states that
any deductions for a breach of contract
which takes place as part of a formal in-
dustrial dispute must be 'fair and propor-
tionate'. Whilst no amount is specified, it
is not legal to make deductions with the
intention of being punitive of those en-
gaging in legal industrial action or with
the clear aim of preventing members of
trade unions from exercising their rights
during disputes. The case of the GMB vs
Harker Ltd (1999) established that where
employers increase the deductions they make
over the course of a dispute, this indi-
```

```
cates an intention to be punitive and
therefore falls outside the law. Unless you
indicate within ten working days that you
will refund all those who have taken in-
dustrial action at Sandford College, the
difference between the 1/365th and 1/202nd
of their salary for each day on which you
deducted the latter sum, we shall bring
legal action against you on behalf of our
members to seek damages for breach of their
rights under the 1998 Act. I would be
grateful if you could also confirm that if
any further industrial action is taken, fu-
ture deductions will be made at the origi-
nal rate. Should you refuse to comply with
this request, we shall seek compensation
both for the excessive deductions and for
the distress caused by this policy.

Regards,
Colin Preston
UCL Regional Officer
```

Tom looks up in disbelief. "He's going to have to refund us for striking?"

"And tell the governors. So all the members who came out get a bonus in next month's pay cheque, and they get paid fifty pounds a day to come out from now on."

"If we keep going, we're going to be better off striking than working." It is the first time in weeks Tom has been capable of irony.

"And this comes out just as our proposals go to the governors. We offer them a way out just as it looks as if it's easier for us to go on." His excitement is that of a child. Tom is uncertain about how to raise the other issue he knows he must discuss.

"I spoke with Colin this morning."

"Oh right, he told you about this."

"Among other things."

"What other things?"

"I really don't want to intrude, but…."

"Come on, out with it. You won't find me in a better mood to discuss it, whatever it is."

"He mentioned your father."

Barry's smile disappears and he sighs, but it is Tom who speaks again.

"Like I said, this is obviously a private matter, but I could probably take on more of what you are doing at the moment if it would help."

"For a middle-class, *Guardian*-reading liberal you do have some decent moments."

"It's probably your influence."

Barry smiles again. "Firstly, thanks. Things look as if they may be getting better. He's got severe arthritis in his lower spine. He's been unable to walk properly for the last three months and because he's a feisty old bugger, he doesn't want any doctors near him. My brother and I have been going up to see him on alternate weekends, and now he's getting irritated because he thinks we're treating him like an invalid. He can't stand up to make himself a sandwich without it hurting, and it offends his dignity when someone tries to help him." Barry's head goes back, and he looks at the ceiling. "Last Sunday, I was rushing around because I had to get the train back down, and every time I was about to leave, he asked me to do one more little thing. I started getting ratty with him, and he went quiet. I said goodbye to him and walked towards the door, and when I turned round, I could see he was crying. I sat down again with him, and he had tears rolling down his cheeks. Said he was sorry, but he couldn't do these things himself, and he hated asking me, but he had no choice. I almost started crying myself, and I had to stay another hour to try and patch things up. Had to pay ninety pounds for another ticket and felt like a complete wanker for the whole trip."

"What's the prognosis?"

"He's eighty-seven, so they can't operate. All they can do is try to numb the pain. None of the painkillers they've given him so far have worked, so my brother is taking him into hospital on Friday so they can give him steroid injections directly into the lower back. If that works, then he could be right as rain for another six months, and they just keep repeating the injections."

"Sounds like a good time for a major dispute."

"Could be that we win and he gets cured at the same time." He pauses. "Look, maybe I was a bit harsh this morning, but there's stuff you need to understand. You're looking for some sort of compromise which the members and management will both buy. That's management's job, and there are major problems if we try to do that job for them. Our only strength lies in our numbers. If we do anything which splits the branch, then we lose any chance of defending ourselves, and talking about pay cuts runs exactly that risk. With a bugger like Dickie in charge and a fire-breathing nut like Liefwint on the governing body, we have to focus on keeping everyone on our side. We have to exert pressure and force them to come up with the ideas. It's the safest way."

Tom smiles and nods. "Ok. From now on we do things your way."

"I knew you were smart. Now get those proposals off to the governors, and we might have a deal."

CHAPTER FIFTEEN

"He wants to meet."

"What do you make of that?"

"Can't be a bad thing. If the governors had simply rejected it out of hand, they would've just written to tell us. Could be they've told him to negotiate something based on what we put to them. In any case, we need to find out what's going on."

"When?"

"Guess."

Tom rolls his eyes. "I'm teaching in ten minutes."

"He says we're to cancel classes. Pick me up on your way."

It is three months since their last meeting. Since then, Tom has barely seen Dickie, who has been spending more time in his office, with ever smaller numbers of staff invited to see him. Even for a man with so little concern for those beneath him the sense of being surrounded by those who disdain him is proving more invasive than he would have expected. He has lost weight, and the tailored suits now sag. The week after the third strike, he was off work for two days. Dan Corporal, the only member of senior management to act as if discussion with Dickie about his ideas were a plausible activity, is now avoided in favour of individual meetings with other senior managers to whom instructions are issued and from whom unquestioning obedience is expected. In the past, Dickie had been content to play the tyrant without seeking any major conflict. Now he finds himself in the midst of a dispute, and he begins to understand a pressure to which he thought himself immune. He is more sensitive to the hatred of his staff than the illusion of necessary toughness can withstand. All those he passes in a corridor look away from him. All letters and emails from parents are critical. He must rely on a small number of his senior managers whose servility begins to annoy him because he can see it for the cowardice it really is. And now he must confront what has happened with the governors. When Sally arrives, he has spent the last half hour composing himself, and he makes it clear that Barry and Tom are to be shown in immediately. When he hears them come into the outer office, he feels his heartbeat quicken. He remains standing when they enter.

"Please sit down." He turns to Bella. "Have you offered them something to drink?"

"I'm bringing them some water."

"Thank you, Bella." He sits down himself and draws a deep breath. "Let me come straight to the point. Your proposals were presented at the governors' meeting yesterday evening. There was an extremely rich discussion of the detail of your document, and it has been agreed that it is in the interests of this college that we come to a compromise which combines the virtues of your own proposals with the realities we must face as an institution struggling to make its way through choppy waters. I will provide you with a written summary of what I am about to say, but the essence is that we now wish to do more in the way of addressing the concerns which, for you, lie at the heart of this dispute. We will increase the value of the voluntary redundancy package currently available. It will not be as high as the figure you suggested, but it will rise to around four months' salary for anyone who accepts it. We will also place a moratorium on the recruitment or replacement of all staff unless it can be demonstrated that those in areas which are at risk cannot be redeployed to take up any free posts. This much is contained in your ideas, and the governors have welcomed them as a move in the right direction."

He sighs once more, knowing that what he is about to say will be the more difficult part. "The governors do not feel they can accept all of your suggestions. It is their view that we cannot draw on our reserves to the extent that you suggest as this would leave us defenceless were we to fall victim to higher than expected costs for building repairs. It was also decided that we must invest to modernise our buildings, or else risk losing students to other institutions with cutting-edge technology. I regret to say that we feel that there must be some compulsory redundancies, but we have agreed to limit the number to thirty-eight full-time equivalent posts."

He turns to Barry, but it is Tom who speaks. This takes Dickie by surprise in that the usual distribution of labour is that Barry does all the negotiating, with Tom only speaking when more technical issues are being discussed.

"You say you will limit them to thirty-eight. Does that mean there could be fewer?"

"Thirty-eight posts will go. The governors are of the view that we must guarantee a certain level of savings in order to ensure the financial security we need. It does mean that, even if we cannot achieve the numbers of voluntary redundancies we hope for, no more than thirty-eight posts will be deleted."

Once more, it is Tom who continues. "The proposals we put forward would mean the college will be returning to surplus after next year. What's the problem with that?"

"There was a lengthy discussion of precisely that matter, and the prevailing view was that it poses too great a risk."

"We have no debts and an annual income of over thirty

million pounds. Any one-off costs could easily be met by taking out a loan."

"That possibility was also discussed, and it was decided that it also posed too great a risk." He struggles to maintain a constant, formal tone. He knows how unlikely it is that he can arrange some sort of deal around this, but the number of staff who will now have to go has been halved since September. Maybe they will consider this enough.

Barry has not yet spoken. Tom looks at him across the table as he continues. "That is unacceptable to us. We are told we have to be more like the private sector, yet no private company would ever set aside the mere possibility of a short-term loan, or running a deficit for a couple of years. This means sacrificing dozens of your staff for no good reason."

Tom's tone is becoming more abrupt. He now seems closer to the bellicose style which Dickie has been accustomed to hearing from Barry. The meeting cannot finish as the last one did, Dickie thinks. Must somehow try to give at least the impression we are moving closer. Have to get these fucking strikes over. "I understand your position, but the one I have set out is that adopted by the governors, and this is the way things must now go. I hope you will at least place this offer before your members. Staff who are to be made redundant will be given an interview time over the next few days. Both of you and any other union representatives are welcome to take time off from teaching to accompany them."

Sally leans forward, tilts her head to one side, and offers a sympathetic smile. "Guys, this is going to be a very difficult time for all of us, but we have to face up to the challenges which are out there and which ain't going away. I hope you will try to understand why we have to do this and that we can all move forward together."

Dickie looks at her and has no understanding of how he could ever have found her attractive. The thought comes to him that he would rather take Barry from behind than go into that bathroom again with Sally. Tom and Barry rise and leave without responding to her. Dickie realises that he must issue cheques to over two hundred teachers in the next few days, and he knows that this will subsidise the next strikes. It is now February twenty-second. The redundancies will take effect on May twenty-fifth, and he can do no more than sit it out as one searing article after another appears in the press and one letter after another arrives on his desk from parents who believe he is eviscerating a college for no good reason.

Sally turns to him. "I think that went as well as could be expected. Perhaps they'll finally come to realise that there's a big, bad world out there which sometimes bares its ugly teeth at us."

Her horrifying stupidity makes him want to mash her face into the table, but there are four and a half thousand people who study and work in his college, and she is the only one who likes him. He knows that all he can do is continue down the path he is already on. "I want the interview times for those to be made redundant to go out today. Barry will be sending out a message, and we may as well get all the bad news out in one go."

When Tom and Barry sit down in the office, they are initially silent. Barry checks his inbox and emails Colin to tell him of the outcome. He then turns to Tom. "You did well in there. I'm sure he would have expected to hear me shouting abuse once he told us what the governors decided, and he seemed more ill at ease this time."

Tom shakes his head. "I didn't see any of that. He didn't have any excuse to start shouting because you didn't provoke him, but it was the same controlling style that he's always had."

"You're probably right, but I'd like to know what went on with the governors."

"I'll see if I can get the draft minutes of the meeting from Deirdre."

"And then you can ask your mate Tony if they're accurate." Barry sees the resistance. "Look, they've halved the numbers they want to get rid of, and we've got three months to grind them down. Even if two percent of what Mr X says is of interest, it could make some sort of difference."

Tom sighs and then nods reluctantly. Barry turns to the PC to beat out a message to the forces, indicating that Tom needs to get on with his part of the deal. He begins by walking to Deirdre's office, taking a route which will avoid his having to pass Dickie's again. When he enters, she is on the phone and motions him to sit down. He gathers she is talking to one of the governors, assuring him that any phrase he objects to can indeed be amended at the next meeting and that this will not be an official record until it has been voted through at the March meeting ... "All right, good-b ..." But the other person has apparently hung up before she can finish.

She puts down the phone and turns to Tom. "I do find Mr Liefwint rather brusque at times."

It is strangely frightening to know that Liefwint has been talking directly to someone in the same room. "Can I take it he was throwing chairs at people last night, and he doesn't feel it needs to go in the minutes?"

"You're not as far out as you might think. I assume you'd like the minutes of yesterday's meeting."

"If they're available."

"I can give you a copy, but I must emphasise that they are

only in draft form at this stage, so they're not yet an official record."

"I'm sure that you've made them as accurate as anyone possibly could."

"Mmmm. I should warn you in advance that it was decided that certain events should not be recorded."

She is obviously reticent, and he doesn't want to press her directly. Is this referring to Liefwint, or is there something else? "Can you give me some sort of general indication?"

She considers this, but then shakes her head. "I'm sorry, but I don't think it's right that I should be gossiping about such things. I work for the governors, and if they decide that certain information is not to be recorded, then I'm not sure it's appropriate that I reveal it."

"Not even to me?" he says smiling in such a crudely flirtatious manner that they are both embarrassed.

"Please don't take this too personally, but I suspect you may be literally the last person to whom I should be talking about such things."

"You're probably right Deirdre. Thank you for this."

He walks out with the seven pages of minutes and heads to the canteen to read through them with an Americano. The union proposals are the first item on the agenda, and the first four pages record the discussion. Tom estimates they must have spent over an hour on them, and once they were voted down, Jeremy Morgan appears to have made some sort of appeal for unity. Judging by the length of this entry, the old fool must have banged on for an eternity on how everyone now needed to rally behind management. Much of the discussion seems to be a predictable back-and-forth over the value of ending the dispute versus the danger of borrowing and moving into debt. Tom tries to imagine at what point Liefwint may have lost it, but he finds himself trying to judge a tone of voice from a written report and realises it is futile. Some of the extracts he reads in the minutes shock him, and he shakes his head in angry disbelief. But he cannot know how important they are without some sort of additional information from Tony. He decides to call him and to demand a meeting immediately, especially after what he has read.

"It's Tom Phelps. I need to speak to you about last night's meeting. Meet me in the union office."

The reply comes in a rasping whisper. "Now you listen to me. You don't call me up and tell me what to do."

"I have the minutes of the meeting. Your name is mentioned, and I think you need to know what is being attributed to you." This is a lie which is entirely obvious to anyone who ever reads the minutes because no one is ever mentioned by name. Tom is counting on the possibility that Tony will be unaware of this because he never reads anything but the set-up instructions for a new laptop.

There is a pause. "I will sneak out, but don't think you can make a habit of this."

Five minutes later, Tom is sitting in the office. Barry has left his mailbox open on the screen. Tom smiles and signs out. The door opens and Tony walks in, scowling in self-righteous anger.

"I do not appreciate the position you're putting me in. You need to think more about the risks I am taking to help you. Now what is it they are saying about me?"

"I'll come to that in a moment, but tell me what happened with Liefwint last night."

"The proposals were voted down, and they decided to …"

"Tell me about Liefwint."

"There was a long discussion. A lot of the ideas were surprisingly well-received. They …"

"Tell me about Liefwint."

Tony's level of anger is increasing visibly as he is denied the performance he wishes to give. He recognises that he may have to delay his speech. "As soon as the letter was raised for discussion, Liefwint said that it needed to be rejected out of hand, and that the entire governing body had to stand behind management's existing plans. One lady, I believe she's the head of a local secondary school, said they had to think about what staff would think of such a response, and before she could finish Liefwint starts banging his fist on the table shouting, 'I don't give a shit what they think – they can fuck off for all I care.' Then one of Dickie's mates starts shouting back at him that he has no right to speak to them like this. Morgan tries to calm them down but they carry on shouting at each other."

"It was one of Dickie's rugby pals who confronted him?"

"He runs some local firm that manufactures pens and stationery with company logos on it, that sort of stuff. Used to taking decisions about how to run things himself and doesn't like some venture capitalist taking decisions behind closed doors and telling him to get in line. Just between you and me, I don't think he likes these finance types generally. Anyway, Morgan eventually gets them to quiet down, but then some of the others start asking why we can't delay some cost savings until next year. Seemed like a price worth paying to end the dispute and all the bad publicity. Liefwint starts shouting again that if they give in, there'll be no end to it and the college will finish in bankruptcy. It took almost the whole evening, but then the vote went in favour of the management plan over the union one."

"The minutes don't say how many voted each way."

"Morgan told Deirdre not to record it as it may inflame matters."

"What was the vote?"

Tony looks down. "I can't tell you that. It's too sensitive. Everyone will know who it came from."

"No one will know it was you, and as you represent staff interests and it's a public body, perhaps you could have the integrity to tell me."

Tony is surprised and irritated by the sharpness of the tone. "Don't you talk to me of integrity. You know the risks I have taken." He pauses in order to reflect on the enormity of what is being asked of him and then looks back at Tom. "It was eleven votes to nine."

"Eleven votes to nine!" Tom shakes his head in disbelief.

Tony looks at him in sympathetic understanding. "I know. I blame myself in part. Perhaps I should have asked to see your proposals before they went forward. I could have edited them to make sure they were better suited to such an audience. Well, too late now. You've missed your chance."

Tom is in momentary stasis, unable to comprehend how close they had come to ending it all. But this thought brings with it the full force of why they had fallen short, and the months of fear and frustration and anxiety and sleep loss now overwhelm him, and they all suddenly seem attributable to this single figure who sits before him. He glares over at his staff governor, and then bellows at him. "You fucking, useless, fat cunt."

Tony recoils, but Tom carries on. "Morgan said at the end of the debate that all those governors who had opposed the management plan needed to rally behind them now, and he pointed out that both staff governors had supported it. You voted to put your own colleagues out of work."

Tony appears in shock at the severity of the attack, and the usual, superior tone is replaced by a wimpish squeal. "Even if it had been ten votes each, Morgan would have had the casting vote and he would have voted against you."

"You don't know that."

"I couldn't have known it would be that close. "

"And I suppose voting on principle was out of the fucking question."

Tony shakes his head and looks up at the ceiling, now recovering some composure and feigning impatience at Tom's lack of perception. "You understand nothing. I couldn't risk letting them know the way I think. They would have excluded me, and then my job might have been at risk."

"You already are excluded, and it's not because they fear your searing business insights. They laugh at you because you're a fucking moron, and I'll tell you something I do understand. I understand how cowardly you are, and I understand how you love playing the undercover agent while the rest of us try to hang on to our jobs."

"You can't speak to me like that."

"I fucking can, and I'll tell you something else I can do. By the end of today, everyone in this building is going to know the way you voted last night and exactly how close it was. And if Dickie finds out it's you who let it slip and you find yourself in danger, then maybe you'll start to understand what it's like to be in our position. Now fuck off."

Tony stands and slowly walks to the door. There is no further attempt to play the misunderstood hero with a good heart. He starts opening the door and is surprised to see that Barry is waiting outside. Tony looks down as he passes him.

Barry sits opposite Tom and sighs heavily. "I go to get myself a coffee, come back to the office, and instead of peace and quiet I hear you yelling abuse at someone. Just for future reference, I'm the one who gets to play bad cop."

"How much did you hear?"

"Everything from the point when you made that rather insensitive reference to his weight."

"You stood outside the door for all that time?"

"No, I heard it from the queue in the canteen. Told them you were practising for meetings with management." He smiles. "Look, this may not be as bad as you think. We'll get something round to members this afternoon telling them the result of the vote, and Jenny might like it over at the *Gazette*. All of this has become a decent local interest story for them, and a deep divide among the governors is an interesting angle. All we need to do is peel off two more governors and we're home."

"Tell me something. How can someone like Tony Coyle be a governor? There's not one person in power in this organisation who is fit to have any authority over anything. They all seem to be in it for themselves, and vanity or money seem to be the only motives which drive any of them."

"That's why people turn to us. There's no point looking to those in authority for any sort of decency, so they feel better off finding someone who can at least give out a good kicking." Barry sees that Tom is still smouldering. "Listen. If you start getting hacked off because the world's full of people in charge who are crap, then there'll be no end to it. Right now we just need to keep going. Half the governors are already desperate to find an end to this, and we've got three months to find a couple more."

Tom nods slowly, and he makes his way up to his office. Mike, Alan, and Tili are all there, and each looks down as he enters. "What's up?"

Tili looks at him. "Are you teaching during the first session tomorrow?"

"No, why?"

"I've been asked to come for an interview with Sally Field."

The appointment is for nine-thirty, and they arrive just in time. Fearing that there might be a queue of people receiving the same notice of redundancy and that waiting with all the rest of them will be like sitting with a group of early Christians as the lions warm up, he and Tili make tortuous conversation in their own office for as long as possible and walk down to the waiting room outside Sally's office at the last moment. At nine thirty-five the door opens. Tom recognises the hospitality lecturer who exits. She is non-unionised, and each time he has deposited newsletters or flyers on the desk of her colleagues, she has gone out of her way to explain to him the moral betrayal inherent in all strike action. It is odd to think that he remains her best chance of keeping her job, but even odder to register that recalling her sanctimony gives no satisfaction. They acknowledge one another, all bitterness gone.

When they enter, Sally smiles and tilts her head. "Tili, do take a seat." She takes a deep breath. "Tili, I am deeply sorry to have to say that the college wishes to release you. I have here a letter setting out the details of what will now happen and a copy of the appeals procedure if you would like to consider that option. This is a terribly difficult time for all of us, but especially for someone in your position, and we wish to do all we can to support you through this process. I'm also enclosing contact details of the counselling service we are employing to help you as well as information on how you may wish to seek other employment opportunities."

Sally's tone is surprisingly polished. It is intended to combine sympathy with clarity, and although it is obviously practised, the delivery is not so saccharine that one wishes to stab her through the heart with the fountain pen Dickie gave her on her appointment to this job, which sits on her desk. They have agreed beforehand that Tili will ask any questions she wishes to and turn to Tom if she is in difficulty.

"Why have I been chosen?" The tone is one of complete incomprehension, which has not diminished since receiving the email the previous day.

"We have used absence from work as the criterion for deciding who is to be released."

"I haven't missed a day's work this year."

"Your record shows that you were off work through much of January last year. I'm afraid that places you in the category of staff we have chosen to look at."

"I had an ovarian cyst removed. The doctor said it was urgent. I had no choice." She looks over at Tom.

"Time off work for illness is something they can legally use to select people as long as they're consistent. They'll have produced some list of all teaching staff with the number of days sick leave we've each taken over the last two or three years and then just circled the number of people they want to dismiss. Maternity leave is the only type of absence they can't use."

Tili looks back at Sally in disbelief. "Does all my teaching count for nothing? Do my fifteen years just get set aside because of an operation I needed to avoid cancer?"

Sally is silent. Her face and neck have become oddly discoloured in patches. She is trying to gather herself. Finally, she is able to offer some sort of response. "I'm so sorry. This is obviously so distressing, and all of us regret that this is occurring." She stops. Tili's head has dropped, and she sobs quietly. Tom takes her hand. He considers hugging her but is unsure if this isn't too intimate, so he and Sally sit there for what must be no more than a minute until Tili lifts her head. She takes a deep breath in order to steady herself, wipes her face with a tissue, then looks straight at Sally. "I'll tell you something. I'd rather walk out of here now than stay in a job I got by letting Dickie hump me from behind over his toilet."

She then pushes her chair back and walks out as both Sally and Tom watch incredulously.

One unexpected consequence of the dispute has been a general sense of civic disintegration. Many simply no longer see any point in putting in the hours they used to. Another aspect of this has been a feeling that normal standards of courtesy can be ignored when dealing with those you see as being on the other side. Isn't this what Dickie has always done anyway? Tom had experienced the same phenomenon as Tili when he met with Tony the day before. What was the point of politeness when someone was shafting you?

Sally shakes her head. "It's very unfair for people to say that sort of thing."

"I know," says Tom. "Wasn't it over the basin?"

CHAPTER SIXTEEN

It takes two weeks for the letters of redundancy to be issued, each one being handed over in an individual meeting. Fifty-three staff make up the thirty-eight full-time equivalent posts. Now there are people who have been singled out. The union selects a number of cases where dismissing someone for absence from work suggests extreme injustice. Aside from Tili, there is a health and social care teacher who missed a month to look after her daughter after she had miscarried horribly in the fifth month. One English teacher had been signed off work for stress after his son overdosed. By the time Tom and Barry have finished with the pulmonary embolisms and the week-long vigils for dying parents, no one reading their press notice is interested in asking if there are any slackers who will throw a sickie every month or so because they feel like a day off.

The journalists just love it. Jenny's reporting in the *Sandford Gazette* remains firmly loyal to the staff, and the dispute now starts attracting wider coverage. The *Times Educational Supplement* and the *Education Guardian* both lead with the story once they receive Barry's press release. The *TES* goes with "Sick and Grieving Lecturers Selected for the Sack," while the *Guardian* restricts itself to "College Targets the Most Vulnerable for Redundancy." When *London Today* covers it, Dickie and Barry face off on air, and Barry wheels out the most emotionally-charged cases of those facing dismissal.

When Dickie cites financial reality, Barry is able to get across that the union has already set out a viable alternative, and the overall impression is one of unjustified aggression by inhuman management. Even the local Tory MP calls for a period of reflection and renewed talks.

Yet the very success of the union's public assault starts setting them back. Four members of the governing body resign. Now that being a governor at the college is seen less as a form of selfless public service and more like contributing to the destruction of the borough's only state sixth form, the local business types cannot quite see the PR value any more. Three of the four who leave are ones they are pretty sure voted for the union plan. Tom and Barry also suddenly find that the *Gazette* has ended its policy of topping and tailing their press releases before putting them on the front page. When Barry sends out a notice listing record numbers of staff signed off on sick leave and submitting their resignations, there is no coverage. Tom calls Jenny and finds out she has been told to focus more on other stories and that the other full-time staffer has been given responsibility for covering the college. The pieces only fall into place when the librarian tells her Unify rep that the college has increased its subscription to the local paper from three copies a week to one hundred. Twelve percent of the paper's entire sales now come from this single source, and that means a near twelve percent increase in sales just when the parent company is looking to close or merge its locals. So the pro-union articles suddenly cease. Go figure.

A month after the governors' rejection of the union plan, Tom and Barry have thus won a clear victory in the battle of public perception, yet are in a weaker overall position due to the loss of key support on the governing body, which they need to overturn Dickie's plan. By the time they reach early April, they are six weeks from the point at which the staff will be sacked, and Dickie has simply dug in, surrounded by a coterie of remaining governors who don't like it but see no choice other than sitting it out in the hope that it will all calm down after May twenty-fifth. The union has to do something to translate that discomfort into a desire to squeeze out of this mess by some other means. They move to a series of two-day strikes which are timed to coincide with any major event they can find. Parents' evenings, open evenings, awards ceremonies, governors meetings which will see governors enter a building emptied of the thousands who should be stuffed in there. There is an optimism generated by how close the vote was last time around and by how much more effective the union has appeared in the public exchanges. But even with the smaller deductions from pay and the strike money from the national funds, this is pushing members hard. This hurts, yet it is less damaging than the other aspect of the dispute which always seems to loom over them and about which they can do nothing: time. Regardless of how convincing they are, or how unjustified the management's policy, there is an unavoidable sense that their opponents need do nothing but wait. Once they have complied with employment law and educational practicality, they can do anything they wish, and the paucity of their case counts for nothing. By the beginning of May, the union has already been out for a total of ten days, and still no movement. They call a one-day strike for May tenth – the day on which local schools will be sending their students for taster sessions at the college – which runs the twofold risk of deterring the students who represent their future income and, hence, of further redundancies if they under-recruit again. The gamble is that Dickie will be more aware of this than anyone and will feel he has to offer some sort of concession to avoid the danger of a financial meltdown. All he has to do is set out a better voluntary redundancy package and delay his plans for modernisation. Instead, he cancels the sessions two days before they are due to take place, writing to tell the local schools that the college's new policy is to hold such events in the summer term so there is no danger of interfering with preparation for GCSEs.

They consider calling off the strike but decide in the end that they can't indulge in playing clever games. Dickie need worry only about a handful of governors, and Liefwint would love the idea of getting rid of more staff and blaming it on the union. Tom and Barry have to bring hundreds with them every time they take a decision, and a last-minute cancelation of a strike which they said was essential wouldn't look like the clear-headed leadership they want to project. So they come out for the eleventh day.

When Tom walks up the road towards the gates he sees the same two people he saw on the first day. Barry and Colin smile as he approaches. It suddenly strikes him that Barry is wearing a sports jacket over a T-shirt, and he recalls their first strike day when they could manage no more than three hours before the low temperatures defeated them. They have now been in dispute through all four seasons and on strike for three of them. "Excellent jacket."

"And you have excellent judgement. Seven-fifteen, Tom. If we go on into the autumn you may start getting here even before us two old lags."

"Much traffic?"

"We got here at six-forty-five to see if we could embarrass a few, but only saw the usual suspects. Richard Tomlinson walked in this time, obviously hoping to get here before us. Had to compliment him on how lucky we were to have senior managers who work such long hours. Humourless git couldn't even crack a smile."

The day now follows the same pattern as so many others. Students have now become so accustomed to almost all their classes being closed that they mostly stay away even if they know one of their teachers will be there. A number of teachers continue to cross the line, but the college effectively closes every time a strike is called, and since the introduction of strike pay Dickie hasn't sent around any further messages about the numbers of staff coming in. The strike is now as solid as it was at the start, and they all know it.

At eight-thirty, Alan Frost comes walking towards them, and Tom prays for some further anecdotes. "Can I infer from your late start that the childcare arrangements are going better?"

Alan stands opposite him, and before he even speaks Tom knows from the look of extreme effort to remain composed what is coming and shakes his head. "No. You can't."

"I'm sorry. I don't wish to, but I cannot come out again."

"You can't, not after all this time."

"We don't have the money to keep on doing this. We're down to paying the interest on our credit cards, we're behind with our mortgage."

"Find the money. Borrow it. I'll lend you something, but you cannot go in."

"You can say that because you have two incomes and a cheap rent. I have one income, a mortgage, and a family. I don't have any more money."

Andy Fortnum is watching this from his hut and walks over, looking only at Alan and carefully avoiding any look which might indicate the acknowledgement of Tom's presence. "Is this man bothering you? Because if there's any intimidation going on, I'll take care of that right now."

Tom's contempt for Fortnum diminishes his ability to persuade Alan to change his mind, and he is tempted to tell the guard to fuck off. He restrains himself, partly from fear of giving Fortnum the opportunity to deliver the kind of physical response about which he fantasises. He continues to hold Alan's look. "Is this the sort of person you want to side with now?"

Fortnum turns in disbelief, but it is Alan who speaks first. "Everything is fine, please leave us alone."

Fortnum looks at both former friends and returns to his hut in disappointment at not being allowed to intervene more thoroughly.

Tom is still in a state of incomprehension. "I represented you, I may even have saved your job. Your family has come over for dinner at my home."

Alan is shaken, and the extreme discomfort is evident. He tries to beat out each word in a tone which comes as close to self control as he can manage. "I'm sorry, but I'm going in." And he walks through the gates with Tom staring after him, unsure what to think.

Alan is right that it is much easier for Tom to stand firm when Sofia could pay for them on her own if they needed her to. Yet this cannot overcome a sense that Alan could find some means to get by. He is not the only one struggling, and whilst some may have been deterred by the prospect of passing their colleagues, most have committed themselves to doing whatever they need to to get by while the union is trying to defend them. Alan has sat opposite Tili for six years, and he is now giving her up. For all the financial arguments, in the end it is this personal dimension which leads Tom to the conclusion that what Alan has done is absolutely unforgivable. Regardless of the outcome, he will try to ensure that Alan is moved out of their office, and he knows that he will struggle with even the most basic courtesy from now on.

He watches Alan walk down the college driveway and into the main building, continuing to look long after he has entered in the hope that he might change his mind and re-emerge. Yet he knows that Alan is now signing the register of teaching staff who have come in for the day and then walking up the stairs to sit in an empty office, where he will wait until the pickets have disappeared, before returning home. Whatever shame he may now be feeling still can't generate the degree of pity in Tom which might make him reconsider his sense that they will never speak again.

After a few minutes, Barry approaches him. "Let it go. He'll not have any serious impact, and it's the wider battle we need to win."

"He's a friend."

"I know, but like I said, there's bigger fish to fry. Right now you need to come with me."

Tom turns to him. "Go where?"

"Café Nero in Sandford town centre."

"Am I missing something here?"

"Yes you are. You, Colin, and I are going for a coffee, and our comrades are going to hold the line for the rest of the day. Now let's go."

The three of them walk the fifteen minutes into the centre, and Barry refuses to explain why. Tom quickly rejects the possibility that this is some means of consoling him for the earlier experience, and it is not until they enter that he begins to understand why he is there. They sit in the armchairs at the back of the café, but they are soon joined by another staff member whom Tom recognises but has barely spoken to. Phil Little runs the post room, but, more importantly, he is the local convener for Unify, who represent all non-teaching staff at the college. Cleaners, secretaries, admissions staff, marketing people, they all come under Phil's watch, and whereas Tom and Barry have to arrange meetings every time they want to speak to their members in different parts of the building, Phil sees all of his people every day simply by virtue of picking up and dropping off their post. A route which should take an hour takes him four as he keeps up to speed with every word of gossip in every area of the college, as well as finding out first anything which might affect his people. If a secretary types something, he will know about it. His near-perfect mastery of all information helps to defend staff from endless threats. Short-term contracts, hived-off services, outsourcing of IT contracts – if it can be done, then management will do it to support staff, and if he sometimes defends them successfully, it is because he often knows of new initiatives even before the managers who are supposed to implement them, and he is able to come up with some sort of preemptive response. The reason he had been unable to tell UCL about the original plans was because Sally Field had taken the minutes of the key meetings, and so Deirdre had been unable to leak them to him.

Barry passes Phil a cappuccino with two sugars, and he carefully makes a hole in the surface through which he pours the sugar and stirs it in whilst preserving the chocolate-covered foam as far as anyone possibly could. When this operation is complete, he looks up, smiles and passes a single copy of an email to Barry. "This was sent out to staff in Student Records and Admissions yesterday evening."

```
Dear Colleague,

As you know, Sandford is going through a
difficult period, and there may be addi-
tional challenges that we face as a result
of the examination period which is now ap-
proaching. I am writing to let you know
that you may be required to do some invig-
ilation. I am aware that it is unusual for
```

```
staff in your roles to have to take on such
responsibilities, but I regret that we must
consider such options in light of the ac-
tions taken by the Union of College Lec-
turers.

Regards,
Sally Field
Personnel Director
```

Barry is the first to react. "Can they force you to do this?"

"No. They can ask us, but no one can be forced to carry out the responsibilities of striking staff. I called one of the national officers, and he confirmed it."

Colin nods in agreement. "There's often some sort of catch-all phrase in all contracts nowadays about staff having to work flexibly, but that's not usually enough to force people to take on something as specific as this. There must be something in the teaching contracts about having to do invigilation, so it's obviously someone else's work they're asking you to do."

Barry leans forward. "Have you discussed this with Sally yet?"

"No."

"So she doesn't know yet that Unify are opposed to this."

"No, and maybe there's no reason why she should before she has to."

"So we have to find a day when there are so many exams that they will need to ask your members to invigilate."

"And I will call a meeting on the day before and try to make it look like one of our regular ones. I will move a motion that no Unify member should carry out any teaching responsibilities, and we can bring in one of our national officers on the day to face them down if they come in to try and make us do it."

"Seeing as you have worked out all the other details of this, I assume you may have an idea of when the best day would be as well."

"May nineteenth. It's the day of the English, maths, and business studies exams. They've even got three of the conference halls in the rugby ground hired out."

Tom is not entirely comfortable with this. "Hitting student exams doesn't look as if it will win hearts and minds."

Barry is unconcerned. "The college cannot allow public exams not to take place. Once Dickie realises that he has no staff to cover them, there'll be no choice but to make some sort of deal. He can offer to postpone redundancies until next year so it doesn't look like a climb-down, and by the time next September comes round, there'll be no taste for another fight. There's no serious financial argument any more. It's all a question of one man's ego."

"So we come out on the nineteenth, and that's an end to it."

"Yes, but not for the whole day. We'll have a half-day strike starting at one o'clock. The exams start at two, and we wait for either Dickie or Sally to state that the letters of redundancy are being withdrawn, and then we march back in together."

"Very dramatic. Maybe you should sell the film rights too. Might fund the next strike."

"That's exactly the sort of creative thinking the trade union movement needs, Tom!"

CHAPTER SEVENTEEN

The nineteenth should have been filled with optimism and a spectacular, final victory.

As he sits on the train, Tom tries to understand the disaster which has just played out. The sheer speed at which events moved and the unexpectedly severe outcome mean that he is not simply downcast but also at a genuine loss in terms of comprehending exactly how it occurred. He tries to reconstruct the precise sequence of events in the hope that this order will reveal to him the causes.

As with so many of the other moments this year which have thrown him, it begins with Laura.

She approached him after class yesterday and asked if she might speak with him. She promised it would be very brief and not require him to spend hours with her as he had before. She asked if they could go to the union office again, but he disliked the idea of the smaller more intimate setting, so he lied that it was being used by the caseworker, and they found an empty classroom instead. She sat first, and he then pulled up a chair and sat opposite her with a table separating them.

She looked down at first, took a deep breath, and then looked up at him. "I spoke about you with one of my friends … not someone from here," she added quickly. "I told her that you were the only person who I felt had really helped me, and she suggested … well … she suggested I should speak to you. I mean she thought it was better to know one way or the other." She now looked him directly in the eyes. "I think you know what I mean."

"I'm not sure I do," he lied, hoping that she would now stand up and walk out of the college.

"Come on, you know," she said imploringly.

He sighed. "It's completely out of the question," he said, trying for something like a coldly formal tone which didn't stray into aggression.

"I know, I know. I just had to find out for sure." She then hesitated and looked at him again. "Can I just know why?"

It crossed his mind to point out that he was old enough to be her father, but aside from it being such an awful cliché, he realised this may be precisely the point of attraction. "I'm your teacher. This means I have a duty of care which is incompatible with what you're asking about. I'm also in a settled relationship." He knew there was something wrong with this reply, but he was now hoping that the two reasons he had given her would be sufficient, and he was not worried about what the correct response should have been.

She smiled at him. "I know you're right." She then looked down, trying to compose herself. There was a silence which seemingly lasted for days, but he was determined to say nothing which may have prolonged the situation. She picked up her Prada bag and walked out. He sat there for a few more moments to give her plenty of time to get away and then returned to his office.

Aside from the extraordinary nervousness of the encounter itself, this need not have been so awful, and he could easily have returned to the relentless pressure of the dispute. It was not until later that the full horror unfolded.

As he lay in bed, he told Sofia of what had happened. She propped herself up on one elbow. "Why did you say it to her like that?"

"What else should I have said?"

"Shouldn't you have told her you didn't find her attractive? Now she might think that when she finishes at the college in a couple of weeks, you might be up for something discreet."

"I should have told someone who is self-harming that she's ugly?"

"That's not what I said, and don't get touchy. I'm just saying that you may not have got rid of her yet."

"Look, I don't see how it makes sense to tell someone in her state of mind that she's unattractive. I may as well start slicing her up myself."

"Don't be silly. If you don't want to discuss this, then I don't know why you raised it in the first place."

"My mistake, sorry." They both lay back, and had things ended at this point, then it would have been no more than a pathetically immature exchange which would easily have been forgotten. But they were each lying there in the dark, smouldering at the thought of the other's insensitivity, and Sofia broke the silence with a question which would lead them to the point where they now stand.

"Do you find her attractive?"

"Oh, for fuck's sake!"

"I'm not accusing you, and you've obviously tried to put her off. I'm just curious. It wouldn't be the first time a middle-aged man got turned on by a schoolgirl."

"This is exactly what I fucking need right now. Thanks a lot." He rose to leave the room for one of those nights that each of them periodically spent on the sofa after a fight. But she leapt across the room with near-Olympian speed and barred the door. "Ok, I'm sorry, I'm sorry. I shouldn't have called you middle-aged."

Unbelievably, he found this amusing. He could only smile at her production of such a line at that moment. She smiled in turn at her own success, and he returned to bed. But this was only a temporary distraction from the spite of what had been said. He was sure that she had apologised only because of what awaited him the next day, and they lay there in bitter silence before a restive sleep. When he left in the morning, he did so without going back into the bedroom to say goodbye, meaning she could not wish him good luck.

So now he sits on the train. He confronts why this should have occurred, and he curses his own stupidity. Why did he react so defensively? What did it matter? The answers which emerge are ones he has known for months and has chosen to suppress. For all Laura's annoyance and the fear she has inspired, what also comes to him is an unmistakable awareness of a scintillating, erotic charge. So much of what she had said to him on that first occasion in the union office had implied a sexual confidence which excited him, and his reaction last night was one in which he feigned righteous anger to mask this. Betraying Sofia is unthinkable, and he knows of the hopelessness of someone like Laura and the terrible vulnerability from which she suffers. Yet none of his rational or ethical concerns can fully extinguish the exquisite sexual appeal he finds in her.

When Sofia asked him if he found Laura attractive, the honest answer would have been there was a sense in which he did. But at this point, the consequences of stating such an answer trouble him less than the implications of what he is now confronting. He has presented himself as the teacher, the union representative, the person who stands up to protect others. Yet here is this thrilling sense of what it would be like to be with Laura. The knowledge that his self-restraint will prevent this is not enough to dim the sense of his own hypocrisy. He struggles to believe that others share the same deviousness, but even if they do, why should that console him?

When he comes to the issue of what he should do, he decides that he can say nothing of the truth to Sofia. By the time the train pulls into Sandford Station, he has made up his mind that he will call her to apologise. He can claim that the pressure he has been under at work had led him to overreact so stupidly. She will understand that. Better to go on as before rather than make things any worse. Better to keep some truths hidden.

He texts his apology and promises to make it up to her. Five minutes later his mobile goes off, and he is so nervous he considers letting it go through to voicemail. He decides to take the call, and before he has the chance to say anything she speaks. "Look, I think what you're doing is amazing, and I was stupid to say the things I did. I'm the one who needs to apologise, not you. I just really admire you for what you're doing, and I should be supporting you."

He gulps. "You're wrong. I'm afraid there is something in what you were getting at. There is a sort of sick sense in which I do find Laura attractive," he decides not to say. Instead he opts for generosity. "Forget it. We probably both said some things we shouldn't have, I'm sure it wasn't just you. You can take me out tonight to celebrate my victory, and if you really want to make it up to me, you can drop a set next time we play."

After they end the call, he isn't entirely sure what he feels any more, but he knows he has a powerful sense of relief that it's over and an absolute desire not to go back into this.

When he enters the office, Alan is already at his seat. He looks up and Tom nods at him in the most minimal form of greeting. This has been the extent of their interaction over recent days, and Alan now gives the impression of being resigned to a coldness which will remain for as long as he does. Tili, who has six days before she is discarded, will not even look at him. Mike is more polite, but the forced nature of their exchanges does no more than highlight a discomfort which allows them to relax only when Alan is absent from the room. Tom was initially unable to comprehend how he could have adapted so fully and quickly to the passive viciousness of his own behaviour, but it has become clear to him that the extremity of what he feels himself to be involved in means that what Alan has done is an irredeemable betrayal. At one o'clock, he will finish teaching a first-year class and then walk out of the college gates. Alan will sit at his desk.

The second of his emails is from Barry. The message reads "75 12." In order to address Colin Preston's paranoia, they have agreed that there would be no language which might make it possible for management to interpret their communications. The message contains the result of Unify's ballot from the previous evening. Sally emailed the same staff as before telling them they would be invigilating on the afternoon of the nineteenth within an hour of receiving formal notification of the strike. Phil has decided that he will send an email to all his members at twelve-thirty informing them that no one should do what Sally says. He will stand in the registry with one of the national officers who will be coming in for the day. Should Sally try to compel anyone, then she will be told that she has no legal right to do so and that any further attempt to force people to do what she wants will result in the national union organising a collective grievance against her on behalf of the ninety-three Unify members working at the college. It is now eight-forty three in the morning, and even after six months of striking the five hours of waiting which lie before them will stretch out like millennia.

He sets a timed essay question for his first class. The thought of trying to focus on teaching is beyond him. As the students write, he sits with a book open in front of him and reads nothing. He thinks about Alan, and he watches the time. He considers how things may go wrong. The class ends, and he collects the scripts which he hopes to mark tomorrow, by which time he expects that one sixth of his colleagues will have been spared. He returns to his office, attempts to prepare for a class he is due to teach tomorrow but realises he will be unable to focus on anything until their victory is confirmed. He goes down to see Barry during the second period, when both are free, but Barry is in a meeting with the other Comms teachers, so he proceeds to the union office, where he can engage in mindless web searches without the embarrassment of anyone else knowing what he is doing. For the final session before lunch, he shows a video on Nietzsche which is almost relevant to the first-year ethics course he is teaching. At one o'clock he returns to his office, where Alan is standing with his jacket on, looking directly at Tom. "I would like to join this afternoon's half-day strike."

"What?"

"I've considered everything, and I think you were right. We've borrowed some money from Mary's mother, and I have a cheque for one day's pay which I would like to donate to the union to cover the day I came into work. If it's all right, I would like to join the strike."

So formally polite. Tom will never know how much this decision has been influenced by the social exclusion which they have meted out to him.

"If you're lucky, then thirty minutes from now the strike will be called off, and I may even rip up your cheque to use it for confetti."

"That's what I'm gambling on. We would much rather use that money for some new furniture."

"Let's see what we can do."

They walk down the corridor side by side and out through the main door of the college building. The plan is for all members to congregate at one-fifteen on the lawn outside this door, just below Dickie's first-floor window. His blinds are drawn, but they know he is there and can hear them. They have worked to bring everyone out. Just one more time. Even those who have drifted back over recent weeks will come out for half a day. The national union has decided to remit a full day's strike pay. Defeat here is something they fear may encourage other principals to take the same aggressive line. If such a branch can be beaten, then anyone can. If such a branch wins, then many others will be safe.

Within moments the lawn fills. The student union leaders approach Barry to give him a copy of the letter of support they have sent to the governors on behalf of the students. By this time, Phil Little is standing in the registry ready to bar Sally from approaching the Unify members.

At a quarter past, Barry walks forward and looks up to the first floor window. "Dickie. Dickie Kilman. It is time to listen to your staff." He turns. "Right, come on." Two hundred and seventy teachers march out of the gates where a dozen photographers and a film crew record every step. Six members of the branch executive take up positions as the official picket, while the others cross the road. They turn, they stand, and they wait.

By now Sally should be in mid-argument with a Unify national officer who is primed to tell her she cannot have the people she wants. Within five minutes, she will already be starting to realise that it is futile to continue, and she will have to tell Dickie. By a quarter to one, someone must emerge to hand over the letter they have demanded which will lift the threat of redundancies.

At twenty to, Barry turns to Tom. "Well, well. Here comes the international support." And he nods to the road which leads up to the college.

Tom thinks at first he is hallucinating but realises that the person approaching them is Sofia. He stands smiling like a child as she walks towards him. She starts to speak but is drowned out by what sounds like the blast of a foghorn. Coming from the direction of the rugby ground is an immense black coach with darkened windows which swings wide and then turns violently to ensure an angle which will allow it to pass through the gates. The blast of the horn is because Barry is standing in front of it. It lurches forward and Barry stands his ground. From his hut, Andy Fortnum shouts over. "Barry, out the way." Barry half turns. "I want to speak to them." Fortnum comes out and shouts again. "Barry, I'm telling you, out the way!" Barry still stands, hands on hips, as the coach driver shouts at him through the glass. Fortnum walks up behind him, hooks a huge paw under each arm, lifts him clear off his feet, takes three enormous strides away from the coach, and hurls him forward where his head hits the ground horribly before Tom and Sofia can catch him. Fortnum bangs on the side of the coach. "Go!" The machine enters the college. Fortnum walks up to stand over Barry, pointing down at him. "I warned you, Barry." Barry is dazed, but Tom bellows back, "You fucking mindless cunt!" Fortnum draws back his right fist to punch him, but he has been told to restrain himself in front of the cameras. In addition, dozens have now crossed the road, and he quickly retreats back to the hut. However soft he thinks this collection of art historians and geologists may be, he doesn't fancy taking on two hundred of them.

Barry struggles to his feet, but it is not Fortnum at whom he looks. Sally is standing by the door of the coach even before it opens. She almost curtseys when the first passenger emerges, and the short discussion suggests this is the man in charge. Big smile and a warm welcome to Sandford.

Dickie has watched all of this from his window, discreetly following it all through a crack in the blinds. "Let this be an end to it," he thinks.

Once Sally raised the possibility that there may not be enough staff to cover the exams, it was clear what the union's final move would have to be. He couldn't rely on the support staff, so he had Sally find an agency for external invigilators and had all correspondence go only to her, using email exclusively. He authorised the cash transfer himself, knowing that the company's name would not reveal the nature of their work to any Unify member working in the finance department. Yet his feeling now is overwhelmingly one of relief rather than triumph. Barry is an old fool, steeped in a rhetoric which he should have outgrown when the sixties ended. Tom is a pretentious twerp who has washed up here because he lacks the ability to make it as an academic. But he feels degraded by the knowledge that he has turned to a thug like Andy Fortnum to ensure everything would work out. He needed someone at the gate who would get the coach through, and this person in turn needed to understand the seriousness of making that happen. When he called Fortnum into his office, he made him only the third person in the college to be aware of what was supposed to occur. Fortnum leaned across the walnut table and gave him an absolute assurance that he would get these people through, and it was then that Dickie understood he was enlisting a man who was salivating at the prospect of breaking others' bones in what he could convince himself was a just cause. Whatever he thinks of Tom and Barry, they are preferable to consorting with this Neanderthal.

Why had he let things get this far? He knows that it was partly because he cannot stomach letting others tell him how to run a college he has steered for two decades. He knows also that money has to be saved and that jobs have to go. But pressing in on him is the sense that he has been fired up by Liefwint when it comes to making tough choices about how to take the college forward. He likes the idea of being strong enough to take on a powerful union to make the changes which are necessary. He knows he has pushed so hard partly because he wants to show he has the will to power through measures from which weaker types would recoil. But when he saw Fortnum tossing Barry aside, all those thoughts just looked like so much shallow, macho nonsense. He found himself wishing for the days when he would hammer out some compromise, and they could all go back to hating each other at lower stakes. He curses the day that Liefwint entered the governing body and insisted on this bolder, braver approach to money, to unions, to everything. On Thursday evening, he will announce to the governors that the dispute is effectively over. In six days, those selected for redundancy will be gone, and the strikes will end. No union strikes to bring back the departed. He will have to think of some measures to smooth things over, and he will have to be around for the start of the new academic year, but he will announce his retirement in the autumn and be gone by Christmas. After twenty years, he will leave in the knowledge that he is hated by all. Better that than stay and endure any more of this. But, well, fuck it, he has won, and he is entitled to have people recognise that. He pulls out his mobile.

They just watch the line of people file out of the coach. No one knows what to do. All two hundred and seventy of them just look on as these people walk off the coach and disperse to supervise students whose teachers stand outside the gates with their jobs melting away. Barry has a thin line of blood which trickles from his temple down the side of his face and onto his jacket. He just watches them. It takes no more than five minutes for all of these people to disappear, and nine months of resistance go with them.

No one knows what to do. One moment they were waiting for Dickie to send out a secretary to deliver his surrender, and the next they are beaten. Barry's phone issues a double bleep, and he opens the text. He shakes his head in angry disbelief before showing it to Tom. "Third time lucky." But now at least some of the fire returns, and he looks at his members. "Right. We can all go back into that building now and sign that register for staff who refuse to strike. Anyone who wants to, go ahead. But there are six days before our friends lose their jobs, and I say we fight for every minute of those six days to prevent it. That starts by showing management that even now we are not beaten. We voted for a strike today, and that's what we'll do, and tomorrow we will have another strategy to win."

There are cheers and clapping, but these responses are ones of artificial enthusiasm. They have lost, and they know it. They turn and walk away from their college because signing that register adds a touch of formal humiliation which they would rather pay to avoid. Ironically, this last strike is the one which has attracted the greatest support. Picketing seems pointless, but Barry wishes to talk with Tom and Colin. Sofia leaves them, and as she does, Barry gives her the anarchist salute from the Spanish civil war. She smiles as she returns the salute. A relic from another defeat.

When they sit at The Garden, it is no more than two-thirty. Tom buys the first round of drinks, and as he waits at the bar, he watches the other two sitting morosely without conversation. Barry has wiped the blood from the side of his face, but the jacket is still stained. When Tom sits down, it is he who breaks the silence.

"Are you serious about trying some other strategy?"

Barry sighs. "Not really. I just couldn't stomach us all walking back in. Now it's just a question of how you handle things for next year."

"Me? You can't step down."

"There's five people in English and Communications who've had their letter. I have to retire to save one of their jobs, and you have to take my place. No one will blame you for what happened. The thing now is to keep the branch together as much as possible and try to get people ready for the next time."

Colin looks over at him. "It may not be as bad as Barry's suggesting. This sort of dispute takes more out of management than you think. Sometimes they get a taste for blood, but more often they're exhausted by it all, and they look to avoid another fight."

Tom reflects briefly on the fact that he was attracted to his position because he liked the idea of four hours a week off his timetable. Now it feels like he must take on a role which would be beyond him even without the day's hideous defeat. "I'm not sure I'm up to this."

Barry shakes his head. "There's no choice. I have to go, you have to stay, and that's an end to it. Now it's just a question of identifying who has to step up to your position. You're the moral philosopher, and I'm sure you know all about moral obligation."

"It's not entirely clear what Aristotle's position is on that question."

"Oh well, not to worry, because as luck would have it, I'm fucking clear what mine is, and you're staying. Now drink up your poncey red wine so I can get you another."

At six-thirty, he is at the bar for the fourth time and is leaning rather than standing. He has now sat through the post mortem of their defeat and the Marxist analysis of how it fits into wider socio-political issues. It is so many years since he has studied Marx that he has forgotten the elegant simplicity of how such theories can account for everything from today's defeat to the global economic crisis, also covering all intermediate phenomena. He is smiling at this when he notices, from the corner of his eye, a woman standing a few feet away and watching him. He doesn't wish to look directly at her, so he checks the mirror behind the bar, but when he finds he is unable to bring her face into focus, he turns towards her.

"Hello, Tom."

It is Bella. The immediate association is with Dickie, but he has never had any sense that she is particularly close to him, and he tries to compose himself sufficiently to achieve coherent speech. "Hello. I didn't know you were a regular at The Garden." He is aware of how badly he is slurring but past the point where he cares.

"I'm not really, I'm meeting a friend for a drink before I go to the … Well, before I go out later."

"Are you going somewhere so embarrassing that you dare not tell me?"

"Well … yes."

"To be honest, unless you're taking Dickie out for a victory celebration, I'm not sure there is anything which could depress me more than what I've already seen today."

"How about if it were with Sally?"

He nods. "Ok, you win. I'm depressed that even someone like her is celebrating today."

"It's not really a celebration. They hired these invigilators from a company in the midlands, and they had to put them up in a hotel for the night. Sally insisted that we should take them out for dinner. The other secretaries and I had to arrange it and, well … I'm afraid …"

He is shaking his head. "God, that's beautiful. To retain the ability for such courtesy at a time like this. Imagine, she not only outwits us, but does it with such good manners."

Bella looks down. She hasn't had the benefit of eight glasses of wine to open her up to the dark humour into which Tom is now slipping. When she looks up again, it is with a look of absolute pity. "Can I just say, I … I'm very sorry it's all worked out like this."

He looks away, struggling to know how he should respond. Even through the haze of his alcoholic stupor he is diminished by that look. The drinks he has ordered are on the bar in front of him. He turns to her. "Well, can I just say I hope you have a very enjoyable evening, and please give Sally my very bes … my very best wishes. Now, I am going to re-join my friends." He is on the verge of tears.

By the time he leaves, he has been drinking for eight hours and has eaten some garlic bread. They had been joined by an IT lecturer who is to lose his job, and he has already decided that he will call in sick tomorrow. Three days from now will be the final Friday before the half-term holiday, and when he returns, Tili and fifty-two others will be gone. He began the day as a liar and a hypocrite, and he will finish it drunk and defeated.

CHAPTER EIGHTEEN

When he wakes, he thinks his head is going to split open. His temples pound with such force that all thought of yesterday is momentarily obscured by a physical incapacity so extreme that mere survival seems unlikely. It is as if any movement will result in his head disintegrating. He is alone and realises that Sofia must have left for work without his even registering any activity. He feels immediately vindicated over his decision to text his manager from the train last night to say he was too ill to come into work. He wonders how many others have stayed home under similar circumstances. After a few minutes, he swings his feet around and sits on the edge of the bed. There is a glass on the bedside table, but it is empty. He must have drunk the water during the night and now needs to achieve enough stability to make it to the kitchen for more. What's the French term for hangover, 'gueule de bois'? Mouth of wood. His mouth and throat are as arid as the desert. He makes it to the kitchen and drinks glass after glass. The discomfort recedes a little, just enough to leave space for a series of images from yesterday, with one returning again and again over the course of the day. He sees Barry's crumpled body lying on the ground as Fortnum stands over him. It is not so much the brutality which horrifies him but the extent of the indignity. That someone like Barry should be tossed around by someone like Fortnum.

Within an hour, the Paracetamol has brought his headache under control, and the feeling of moderate physical recovery is one which allows him to begin the day. He turns on *News 24* and briefly follows the items on the economic downturn in southern Europe. He is struck by how unconsoling it is that his Greek and Spanish counterparts are so much worse off. Indeed, there are many respects in which his own position will remain largely unaltered. His job and salary are almost certainly safe. He will continue to teach a subject he loves. He will be better off than so many, but why does this count for so little? There were moments of beauty. Alan walking out with him. Sofia coming to support them. But in the end, it is the thought of Dickie which he cannot get past. He would rather have his pay cut and his colleagues saved than cede victory to this man who screws up the college's finances, forces others to pay for it, and congratulates himself on a job well done. How much will his bonus be for what he has done? How warmly will Liefwint congratulate him for such strong management? He will dismiss all the union has said as unrealistic, sentimental nonsense and will therefore never have to confront the true nature of what he has done. And it is this which ultimately generates a bitterness in Tom which means nothing will compensate him for what happened yesterday. It is not only the sickening injustice but the fact that those responsible will never pay for it, or even acknowledge it as such. In a climate of general destruction across the public sector, Tom is aware he is unlikely ever to find a job elsewhere and may well come across the same thing even if he were to escape. Yesterday's defeat means he can do no more than adapt to a harsher and more humiliating environment.

He channel hops, but even here it feels like selecting from different forms of obscenity. He is offered programmes in which celebrities fetishise the food they concoct for other celebrities. He can receive helpful advice on which designer clothes he should wear, or how best to reform rooms such that functionality is trivial when set against the aesthetic priority of stylish subtlety. Sports news includes an item on a premiership player who won't sign a new contract with the club that first discovered him so that he can leave without any transfer fee and thereby better his current salary at a rival club. Tom calculates that his own annual salary is two days' pay for someone who complains of not earning enough and seeks sympathy for his need to ensure his family's future. In the end, he settles for watching an episode of *The Sweeney*.

In the evening, he is due to play his match in the opening round of the club's summer tournament. He has recovered sufficiently to be confident of the relatively harmless release of aggression against one of his friends from his doubles on a Tuesday night. Andy South is a fundraiser for Shelter, and drawing such a weak opponent means that Tom will advance to at least the third round, as both the second-round prospects are even weaker than Andy. When he reaches four-one in the first set, he cannot play a forehand. It is not simply that he is over-hitting or needs to exert greater control, he simply cannot remember how to play the shot and no matter what he tries to recall from the lessons he has had over the years, he can do nothing. Andy realises this almost instantly and hits everything to this weaker side. After twenty more minutes, he has lost nine games in a row but begins to regain something close to his usual shot. He brings the score back to four-five in the second set but then drops his serve after hitting three double faults. He walks to the net and shakes hands. He then turns and smashes the racket against the ground with all his force. He hopes for a clean, satisfying snap, with the top half flying high into the air. Instead, the head is broken half way down each side but is firmly attached to the shaft by the strings. It is a one-hundred-and-thirty-pound racket which Sofia has given him last Christmas. The courts are full, and everyone stops to look at him as he stands there watching his racket. Mitch is playing a doubles two courts away and walks over.

"Andy, do me a favour. Take the place of a tired old man while McEnroe and I get a drink."

Play resumes on all the other courts. All banter stops. They are waiting for Tom to leave. He feels almost as humiliated now as he had done outside the college gates yesterday. When they sit in the bar, Mitch buys them both a glass of the Spanish red wine he has had the club order in since Sofia brought it around for dinner one evening.

"I saw the footage on *London Today*. Security guard pushing a picket out the way so the strikebreakers could get past."

"Actually, he didn't push him. He lifted him and threw him." Tom's tone is resigned. He is just stating the facts. He sips the wine. "This is very good."

Mitch pulls out his iPhone and goes to one of his tennis websites. "I've told you before that those Wilson rackets lack rigidity. I'm going to order you a Head, one which I think will work better for someone who hits with your sort of topspin."

"Mitch, I can't let you do this. I'm humiliated enough as it is."

"It's great isn't it? Makes me feel like Viv Richards." He taps a few more times on the screen. "There. Not happy about getting you the same one as Andy Murray, but at least you share the same temperament."

"I don't know what to say."

"I've told you before, my top priority is to keep Sofia happy, and you're just a useful means of doing that."

"Good to know I'm useful for something."

"Hey, don't start talking like that," he snaps. Tom is surprised by the sharpness of this, but then Mitch puts a hand on his shoulder and softens his tone. "You want to know the real reason I'm doing this. When the National Front started marching through London in the seventies, it was the unions who stood up to them. This arsehole at your college will be gone sooner or later, and you'll get someone better. In the end, these sorts of people always lose."

"I'm afraid I don't share your optimism."

"That's why I'm the successful businessman, the club chairman and the one who's buying the drinks."

Tom smiles for the first time today. Even now, there is something infectious about this man's belief. "When he goes, perhaps you'd consider applying for the job yourself."

"Christ, you mean take a pay cut and deal with those public sector unions?"

"Good point. Better stay here and keep me in rackets."

By the time he leaves, Mitch has contrived to make him feel better, and he is actively looking forward to receiving the new racket. Maybe he is right. Maybe Dickie will be gone soon. Better not count on it.

CHAPTER NINETEEN

It turns out that Wednesday had seen the greatest number of staff absent that anyone could remember. Even those who hadn't been on strike called in sick because they couldn't stomach the thought of Dickie's triumph.

When he comes in on Thursday, he expects a wake but encounters only the best of gallows humour. On starting any computer, it goes to the college's updated homepage, which is a black screen accompanied by the Funeral March. It only takes till nine-fifteen this time before it is transformed back to the happy faces of the college's contented, successful, and socially perfect students. The fifty-three staff whose last chance has now evaporated must now deliver their final classes to their second-year students, all of whom finish their studies on Friday and will sit their exams after the half-term holiday. This usually signals a time of absolute relief for a staff whose year is essentially over, except for many it is now their time to leave the college as well. Tili gives Tom a bottle of wine to thank him for what he has done. She is applying for jobs anywhere and will commute if she can. If she can't, she will stay in the cheapest B&B. There are no jokes about how unfortunate it is that no one can beam her down to wherever she needs to be. Personal jokes are now only at the expense of management. What's the difference between Sandford College and a bad brothel? Everyone gets fucked at Sandford.

Boom, boom. All laughter is forced. It is a trivial form of resistance, but even those who are beaten can engage in it.

It rains on Friday. A steady, relentless drizzle coats him as he walks to the Junction and falls with the same, slow saturating force when he gets off at Sandford. He decides for some reason to buy a *Guardian* instead of reading it online. He is dissatisfied with the book he has with him. As the pressure has risen during the year, he has been unable to read either serious philosophy or serious literature. He has therefore decided to turn to good thrillers in order to find something which will hold him instantly and without effort. He has read the first three pages of a Scandinavian bestseller which he finds so awful he resents the one penny he paid for it on Amazon. He no longer has the capacity to know if this reflects the quality of the book or the extent to which his outlook has become too twisted to appreciate it.

Out of perverse curiosity, he also picks up a copy of the *Sandford Gazette* to see which pictures they would carry of Tuesday's events. He reads the headline and experiences something quite specific which he knows he has felt before. The memory of this recognition returns to him at various points over the day, and it is not until late in the afternoon that he finally places it. There is a moment in tennis more sublime than any other, one which redeems the mediocrity often surrounding it. There are doubtless similar ones in other sports, but it is from the tennis court that Tom knows it. Sometimes you throw the ball up for a serve, your arm swings smoothly, and you strike with such precision that the contact is barely perceptible. But this is not it. On a far smaller number of occasions, the ball flies over the net and passes an opponent who cannot touch it. On such points, there is the merest of gaps between the bounce of the ball and the time when it passes the opponent, and it is here where perfection lies. There is a millisecond when you are aware of exactly what will happen, and you know that things will move in your favour before they have occurred. And it is this oh-so-fleeting sense of seeing with absolute clarity a future that is yours which Tom receives when he reads, "Kilman to go in Local College Shake-up." He understands before even looking at the main body of the article that they have won. He doesn't know how and doesn't yet care. But he knows. Rather than hunt for one of the hundred copies which will be scattered around the college, Tom buys his first ever copy of this paper, perhaps unconsciously thinking that he may keep it, and reads it right there, in the rain.

He pulls out his mobile and calls Barry. "He's gone."

"Who?"

"Dickie is gone."

"I'm on the train. Speak up. What do you mean?"

Tom is now standing in the middle of the concourse in front of the station with no umbrella and shouting at the top of his voice. "Richard Kilman has left Sandford College. He is not coming back."

"Where've you got this from?"

"I'm reading it in the local rag as we speak. It says the governors decided last night that they no longer felt it appropriate that he remain at the college. It says he's stepping down with immediate effect. Immediate effect."

"What the fuck happened at the governors' meeting?"

Tom scans the article again and shakes his head. "It doesn't say. It just says the governors decided he should leave."

Tom is tapped on the shoulder. He turns to find a policeman looking at him. "Would you mind moving on please, boss. You're blocking the way, and you might consider being a little more discreet with your shouting."

Tom looks back at him. "Dickie's gone."

"Well maybe you should join him."

Tom laughs, turns and begins jogging towards the college. As he approaches the gates, he begins to have doubts. But they couldn't get a story this wrong. Even if he's still here, he must be leaving. Get in, find out more. By the time he reaches his office, he is exhausted, but fortunately he is the last one there. Alan and Tili are standing behind Mike. They all look at him and smile when he comes in. Mike rotates the monitor as he walks over.

```
Dear Colleagues,

This has been a time of tremendous diffi-
culty for this great college, and I believe
the moment has come for me to pass the
baton to someone else to move the college
forward. I shall therefore be leaving Sand-
ford after twenty-two years as principal.
I do so with great sadness but also in the
belief that I have steered us through some
rough seas and that we are a stronger col-
lege now than we were when I first took the
helm. I know that many have been unhappy
with many of the measures I have intro-
duced, but I would like you to know that I
have always acted in what I believed to be
the best interests of the college. I wish
you all good fortune and thank you for all
you have done to help me in making this
college what it is.

Regards,
Richard Kilman
```

Mike looks at him. "Bella called. She says you and Barry should come to the principal's office at eleven-thirty."

"To meet Dickie?"

"Don't know. She wants you to confirm by email that you'll be there."

"Is he definitely gone?"

Tili nods. "Looks like it. The security guard on the back gate said that, as he was leaving last night, Dickie thanked him for his work at the college and said that was his last day."

Despite all the mounting evidence, he still struggles to believe that this is not a sick conspiracy to raise their hopes one last time. He goes down to Barry's office. Smiles from wall to wall. Barry is surrounded by the troops. "I'm telling you, it's because they realised the college couldn't function if I retired." He looks up as Tom walks over. "Well done, comrade."

"Who are we meeting at eleven-thirty?"

"We'll see in three hours, but I tell you something, I fucking hope it's Dickie. Can't bear the thought I won't be able to wish him farewell. But just in case, let's make sure he doesn't miss out." He calls up the text he received on the picket line and hits reply. With painfully slow precision he types out, "He who laughs last, Dickie," and shows it to Tom.

Tom smiles but shakes his head. "Don't send it."

"Why not?"

"I don't know. There's just something wrong with it." He reflects for a moment. "Have you ever seen *When We Were Kings*?"

"Ali and Foreman in the jungle."

"Do you remember the scene when Ali finally puts him down?"

"He turns to see him falling, pulls back his right but doesn't throw the punch."

"Mailer said it was because he didn't want to ruin the aesthetic of his victory. There's something cheap about acting the same way Dickie has simply because we're powerful enough to do it."

Barry sighs, shakes his head and cancels the message. "All right, but the price you have to pay is that you will not even be considered for the highly prestigious post of executing the enemies of the revolution after today's events inspire the whole country to rise up."

Tom smiles at a prediction which he knows Barry takes semi-seriously. "Do we know what happened?"

"Governors must have decided in the end that kicking the shit out of innocent pickets was not their idea of progressive education. If you hadn't been so unkind to Mr Coyle, you could've asked him." He hesitates for a moment. "Tell you what. Get down to see Deirdre Platts. Tell her you're interested in the draft minutes of last night's meeting and see if she'll give you a hint as to what happened."

"Isn't it your turn to try and squeeze information out?"

"They all love your middle class accent. Hurry up. Might be important before this morning's meeting."

Tom nods reluctantly and makes his way to Deirdre's office. When he enters, she looks up and shakes her head.

"Please tell me you're not after the minutes already. I've barely sat down. Haven't even pulled them out to type them up yet."

"Of course not, Deirdre." He is unsure what move he can make next, and out of sheer desperation he goes for honesty.

"We're meeting with someone in senior management this morning, we don't even know who. We just wanted to know what happened yesterday evening. We thought … just thought it might be useful for us to know."

She looks at him with a sort of maternal pity. She turns her monitor towards him and motions for him to sit in the chair opposite her. She opens her inbox and then goes into an email from 'hot_little_number'. The email contains the single line, "Thought you might find this interesting." Beneath it is a link which Deirdre opens. It is grainy video footage from a mobile. It is interior and badly lit, yet the person in the frame is clearly Sally. She is holding a drink and laughing. Someone is speaking to her from off camera, and she laughs again. Another question, and she laughs again, giggling in drunken embarrassment, loving it. She finally manages to compose herself, and when she speaks, there are subtitles imposed over the images. "Ok yes, I did shag Richard." More giggling. "But it was only once in the office. Only once." This evokes laughter from all around, and the clip ends. It is no more than thirty seconds.

Deirdre shakes her head. "Such a silly woman. After they finished Tuesday's dinner with these people from Walsall, she went to the Bar on the River with some of the staff from here. She had one too many Mai Tais, and a student caught her."

"A student?"

"Half of them work, and bar work never interferes with their classes. This was sent to the entire governing body yesterday morning."

"And they confronted Dickie with it last night?"

"It was farcical. Only half the governors had seen it, and the projector in the classroom we were using didn't work. So we all had to decamp next door, it took ten minutes to switch on the computer, and then we all sat through Sally's little performance. They asked Richard, Sally, and Dan Corporal to leave the room, and they decided that they had to get rid of Richard for fear of what the press might do with it. Lots of awkward questions about the timing of Sally's promotion."

Tom shakes his head in disbelief. "So they're prepared to let him destroy his staff, but nailing Sally is a step too far, and they sack him."

"Oh they didn't sack him. He and Sally are both going immediately, and they both get their full salary for the duration of their notice period. Richard will be on his normal pay for another six months, and then draw his full pension." She hesitates and then considers things before continuing. "I'm not sure they'll pay his bonus for this year. Rather oddly, it was one of the staff governors who suggested that he step down."

"Richard Tomlinson?"

"No, Tony Coyle. It was almost the first time he's spoken in the two years he's been on the governing body, and his first serious contribution was to suggest that the principal needed to go."

"What about Liefwint?"

"He and Morgan are both going to step down in the autumn. They don't want to make it look like the whole ship is sinking, so they plan to leave quietly in September."

"Did they say anything about the redundancies?"

"No. They just agreed that new management would have to present recommendations about how to move forward. Now, the governors have scheduled an emergency meeting for next week, and they want the minutes as soon as possible, so you'll have to leave me."

Tom turns to leave, but as he reaches the door Deirdre speaks again. "You know something strange. When they told him they wanted him to go, he didn't really seem that resistant."

Tom smiles at her. "He's too vain to show what he really thinks, but someone like that will die without a place like this to tyrannise."

They arrive early, and so they wait once again in the outer office. They hear a woman's laugh from inside, and Bella comes out at exactly eleven-thirty to usher them in. Dan Corporal is sitting in exactly the same chair which Dickie used to occupy. They sit and he begins. "Let me come straight to the point.

The governors have asked me to be acting principal until a permanent appointment is made, and they feel it is essential that a line is drawn under the events of the last nine months. I'm therefore charged with trying to find a means of ending the current dispute in a way which will leave us financially intact."

Barry nods sympathetically. "That all sounds exactly like what we want. Have you got any specific proposals to put to us?"

"I'm offering to withdraw all the letters of redundancy which have been issued in return for an end to industrial action. I'm going to recommend that plans for modernisation be implemented over a much longer timeframe, which will mean the savings we need to make in the short term are not as great."

"We'll have to put it to the members, but it sounds like a reasonable offer." Even now he restrains himself from showing any warmth or enthusiasm. Management is still management no matter who is sitting across from you.

"I'd also like us to issue a joint press notice. I think it would be a good idea if we can create the impression of peace having broken out."

"You do know that the *Gazette* has been sent a copy of that video clip? Jenny Skelton called me this morning for a comment on Dickie's departure. I hadn't seen it by then, so I said we'd issue something later. Looks like they delayed using it so they can spin out the story till next week."

"So I hear. We've increased our subscription to one hundred-and-fifty copies a week. We'll cut it back to something more reasonable in the autumn when enrolment is finished and everyone's forgotten about the strike. In the meantime, I hope that even a local editor will work out what will happen if they go out of their way to embarrass us, and I'm not sure they will risk such a huge decline in sales."

"Very astute."

There is further discussion around some of the more technical aspects of the union's February proposals, but after half an hour the deal is done. Barry will recommend to the branch that they formally end the dispute in return for no compulsory redundancies. Tom and Barry both know that this may be no more than a delayed execution, with God knows what further problems they may face in the new year. But for now, fifty-three people get to continue teaching in a leaky, crumbling wreck, and that's as good as it gets.

They shake hands, and Dan asks them to arrange another meeting for the first days back after the half-term so they can discuss the governors' response. Barry goes off to teach his twelve-forty-five class, leaving Tom to arrange the meeting time with Bella. She sits at her desk in the outer office. The other secretaries are at the retirement lunch for one of the receptionists, so they are alone.

Tom offers her some times when he knows that both he and Barry are free on the first days back, but he cannot pass up the opportunity to ask her.

"Have you seen that clip of Sally?"

"Yes I have."

"They're saying a student did it. Did you recognise any of our students working there?"

"I wasn't really focusing on the waiters."

"Waiters? I didn't realise the Bar on the River had table service now. You had to go up and get your own drinks when I was last there. Maybe it wasn't someone working there. Maybe it was someone who sat down next to you. It just looked as if someone was shooting the video from hip height."

"Mmmm ... Maybe. Who knows?"

"Subtitles as well. I've tried and failed for years to sync them properly on the stuff I download. I'm guessing whoever shot the clip was pretty clued up. You might even have to know someone like the IT lecturer facing redundancy that you met at The Garden before you went out with Sally."

She looks up at him. No look of pity now. She's not just uncomfortable, but scared. "Aren't you pleased that they're both gone?"

He smiles at her. "Yes I am. Pity I'll never get the chance to thank the person who did it." She smiles back at him, and he walks out of her office. It is the first time he has ever left there without a sense of extreme unease.

He wolfs some lunch before once again making the bizarre journey from union officer to ordinary teacher. It reminds him of how it felt sipping wine in the back garden of the flat whilst listening to the news about the looting of Clapham Junction half a mile away, knowing that he had passed through there earlier and would do so again the next day. One world seemed absolutely removed from the other, regardless of how close they were in reality.

Within an hour of seeing Dan, he walks in to see 2Phil1 for the last time. As soon as he sits down, he realises he has forgotten one of his handouts in all the confusion of earlier in the day. He is aware of being more distracted now than he was at any time during the dispute, and he takes a deep breath to compose himself.

"Consider this. Is there a difference between being wise and being intelligent? What does the wise person know which others do not? Could someone be wise and immoral? Miles?"

He looks up in surprise. "Well … uh … I think wise people are probably intelligent, but it's not the same thing. I think you have to be experienced to be wise, but you can be young and intelligent."

"That is also Aristotle's view. We can think of someone being a genius at maths or physics, or even being very gifted at philosophy at a very young age. But it seems much less likely that one would seek advice from a brilliant young mathematician on the sorts of issues where wise people might help us."

Joe's legs reduce in speed as he looks up. "What issues are those?"

"Aristotle believes that those who are wise are able to answer questions on how one should live. They are older, they are experienced, and they are morally virtuous."

Now Maya raises a hand. "So you have to be morally virtuous to be wise?"

"Aristotle makes the radical claim that you must have all the moral virtues to be wise. He thinks that the virtues help us to know what we should try to achieve, and wisdom tells us how we should achieve the aims set down by the virtues. So if we are courageous, then we have the aim of acting bravely, and the wise person will be able to say what actions this requires in specific situations."

Maya shakes her head. "If he's saying that you must have all the virtues, then is there anyone who has ever been wise?"

"This is very difficult to answer, and it may be he is defining wisdom in ways which are too demanding. But the general point is that moral goodness and wisdom are inseparable. The wise person acts in morally good ways and advises others in the same way. She knows this is the most effective way of leading a good life."

"So if you're wise, then you'll be happy?"

"No. Happiness also requires a degree of good luck. Without that even the best people may find themselves losing out due to factors beyond their control."

"But if you're wise and you're lucky, then you'll be happy."

"Yes."

There is a general silence as they consider this. It is Laura who raises a hand first. "So if wise people have all the virtues, then they are kind, and they know they have to act kindly."

"That's right. They also know that there will be areas where they lack the expertise to provide the required help, and the kind action is to turn to others."

Miles now shakes his head. "How do you actually know if someone is a wise person? Someone could be experienced, and they think they're good, and everyone else thinks they're good, but they're basically getting it wrong."

"This is also a major problem. We can't test for wisdom in the way you test for competence in medicine or mathematics. The question of how best to lead a human life is too complex and open-ended. Even those who believe themselves to be wise need to have the humility to recognise they may be getting things wrong and to rely on their having the virtues to guide them."

"It doesn't seem very satisfactory."

"Better to acknowledge our limitations and do the best we can. This is better than foolishly trying to reduce these questions to some sort of calculation of the quantity of pleasure an action will produce, or else rely upon those who claim to have a perfect understanding of goodness based in some perception of a mysterious otherworldly realm."

He pauses and sighs. "In the end, this is probably not as hopeless a situation as some of you seem to be suggesting. If qualities such as kindness, courage, generosity, and self control have often been thought of as virtues, then it is because those who possess them have been generally more likely to lead a flourishing life. Rather than radically challenging such ideas, the wise person is more likely to have good reasons to endorse them."

He gives them a final extract to read, and that is that. A year of studying the most important work of ethics ever written is at an end. He thanks them and assures them that there is no question they will be unable to answer. Joe interrupts him to hand over a bottle of wine and a card they have clubbed together to buy him. He smiles at them as they leave. Laura does not look at him as she passes.

By three-thirty he is on a train. Seven hours earlier, he arrived in hideous defeat, and now he leaves with the prospect of a week's holiday which will be the best of his life. On the other side of the aisle, two fourteen-year-olds are listening to Price Tag on one of their mobiles. This morning this intrusion would have irritated him, but now the world is a different colour, and he finds beauty in the memory of Sofia dancing to this with her eight-year-old niece at a family dinner in the Valencian countryside last summer, the girl ecstatic as they mimic the dance moves from the video.

When he arrives home, he sits and thinks about what has happened and what needs to happen. It becomes clear to him what he must do, and it takes only an hour for him to arrange it. When Sofia comes in, she casually drops her keys in the bowl by the front door and smiles sympathetically as she sees him sipping a Kir. He pours one for her. She thanks him. "How was it?"

It suddenly strikes him that he has completely forgotten to call her about the events earlier in the day. "Not too bad, really. Saw my second-years for the final time. Found a couple of good films to download. Oh, and Dickie was fired last night, and no one is losing their job."

She sits there open-mouthed.

"Well, not fired exactly. Just leaving immediately. So is Sally, and Barry is no longer retiring, so I don't have to take over. Means life should be a little less strained next year."

"What happened?"

"One of the secretaries used her mobile to film Sally talking about when she shagged Dickie, and sent the clip to the governors. Rather bizarrely, she decided not to put it on YouTube, so I'm afraid I can't show it to you until it leaks out over the next few hours."

"Oh, my God." She shakes her head in disbelief. " Can you beat that?"

"I think so." He tries to compose himself, desperate not to stumble. "Marry me."

"What?"

"In Valencia, on September eighteenth."

"Why?"

"Wow, that's a much better reaction than the tears of romantic joy I'd hoped for."

"Hold on, I'm just in shock, that's all."

"We can do it at the town hall near your mother's house and go on honeymoon to the south."

"Look, this is romantic, and you know my feelings about all this. But … you don't think we should try to get a place first?"

"I looked up the places you saved when you did your searches last year. Half of them are still available, and two of the ones you really liked have reduced the asking price. We're seeing them tomorrow morning."

"Buy a flat and get married in the same year."

"We'll probably both be redundant soon, so this is the last chance to find a mortgage or pay for a decent honeymoon. And once you tell your mother, she'll forcibly take over all arrangements for the wedding anyway."

"I'm slightly struggling to deal with all this organisation. Is this what it's like living with me?"

"Not even close."

She smiles. It is the same irresistibly infectious way she always smiles at him when he surprises her. "Are you sure this is wise?"

"I've never been more sure of anything."

She is still smiling, still happy. "Oh, all right then."

They kiss and then hold each other. He looks down at her. "I've booked a table for eight o'clock at Tapas Variadas. May as well start celebrating as soon as possible."

"You were pretty sure of yourself."

"Well, I know you're desperate, and I thought I could always cancel the booking if you made the wrong decision."

They both drink. What a day. They each wonder how many more good ones there may be, but neither says anything. Not today. Not today.

ACKNOWLEDGMENTS

Firstly, enormous thanks are due to Michael Eskin and his colleagues at UWSP. Not only were they prepared to give an opportunity to a previously unpublished author, but they provided countless suggestions about how this book might be improved. Whatever faults remain are far fewer in number than those contained in the manuscript they first read. My agent Darin Jewell also offered considerable support, and I am grateful to the anonymous readers who gave me a series of very helpful suggestions. Finally, I must thank Jana for reading my work and providing constant encouragement.

AVAILABLE FROM UWSP

- *November Rose: A Speech on Death* by Kathrin Stengel
  (2008 Independent Publisher Book Award)
- *November-Rose: Eine Rede über den Tod* by Kathrin Stengel
- *Philosophical Fragments of a Contemporary Life* by Julien David
- *17 Vorurteile, die wir Deutschen gegen Amerika und die Amerikaner haben und die so nicht ganz stimmen können* by Misha Waiman
- *The DNA of Prejudice: On the One and the Many* by Michael Eskin
  (2010 Next Generation Indie Book Award for Social Change)
- *Descartes' Devil: Three Meditations* by Durs Grünbein
- *Fatal Numbers: Why Count on Chance* by Hans Magnus Enzenberger
- *The Vocation of Poetry* by Durs Grünbein
  (2011 Independent Publisher Book Award)
- *The Waiting Game: An Essay on the Gift of Time* by Andrea Köhler
- *Mortal Diamond: Poems* by Durs Grünbein
- *Yoga for the Mind: A New Ethic for Thinking and Being & Meridians of Thought* by Michael Eskin & Kathrin Stengel
- *The Wisdom of Parenthood: An Essay* by Michael Eskin
- *Health is in Your Hands: Jin Shin Jyutsu – Practicing the Art of Self-Healing (With 51 Flash Cards for the Hands-On Practice of Jin Shin Jyutsu)* by Waltraud Riegger-Krause
- *A Moment More Sublime: A Novel* by Stephen Grant
- *High on Low: Harnessing the Power of Unhappiness* by Wilhelm Schmid
- *Potentially Harmless: A Philosopher's Manhattan* by Kathrin Stengel